The Banker's Daughter

Emran Mian

W F HOWES LTD

This large print edition published in 2013 by
W F Howes Ltd
Unit 4, Rearsby Business Park, Gaddesby Lane,
Rearsby, Leicester LE7 4YH

1 3 5 7 9 10 8 6 4 2

First published in the United Kingdom in 2012
by Harvill Secker

Copyright © Emran Mian, 2012

The right of Emran Mian to be identified as
the author of this work has been asserted by him
in accordance with the Copyright, Designs and
Patents Act, 1988.

A CIP catalogue record for this book is available
from the British Library

ISBN 978 1 47122 771 4

Typeset by Palimpsest Book Production Limited,
Falkirk, Stirlingshire
Printed and bound in Great Britain
by MPG Books Ltd, Bodmin, Cornwall

MIX
Paper from
responsible sources
FSC
www.fsc.org   FSC® C018575

TIME OUT, BEIRUT

Social Scene
Beirut this week

Thursday 13 March 2008
Summer collections arrive at Le Balcon des Createurs

One of our favourite boutiques in Gemmayze, this is a meeting point for the creativity thriving in Lebanon. It brings together exclusive collections by eighty local designers. The clientele already includes models, television stars and singers. Now we're told that Hanna Mehdi, daughter of Mateen Mehdi, the former boss of IBCD, has become a big fan too.

The father and daughter are reputed to be worth tens of millions of dollars and have been living in the nearby Saint-Michel hotel since the bank collapsed in 2006. Our girl in the know says Hanna made a whirlwind tour of the boutique last week and walked away with stunning pieces by some of Lebanon's best up-and-coming designers, including some very revealing swimwear.

Summer is just around the corner and it seems that Hanna for one intends to enjoy it in style.

BEIRUT

CHAPTER 1

I'm looking at a photograph. It's hard to look at it. It's hard to look away. For some minutes now, I have placed my hands, palms down, against my knees, like I need to keep them away from my face, or I will wring my neck, or I will blot my eyes. In front of me there is a garden; and a table; and on that table, a head with no body underneath it.

I don't know when the photograph was taken but I know the garden is here – in Beirut. It's a part of our new life, not a remnant of the previous one. I'd like to believe that it's a news photograph or a special effects production. I'd like to believe that it represents some ancient scene, distant from me by many years, but it doesn't. The garden belongs to Baba's businessman friend Rami, who has lived in Lebanon since he was born, through the wars, despite the assassinations, the tyre-burnings, the Israeli jet planes (he stayed for profit not for courage, I should say). I recognise the rose bushes. I recognise the table. The table is made of stone and I've sat on the matching stone bench, listening to Rami's stories. I've drunk

wine and eaten cherries at that table. In the photograph, the head bleeds over the edge onto the
ground where Rami's cat lurks when there are
guests waiting for scraps. My hands escape and I
cover my mouth. I feel something shift in my gorge.

Beirut was supposed to be our safe place. For
two years, it has given Baba and me safety. We
came here from London, trying to get out from
underneath a collapse. But the photograph on the
laptop screen in front of me changes how I will
live in this city. It is a secret that I can't keep away
from like the others, my first Beiruti secret. I want
to turn away. But I don't. I keep looking.

The man's nose is spotted with blood, his eyes
closed like he's listening in concentration, his hair
matted with his own sweat. When the head is
carried away from the table, I wonder, will it be
taken by someone in their hands, or gathered up
in a cloth?

I have never suffered violence before in my life.
After a gallery opening about four years ago, I
went for a walk in a part of London that I didn't
know. I wandered under a railway bridge. A car
drew up next to me and a man got out of it, tried
to grab me. I slipped from his grasp and ran.
That's as bad as I've ever had. And yet I've seen
pictures and art installations that portray acts like
this, acts of cutting, acts of dismembering. I wrote
a thesis on Caravaggio in the final year of my art
history degree. I have looked at my mother's body
in a coffin. I've driven past a traffic accident

fatality. I read a newspaper story about one of the assassination attempts on the army chief Musharraf while he was president of Pakistan, how the head of the man with a bomb strapped to him popped off when he detonated the device, and was found intact at the scene afterwards. Three months ago, Baba and I went to Damascus for a day. Baba is Shia Muslim, Uncle Yani is too, as well as Sherpao, the founder of their bank, the IBCD. The large Umayyad Mosque in Damascus contains a shrine for Husain, one of the first martyrs in the Shia tradition. The shrine is built on the spot where Husain's head was kept for two hundred years. The head was removed from Husain's slain body after a war between Sunni and Shia and brought to the governor of Damascus, a Sunni, as a proof of victory. It's an odd monument. It's a monument to Sunni prowess, total victory over Husain's army, the decapitation of its general; it's not a celebration of anything glorious or powerful about the Shia. But that's okay because there is no glory or power in Shia Islam, there's not supposed to be. The most they want to celebrate is the improbable fact of their survival despite everything that has been done to them. Baba sat for an hour on the floor in that shrine talking to other pilgrims who had travelled from Iran, Bahrain, India.

So I do know that heads get removed; I know that it has been done, that it can be done, what it might mean. I also know many of the things

5

that Baba has done with his bank and how my uncles, the friends who worked most closely with him, helped him. I know they sold Thai sovereign debt short to compel the government to take a loan from them. I know they ignored international sanctions and made deals wherever they wanted. They built a giant bank from nothing within ten years, the International Bank of Commerce and Development, though I know that others call it the International Bank of Charm and Deception. And, when it fell, prompting Baba and me to flee London and come here to Beirut, I know that millions of depositors in over fifty countries lost their money, the tens of thousands of people who worked for the bank lost their jobs, many of them lost their homes as well, which the bank had helped them to buy. There were dozens of other businesses that collapsed because the bank fell, the government in Bangladesh had to resign in the face of criticism about the access they had given IBCD to their country, a brother and sister in Edinburgh committed suicide because they couldn't withstand the ruin it brought their family. I am not ignorant about the damage that takes place in the world, nor my father's part in it. But this is something different. I am not prepared to see among his emails a picture of a head, or to be compelled to imagine the body that carried the head around lying slumped, out of the camera's sight, in a corner of Rami's garden, like an old coil of rope, like a yellowing

6

leaf fallen from one of the garden's many palm trees.

The laptop screen goes into power-saving mode and the photograph disappears. Here is a chance. If I hadn't come into Baba's hotel suite this morning, into his study, then I would never have seen this photograph. I fold down the screen and stand back from the desk. I can walk away now. Baba is swimming in the pool on the roof. We argued earlier about whether I would join him. I don't like swimming. He knows that, but he keeps asking. 'You swam just last week,' he claimed when we spoke on the phone this morning. I was in my bed, he was perhaps in this study. 'I saw you swim into the sea,' he said, 'straight down the throat of a whale.'

'It wasn't me,' I told him. I knew this game.

'I saw you in a film,' he said, 'in a chic one-piece swimsuit. You jumped off the diving board, narrowly missing a plump young man on your way into the water.'

'It wasn't me,' I repeated.

'You were on the last leg of the winning relay team at the Olympics. You swam backstroke faster than any of the others swam freestyle.'

'It wasn't me, Baba.'

He hesitated. 'Did you put on weight?' he asked in a tone stripped of the prior playfulness. 'Is that why you don't want to swim?' He finds a moment to ask me this question roughly once a week. Every time I wear a close-fitting dress to dinner,

7

he examines my middle when I greet him and doesn't respond until he is satisfied that I am maintaining myself. When I wear a loose-fitting dress, I know that the question about my weight is close by.

'No, Baba,' I told him. 'I didn't put on weight.'

'Just up to the pool,' he said. 'Not out in the boat.'

'Let's talk later on,' I said.

Instead of swimming with him, I had a coffee with Ghalib. Ghalib is Yani's son. He visits us every few months when he is in the Middle East on business. He always brings a recent photograph of his father with him. Yani is living in Casablanca. Baba and Yani don't contact each other since the collapse, supposedly it's too dangerous. They are wanted for the crimes, felonies and infractions of their bank. Baba was the chief executive and chairman. Yani was his fixer and breaker, the manifestation of his will, his sharp end at the sharp end. On this latest trip Ghalib hasn't brought a photograph. 'I'm not on speaking terms with my father right now,' he said at dinner last night to my father. 'You and he are up to something. You're talking. You have something.' Baba looked blankly at him, then at me.

'You're wrong,' he said. 'I haven't spoken to Yani since 2006.'

Ghalib shook his head. 'I don't know what the transaction is,' he said, 'but you have something.

My father has that creepy look he gets when he's working on a deal.'

'Perhaps he's chasing a woman,' Baba said.

'You're putting Hanna and me in a very difficult position,' continued Ghalib, pointing to me, staring intently at Baba. 'We have been loyal to the two of you. She's moved her life here to Beirut for you. Me? There's no financial institution in the world that will hire me. Because I'm Yani's son. But that's fine. I live with that. If you're back in business though, the two of you, after all the shit that you've already brought down, why exactly are we making any sacrifices for you?'

'Don't be disingenuous,' replied Baba. 'What have you sacrificed? UBS? Goldman Sachs? You don't want to work for anyone else. You've never tried.'

Over coffee this morning, Ghalib repeated his suspicions to me alone. 'They have something,' he said. 'Yani is in deal mode. And he wouldn't make a move without your father. They're talking to each other.'

'Why?' I asked him. 'How can you be sure?'

'He looks like he's not sleeping,' he said. 'And during the day it's like he's got a tiger's paw in his pocket. Something he must keep all to himself.'

'That doesn't sound like a lot of evidence,' I replied.

'I've been trying to contact Terry,' he said. 'But I can't get hold of him.' Uncle Terry was the third member with Baba and Yani of the axis that

9

controlled IBCD. He was their strategist, their maven, ex-Bank of England, ex-Her Majesty's Treasury, their connection to the old world, formally designated the chief risk officer for public relations purposes, but in fact the deviser of all their riskiest operations, their furthest-flung interpretations of the letter of the law.

'Terry is retired,' I told him.

'Don't be like that,' he said. 'You know how they are. You know the look just as well as I do.'

He's right. There is a look. There is a look that they bear when they're into their work. I've known it since I was a child. I remember for example that they had it for days and days during the frenetic circulation of IBCD cities that they made at the end of each financial year. Before I started in school, I was allowed to go with them, city to city, hotel to hotel. The idea of the financial year was an exciting idea to me. I had known one kind of year and then I discovered that Baba and Yani and Terry knew a different one. In the days before their year changed, in Riyadh, in Dubai, in Kuala Lumpur, in New York, in Buenos Aires, in Zurich, in Geneva, in London, Baba winked at me when he saw me. There were usually papers under his arm, people waiting to talk to him as soon as he stepped outside the hotel suite. I heard him murmuring in the other room on telephone calls until late into the night while I was in bed. He was out in the morning before I got up. He moved too quickly for any of the questions that I wanted to ask to land on him. And all the time he had a look. Then 1 April arrived, and there was a sudden alteration. There were no more papers under his arm. There were long breakfasts. There were trips to places that I wanted to go.

Does Baba have the same look these last few days? I must have felt he does. Or Ghalib persuaded me. That's why I opened up the laptop and started looking around.

It was easy to come into Baba's room today. He will stay out of it until the evening. It's the day when the carpets are changed. It happens every three months. He asks for the change and he chooses the carpet. On the whole, he is an easy guest. Though he wakes up at 5am every day, he makes no fuss that the breakfast room of the hotel doesn't open until 6. The staff are used to guests unlike Baba here, Sammy Aboud for example, who they say deals in diamonds dug by bonded labour, men branded on their cheeks with obscene signs, which is meant I think to make even the prospect of freedom seem desperate. Aboud has a suite on the same floor as Baba and plays gypsy music at top volume when he has insomnia. He asks the staff to buy drugs for him and then he compels the management to fire the staff who serviced him so that they don't get used to making money from him. Baba could make a big deal about waiting for his breakfast, in fact he has never mentioned it to anyone. He turns up at six as if that is the perfect time for him. He goes into the lobby afterwards and dawdles a while outside the hotel, watching the traffic, feeling the weather, whatever it may be, on his face. Then he walks back up to his suite by the stairs. The staff know that this stroll, made gently, with breaks, is part of the daily system by which Baba sets himself to the world, and the ones who like him sometimes find an excuse to join him for part of the journey. There's a lot of bad behaviour in this hotel. The staff tell Baba the highlights of what's been going on, floor by floor. The Saint-Michel is one of the grand old hotels of Beirut, popular with wealthy men from across the Middle East. I get winked at in the lifts by men in Arab robes and I have some ideas about what they like to do with the women who wink back at them. Ghalib has been to the parties, where they give the women drugs and watch them getting shagged by man after man; he said that he saw one prince lift up his robe and piss on a woman while she was giving a blowjob to a gigantic Ethiopian who was a family driver, but that might have been an exaggeration. There are the European guests too, holidaymakers and business people. They behave very well by comparison, but they don't have the eastern habits that are better suited to living in a hotel, like tipping properly. Baba tips highly properly. He has it as a point of principle to tip a set amount every Friday rather than make the staff anticipate his tips like a royal favour. Baba, I've heard staff members say, is the customer that always does right.

There's a routine to carpet-changing days. The firm comes in the morning and they clear the furniture from Baba's rooms. Baba is supposed to tidy himself away before they come. He doesn't have much to tidy, he has been cured of collecting since he came to Beirut, but I worry that he might be careless. So, before the carpet arrives, I make a check of his suite. I live on the other side of the same floor. I drop in while Baba isn't here, because he shoos me away if he is inside. There are people they pay to do that, he says, whenever I do something domestic, serve him a coffee or put a book back on the shelf. He has it clear in his head. Two years here in the Saint-Michel, and he has never been confused for a moment into thinking that it's his home, though he has said to me a couple of times that it may be the place where he lives until the end. When he is sleepless at night, I know that he sits here in the study, playing cards. I've told him that it's odd to sit in this box room when he could pull up the blinds in his lounge and look out at the city. 'You could walk,' I say to him. He looks at me with a frown. 'I haven't been outdoors after midnight since 2004,' he says. He likes these facts. He quotes them at me all the time.

After my coffee with Ghalib, I came up here to Baba's suite. I told myself that all I was doing was checking his room before the carpeting firm arrived. But I was looking for something as well:

13

proof that 'the look' really had come back, any hint of betrayal. My first discovery was a piece of paper on the dining-room table. That's all there was, where sometimes there can be whole files and cut-out magazine articles on that surface; it was a scrap with a restaurant telephone number on it, the place where I went with him for dinner two nights ago, before Ghalib arrived. I wrote the number into his address book and discarded the paper. Then I went into his bedroom. He was well tidied away. He had lifted his slippers and yesterday's jacket from the chair by the bed. His medicines were all enclosed in the cabinet in the bathroom. Then I came into the study and saw this machine, this unexpected machine, not the same laptop that I see him with every day. I opened it and the screen powered up. There was no password needed to unlock the contents. There was an email program already open and a single message in the inbox. The address of the sender was a string of numbers. There was no text in the message, just an attachment, a photograph. I clicked on it and it opened up. It opened up, this entry into a medieval world where heads are removed, a line of sight to what Baba's real life looks like, the elements that can't be locked into cupboards when the carpets are changed.

The day when we ran, as soon as he knew what was happening to IBCD, Baba called me from work in whispers. He spoke quietly but with the fervency of a converted man, which, in a way, he suddenly was. 'We have to go,' he said. 'There's no safe haven for us here. No one will answer my calls. Quickly,' he said. As soon as I got off the phone, I started looking for money. I felt that I had to have money. Not the means of access to money, not a cheque book or an American Express card, but cash. I sought out the places in my flat where I had hidden money from myself, drunk, at night, usually after dinners with Baba, which he concluded by turning his pockets inside out, finding a toothpick for himself and a miscellany of banknotes to press on me. While I looked for money in my flat, I kept pausing on other things. I saw the antique backgammon pieces that Sherpao, Baba's boss, the founder of the bank, had left as a gift when I was unborn, when the flat belonged to my young father and young mother, their first home in London, with their young *cave* of wine, and young laughter, young cigarettes between young fingers, young splashes of gin in tumblers that were wedding presents too, young breakfasts of chapatti from the night before, two sips of coffee and a kiss. But I couldn't take those backgammon pieces with me. Nor could I take the gold and lapis lazuli that I kept in my bedroom in a beige suede stetson that my cousin Mudassar had given me on my eighteenth birthday. Just cash, I kept reminding myself. Baba had told me to be ready, absolutely ready to go, when he arrived. I threw on more clothes. I put on the television and clipped through the news channels. I suppose I wanted

15

corroboration for what Baba had told me. 'They're crashing metal baseball bats against my bank,' he said on the phone. 'They're breaking her ankles. They're bringing her down. Next they'll be looking for me.' I wanted to hear this described in plainer terms, by a journalist with a professional manner, someone who had never flown in the bank's private plane, who didn't know the name of the velvet that was used to line the inside of the deposit boxes in the vault in the headquarters, who wasn't there when the bank opened in Ghana and Sherpao played the trumpet and I kissed the president of the Republic's son. But it was Baba's own lurid sentences that kept running in my head as I found a cardigan, a jacket, a coat, multiplying the places where I could hide my shaking hands.

It had happened before that Baba turned up at my flat and asked me to go with him on a trip straight away, and always he expected me to say yes. Often I did. After my mother died, always I did. I am Baba's family. There's only me. But this time we weren't leaving for a short jaunt, we were escaping. I looked around the flat that I had lived in for five years, the flat that had belonged to my parents before, and suddenly it seemed obvious to me: I had always been leaving. I had painted the study. I had tins of tuna and packets of pasta in the cupboards. I had a steady cleaner who came twice a week. But I had always been leaving. When the odd friend happened to visit my flat, the first comment was usually something like: 'Is

16

this really your place?' In fact there was hardly anything of mine there. Though there was, in the room where I slept, a stack of paintings wrapped in sheets of plastic bubbles; they were my little trading business, paintings by a small group of Pakistani artists who were making the new art of a young republic. Every few months, I went to Karachi, and Lahore, and Islamabad, and occasionally some new settlement in the picturesque north where three rich families had built villas on a hillside to give the artists in their midst a place to reflect and work, and, after a few days, when I had returned to London, the packages began to arrive. Then I went to Manchester and Glasgow, Houston and New York, Hamburg and Paris, every city where I had found a handful of Pakistanis who, despite living overseas, were willing to renew their visions of Pakistan with these paintings. The latest assortment would have to remain unsold.

Once I had been looking for a high place to stow the letters my mother sent me when I was at college. I climbed precariously onto a chair I knew had come from the first auction at Christie's my parents went to together and there, on the highest bookshelf, I found, printed in the dust, Baba's handprint. It could only be his, because my mother had such small hands, and I recognised the shape of the ring that he wore on his little finger. Afterwards, I often expected to find that handprint again in other places, expected that I might lift a pot from the table and see it branded into the wood underneath, that I might run hot water in the sink to wash my face and look up to see Baba's hand in the mist on the mirror.

When the doorbell rang, and I opened the door, I understood right away, from his expression, the extent of the danger that we were in. I pulled him into the flat. I pressed down his hair where his hands had been through it.

'Don't you ever look in a mirror?' I said.

'I haven't looked in a mirror since 1987,' he said, taking off his glasses and wiping them on my coat-sleeve. It was me who monitored how many white hairs he had, who watched for the emergence of moles or the patches of vitiligo that develop on the faces of many older Asian men. Baba never looked, so it was up to me. 'I saw Veer set fire to things,' he said. 'I saw him stamping on a box file until it broke, then he took what was inside it and added it to a small fire that he had started. There was no alarm. Did someone switch off the fire detection? Isn't that dangerous?' Veer, I knew, was the bank's vice-president in charge of new operations in South America. Baba had hired him from a rival bank ten years ago. I had removed his hand from my thigh in a rooftop bar in Muscat when I was nineteen.

'Did you speak to him?' I said.

'He wouldn't speak to me,' he replied. 'He was furious with me. They all were. My secretary called security to escort me out of the building. I left with three guards. They didn't let anyone else into the lift on the way down. We practically ran through the lobby. Listen,' he said, 'do you have money?'

'Yes,' I told him. 'I have cash.'

'Good.' He nodded. 'I have to leave,' he added. 'I really do. I need to leave London. You can stay here if you prefer. I checked: Habib is here right now.' Habib is the accountant for my mother's family, except he's more than that: he manages everything for them. My uncle, Bilal, my mother's one sibling, has a house in London and his wife stays here for most of the time. Habib shuttles back and forth between Lahore and London, keeping everything in form, paying necessary expenses, choking off unnecessary ones. Baba says that, without Habib, Ma, my grandmother, and Bilal and his family would have become destitute years ago. Baba has always liked Habib and trusted him and has never had anything more than a word of salaam to say to Bilal. Even after my mother died, Baba spent afternoons together with Habib from time to time at a racecourse or in a betting shop. Habib is a bit of an expert about racehorses, though Baba says he never bets more than £50 at a time. 'I could call Habib,' Baba continued. 'He will look after you.'

'On the phone you said we have to go. Both of us,' I replied.

'Yes,' he said absently. 'Yes, I suppose I did.' I

19

noticed that he was looking around the flat. It was where he had lived with my mother when they were a young couple. This link with her was about to snap as well. I stepped briskly out of the room. One night the glass globe over the dining table slipped and broke, and I improvised a light-shade by clipping three sketches that the great Pakistani artist Gulgee had made of my mother to a wooden coat-hanger. Gulgee made them when my parents visited his studio to view a large work that IBCD had commissioned for the Pakistan HQ. I took down the sketches carefully and slid them into a plastic portfolio. 'Now let's go,' I said, handing it to him. My father took the sketches and held them to his chest. I put my hands in my trouser pockets.

'Hanna,' he said, 'is there any reason that the police would pursue you?'

'What do you mean?' I asked.

'Did you ever get stopped with drugs?' he said. 'A friend's drugs, they may have been? Did you ever drive away from an accident?'

'Am I a liability, Baba, to your escape plan?' I replied. 'Is that what you're trying to work out?'

'No, no,' he said. 'Of course it's not that.'

'Baba,' I said, taking his hand. 'You said we have to go.'

As soon as we were out of the door, he had momentum again. We travelled for two days, arriving in Beirut by boat from Cyprus. Since then, Baba has lived in this suite, isolated from his

20

former colleagues, his old powers dispersed. Or so I thought. With my hands in my hair now, I stare again at the photograph. It's hard to look at it. It's hard to look away.

CHAPTER 2

When I return to my room, Annette is inside. I am startled to see her, but then I remember that this is the time when she comes every day. Annette has made my room since she started working at the hotel eighteen months ago. Now she makes Baba's room as well because his previous girl left to get married. She is cleaning out the grounds from my espresso machine. 'Good morning, Annette,' I say. She doesn't reply. She gets up onto her toes and peers into the machine to check how thorough she has been. Once she asked me if she could take the ends of the packets of coffee that I throw away. Clumsily I offered to buy her coffee instead. She withdrew her request. 'Who was new last night?' I ask her. It's our favourite topic of conversation, arrivals to the seventh floor. Again she doesn't reply, busy reassembling the coffee machine. 'Annette,' I repeat, 'no one new last night?' She glances towards me. Her hand goes up to her mouth.

'Good morning, Miss Hanna,' she says, then takes out two earphones. 'I am so sorry not to speak to you.'

'Oh that's fine,' I say. I put the laptop down on the table in front of her. On impulse I took it from Baba's room when I left. Now I wonder what I'm going to do with it. I could throw it into the sea I suppose. I could give it to Ghalib so that he can prove his suspicions. If he were to look, I think he would find the same photograph in his father's records. If Baba has done what I've seen in the photograph, then he will have done it with Yani. Or if the photo has been sent as a threat to Baba, then it will have been sent to Yani as well. As I lift my hand from the laptop, I want to ask Annette if she has seen it before; instead I watch her for a reaction to it being in my possession.

'Is the carpet come?' she says, putting the earphones away into a pocket of her uniform.

'Not yet,' I tell her, sitting down. She shakes her head.

'What a colour,' she says. 'I hope it look good.'

'It's purple, isn't it?' I ask her. Baba told me it was going to be purple. He chooses a new colour every time that the carpet is changed.

'Purple,' she repeats. I watch her thinking of something else to say about it. The problem is that there is nothing else to say about purple carpeting except that it's a rich man's folly, and she can't say that.

'Did you see him?' I ask her. 'He went swimming?' She nods. 'He left this out,' I tell her, pointing to the laptop.

23

'Do you want me to put it somewhere?' she asks. I wonder why she asks this. Is it possible she knows that it must be kept in a safe place? Or that specifically I was never supposed to see it? Annette knows things about Baba that are hidden from me. She knows if he has vomited his food; it happens not infrequently because his gut is intolerant of many different foods yet he won't refrain from eating them. She knows if he has smoked. She told me that he has started to hum while he peels fruit. But none of that is proof of any sort of collusion.

'I'll see him later and give it back to him,' I reply, picking the machine up again.

I lie down on the couch in front of the television and set the laptop in front of me on the table. Why do I want to keep it with me? I suppose I know that it is going to change something. But I don't know what that will be. Do I hope that looking again at the photograph will tell me? It can't. It's the proof of a horrible, violent act, but it doesn't tell me who did it. I don't even recognise the face on the head. Must I leave Beirut because my Baba is a murderer? Or must we both leave because the photograph is a threat, a premonition of what someone wants to do to Baba, a terroristic device?

I switch on the television and turn up the volume to a level where it beats back the thoughts coming into my head, scattering them into pieces small enough that I can be inattentive to them. I cycle

24

methodically through every channel. It doesn't work. The photograph won't leave my mind. I watch the mouth on the severed head break into a grimace that broadens slowly; I hear the jaw crack. Fresh blood stains the teeth. Then Baba is there, standing beside the head, facing away. He slides the eyelids down gently with his fingers, then places his hand on the hair. There is a large red ruby ring on his middle finger. He makes a gesture and other people enter the scene with a large silver tray and take away the head. He begins turning towards me. I cry out.

I look around for Annette but she isn't in the room. I can't tell if I have made a noise or only within my mind. I turn up the volume on the television even further. After a few minutes, Annette reappears, coming into the lounge from my bedroom. She lobs a smile at me before passing into the guest bathroom. Even if she did hear me cry out, the truth is that Annette has seen worse than this. She has seen me not getting out of bed until the late afternoon because I stayed up all night looking through the latest gallery catalogues to arrive from Paris and London in the post. She has seen me come in from a morning coffee with Baba, where he talked about my mother, and burst into tears as soon as I was inside the suite. She saw me on the morning of my last birthday throwing eggs off the balcony, remembering how I did the same with Uncle Yani when we were staying at a hotel in Davos in Switzerland. Annette

25

is still in the guest bathroom I think when I fall asleep, holding a cushion tightly against my chest.

When we arrived in Beirut, at the Saint-Michel, after short flights in small planes and a motorboat ride from Cyprus, Baba told me not to talk to any member of the hotel staff about where we were from; to lock any personal items that may reveal my identity in the safe in the room; to call him once every hour, on the hour, except, if I was sleeping, between midnight and 6am, from my room to his room; but not to come to his room, or to approach him anywhere else in the hotel. Throughout the trip, I had imagined that the people who helped us might turn us in. I tensed every time someone reached for a mobile phone. As we left the bay in Cyprus on the motorboat, I thought that we were like a whale trailing blood in the water and that it was only a matter of time before the sharks arrived. In the hotel, I spent the hour between each call to my father performing a complicated routine. I started by checking the locks on the door; I popped open the safe, made sure all my stuff was there, then closed it again; I stood at one end of the long window in the lounge and peered through the blinds that I was keeping shut all day, looking for a glint of light on a tele-scope or camera lens pointed towards me; then I picked up the phone to Baba and told him I was okay. Sometimes I had a terrible feeling of premon-ition, so I called again, before I was supposed to, to check on him. I waited for him to clear his throat, waited for him to breathe, then put the phone down before I had embarrassed myself further. I remember picking up the phone to call reception from time to time to hear them say 'Hotel Saint-Michel', as if it weren't enough to check that my father was in place, but I had to check that *I* was in place as well.

A burst of noise from the television wakes me. I swipe the hair out of my eyes and look at the screen. It's a news programme. The commentator's voice is very loud and excited. I sit up and rub my face with my hands. I don't understand Arabic, despite Annette's best efforts, despite a run of classes at Berlitz, despite the congruence with Urdu. I don't know what the commentator is saying, except there are sudden jerks in his voice, like the interruptions that come from keeping back sobs. The camera moves around the outside scene skittishly. It stops on a car that has been stripped back to a bare metal frame. There is a bus that has been pulled down into a hole in the ground. The camera lingers on rising smoke. The commentator takes a longer pause. The camera moves through the smoke and a building emerges on the other side of it. It's bigger than the shot can accommodate. Many of its windows are smashed. The commentator is speaking again. The camera picks out an ambulance moving in. A man covered in soot moves towards the ambulance. He is gesticulating slowly, like he doesn't think it is possible for anyone in the world to understand him now that there has been this bomb. My heart starts to pound, like it's suddenly enlarged five times in size. The building with the smashed windows, I realise, is this building. The camera is on the Saint-Michel. What it shows on the street is what is visible from Baba's windows.

I stand up. I move closer to the screen, as if by moving closer I can look outside what is framed by the camera. The building is this building. I've lived here for two years. There's no question about it. We're in danger here. I call for Annette. No answer. She must have left for the next room. I rush out of my door and run across the corridor towards Baba's room. I pass Sammy Aboud's door and I imagine that Sammy and whoever the other people in his suite today might be are covered in soot like the person outside in the television footage, lacerated by glass from blown-in windows, on the floor dragging themselves towards the doors, a bloodied hand reaching up towards the handle. I try to stop this line of imagining. We're too high up. The blast won't have reached us. My room isn't damaged.

I crash into Baba's door. I won't call for him. That will increase the panic. I crash into his door a second time. I put my ear to the door and listen. There is no noise inside. Then I remember that he isn't there. He was going to swim on the roof. I run directly to the stairs. What a rational decision to take the stairs rather than the lift. Even if it were working, it would be foolish to use it. I climb the stairs quickly to the roof. I haven't thought ahead to what I will do when I get there. But I want to be with Baba.

When I come out into the open air, it seems oddly quiet considering there is the aftermath of a catastrophe downstairs. I want to hear a helicopter overhead, watch the crew throwing down a rope ladder for us. I panic when I see that there are people still in the pool. It will take too long to get them out if the building starts to fall. Where is Baba? I look for him among the bobbing heads in the pool. He isn't there. I find him in the solarium, sitting at a table on his own with two glasses of water in front of him. A doctor told him years ago to drink lots of water after swimming. Baba hates to drink water but he does it as instructed. He sees me approach. 'Too late,' he says, 'I've already been in the pool. We can't practise our synchronised swimming routine.' I move my hands in front of me as if to clear away anything other than what I want to say.

'Didn't you hear it?' I ask him. He raises an eyebrow and peers at me with a narrowed gaze, like he's trying to remember if this is one of the jokes we do. 'There's no television up here?' I ask. He points to a television. It's showing something else, sports.

'They should all have it on,' I mutter quietly. I find another television and it's also showing sports. For the first time since I was downstairs in my room I review what I saw on my television screen.

29

This is a city where bombs go off, in the city centre, in the hills, by remote control, strapped to individuals. A bomb, it must have been a bomb.

'New sleeping pills?' remarks Baba. He asks me the question then stares at the first of the two glasses of water on the table in front of him. It's as if he wants to send it skidding from the table by the force of his stare. He picks it up and drinks it empty in one shot.

'I don't take sleeping pills,' I reply dumbly. Actually it's not true. I take sleeping pills several times a week. I have done since I was fifteen, when I first discovered them in my mother's bathroom cabinet.

'Annette thinks that you can be an odd person sometimes,' says Baba. He is staring at the second glass of water now. 'But Annette is odd as well,' he adds, glancing up at me. 'I ought to speak to an independent source.' I look again at the two television screens close by. They still haven't switched to the scene that I saw on the television in my room. I start to think it over again. Hariri, the Lebanese prime minister, was assassinated in a bombing close to this hotel. It happened before we got here. I've read about it. The United Nations set up a tribunal to find out who killed him. Hariri had helped to agree the peace that ended the civil wars. After that bomb, the Saint-Michel was a wreck, rumours flew and protests built and a change came on in this country. It was called the Cedar Revolution. By contrast this is a normal day in the hotel. There are people in the pool. Waiters are juicing fruit behind the bar. I watch Baba drink the second glass of water. Then I realise. What I was looking at were pictures of 14 February. The television was replaying pictures of that day. I should have recognised them but perhaps the photograph I saw earlier has jolted me into a state where I see danger everywhere.

'Stay for a glass of water,' says Baba. 'It's the finest.' I shake my head and leave him.

As I go down the stairs back to the seventh floor, I see the photograph in my mind again. I look at the head. I look at the hair. I look at the eyes. I don't introduce Baba into the image this time, I leave it as it is. Why is it only the head that is in the photograph? Is it possible that the photograph is not a document, it's a threat? This is why I felt afraid for Baba when I saw the images on the television, this is why I made my stupid mistake. The photograph came to Baba in an email from an anonymous sender. Baba might know the man who was killed and the sender might be the killer. He might want Baba to know that he can reach into Baba's network and enact violence. And, more than that, that he can do it in a garden where Baba goes to relax, where he has eaten lunch, where he has snoozed in the afternoon.

I open my door and go to the table by the television. The laptop is still there. The not-bomb coverage is over. I switch off the television and regard the laptop. I call out to Annette. I walk between all of the rooms. She has gone. She won't be back again today. I pick up the laptop and then I put it down. Which apparition is true? Is Baba the solemn and cruel Mughal king or is he the prey?

CHAPTER 3

I have an appointment with Baba for afternoon tea. It is the ritual of the days on which the carpet is changed. I have tea with him in the hotel lounge and then he takes me upstairs to his suite to show me the new carpet. I'm early, even though I took a shower before coming down, even though I paused to refill the coffee tin that I keep in the fridge, even though I walked, rather than taking the lift. I hid the laptop before leaving my room. I slid it into a shoe bag, then I lifted the lid of the cabinet that conceals the flush tank in my bathroom and put the bag on top of the tank. I used to hide my passport in the same place when we first moved here. I stopped doing that after we were found. The men with badges were the first to arrive, sent by their governments to persuade Baba to answer their questions. There was no chance that Baba would do that, not unless they came with an arrest warrant for a criminal offence, and they didn't have that, but they came anyway. The British were the most persistent. They stayed for three weeks. They took a room in the hotel. They put on their suits and came and knocked on Baba's door every morning. Every time Baba left his room, they followed him. When he asked a porter to go and fetch him something, they followed the porter too. They sat, a block of four of them, on the table next to me whenever I was in the hotel restaurant. They hustled me into a corner of the lift, made me push past them to get out at my floor. But I followed Baba's lead and said nothing to them. One evening, they turned up at dinner with pornographic magazines. They told me that the pictures in the magazines were of Asian girls. They nudged each other every few minutes and said 'Great tits' or 'I would fuck that arse until it was sore.' Next came the journalists. They had different objectives. They recited unbelievable stories at us and waited for reactions. I remember one of them told Baba that he had been linked to terrorist attacks in Mumbai. Another suggested to me that I had organised orgies for Baba and my uncles. We didn't falter, Baba and I; despite the provocations, we never said a word to them. In the end, each one of them had to settle for a few snatched photographs and that was it. There's a particularly choice one of me, which made it as far as the front page of the *New York Times* weekend magazine: I'm holding a champagne flute and laughing. The headline was something like 'Incognito In Style', and the write-up featured me and an heiress based in the Maldives whose father had sold arms to African warlords. The writer had found the boutique in the

Gemmayze district where I go every few weeks. I don't like shopping, that experience of putting myself together in public view, yet I feel that I need to dress to a standard for Baba, for the hotel, for the boat club, for the places where we have dinner, so I go out every few weeks and buy a dozen pieces at a time, always from the same boutique. The owner hadn't said anything but one of the sales-girls blabbed and the article contained a page of photos of dresses that I had bought.

That article was the only one to focus on me. There have been many more about Baba. In the same style as the *New York Times* magazine piece about me, there was a big profile of Baba in *Vanity Fair* four or five months after we moved here. Their correspondent wrote about what wines Baba drank at dinner, the fine shoes he wore, the price of his watch. He loved the fact that Baba was a liberal Shia Muslim, that he lived in a hotel suite, that the staff revered him, that he had once been rude to the US Treasury Secretary in front of television cameras, that his chairman, Sherpao, the founder of the bank, the man who discovered Baba, left the bank because he couldn't stand Baba's behaviour any more. In his eyes, Baba was brilliant, rich, impetuous and arrogant. And IBCD was a subaltern riot. Together they gave him a great article to write. Uncle Terry suffered in a similar way with the press. He didn't run when the bank fell over. He couldn't run. He was a former Bank of England official, ex-government too, a professor.

Where could he run to? He was fired from his academic positions and banned from working in finance. He was put on television in front of a parliamentary committee and told everything that he had done wrong. The newspapers printed stories about how much money he has and photographs of his son with prostitutes. Eventually it stopped. The media got bored with him.

With Baba it goes on and on. Every time a new piece of the wreckage of IBCD is found, his name is there etched upon it and a new run of articles begins. As many are enthralled by his achievements as are outraged by them. There was an article a few weeks ago about a set of commodities transactions Baba authorised his traders to run in 2002, picking up and then dumping within days very large quantities of eight different commodities in five different countries. The article alleged that Baba wanted to create instability in the market and change the behaviour of the farmers, who were also clients of the bank, primarily to make them sell their produce en masse and pay back their loans from the bank. 'It was manipulation,' I told Baba after I read the article. 'The article doesn't use that word,' he replied. 'What do you call it?' I asked him. 'Okay,' he said, 'we were forcing farmers to make decisions, but the right decisions.' The article quoted an expert from a think-tank who took the same view. The bank's aggressive trades, the expert said, highlighted a price risk that existed whether those specific trades had happened or not and it encouraged farmers not to hold that risk any more.

This is what has changed in Baba's life. For years he made these large, laden choices every day that won or lost massive sums of money for the bank, that affected the lives of thousands. Now he reads other people arguing about his past choices. And the choices he has left are small ones, like the colour of carpet in his room. He tried to stay on some of his other turf, when we first came here. He bought Shia Islamic objects from antique dealers: manuscripts, prayer beads, incense holders. His house in London had been full of these. But word spread among the Beiruti dealers as to who he was and they began to shift up the prices they quoted him. Baba collected art as well in London. But he told me a few weeks after we arrived, after he had met government ministers over dinner, when he was sure that we were safe, that he was going to leave me to discover and know and support the art scene. It was like an old-fashioned colonial conference when he spoke to me, a dividing up of the city between us; art was his gift to me.

I haven't done that much with it. I used to go a lot to a gallery in a warehouse by the port. I became sort of friendly with the owner and she asked me to give a talk on Pakistani art to her staff. I still felt good at talking about art in the months after we arrived here. My knowledge was current. I had done well with my little business in dealing art in London, and before then in university, though only in the theory classes; I had never made a piece of art that was worth keeping in any of my studio classes. Alain, my former boyfriend, used to tell me that I was a Shia critic-mystic from early on. The Shia faith tends to place the interpreter above the creator – Muhammad, the messenger, above Allah, Muhammad's successors above even him. I was the newest manifestation of this tradition, Alain said, naturally more gifted as an interpreter of art, than as a maker of it. In any case, it was uncontroversial, I thought, to argue in my talk to the Beirut art-gallery staff that a gallery is part of the critical apparatus of art, that a gallery has responsibilities. My university friend Pen and I used to talk about this a lot. Pen is very clever, much cleverer than me. She has dense blonde curly hair, it's almost white in fact, and she moves her hands so much when she's talking about art that it's as if she is recreating the inner system of the piece in thin air as she goes. We haven't been in touch since I left London. I think of her more than most people. I look her up on the internet from time to time. She runs her own gallery now.

Anyway, the challenges I described to the team at the Beirut gallery were the same ones that I have heard Pen talk about and that I have talked to artists and critics about in Pakistan: presenting a world different from the established western world, with its authenticity intact, but without the carnivalesque spirit of the new or the oriental; creating a true account, but not a folkloric one; and, crucially, from the artist's point of view, finding the language to eke out a personal truth aside from the political one, imbuing the practice of art with character as well as geography. None of it was startling stuff. I didn't make it up on my own. Nevertheless, the effect of my talk was that the gallery didn't have another show for a year while the owner travelled to galleries in other countries and revisited all of her artists, seeking now to express her responsibilities. Baba teased me a lot for that: my annihilating debut in the Beirut art scene, he called it.

I haven't regained the will to reinvolve myself with this city since then. My life is Baba and the hotel, the hotel and Baba, super-routine. We watch television together. We eat meals together. After lunch, often he reads lying on the couch in his room and falls asleep. I sit in the rocking chair that he doesn't like by the window and listen to music on headphones and go through art magazines. Sometimes he gives me a list of books and journals to order for him from internet sites and I do it while he sleeps. All I have ever seen him do on a laptop is to read the news and check market prices. Though he doesn't even invest any more. His money is handled by other people. It has to be. He would lose it if the regulators found his marks on it.

Now I wonder if this second laptop is not solely

a repository of a forbidden photograph but the wider means by which he has cheated on me and kept in touch with Yani and Terry, my 'uncles' as I used to call them, and his previous life. I remember in Damascus, after Baba visited Husain's shrine, we travelled to the building that had housed the sole Syrian branch of IBCD. He asked me to go inside to look at it before him. 'If it's too sad,' he said, 'come out and get into the car. Don't say anything.' IBCD had owned the entire building. Since its fall the upper floors had become flats and the ground floor had become the salesroom of an upmarket maker of traditional Syrian sweets. When I walked in, I saw there were orders ready for collection on shelves behind one counter in large white plastic bags with slips of paper hanging off them on sticky tape bearing Arabic writing in blue biro. All the staff were men wearing khaki shirts with no pockets and brown trousers with black belts. I tried hard that day to see as Baba would see, as a boss of men would see. But when I think about the secret photograph and the laptop with the hidden uses, it seems silly to have attempted to be Baba's eyes. Doubtless I have my uses. But I am not intrinsic to how Baba perceives the world.

Baba must have noticed by now that the laptop has gone. He must be wondering who has taken it. We have a mild suspicion that the boys from the carpeting firm stole a pair of Baba's shoes the first time they came. But Baba thought it was possible he had left them on the boat. Probably now he thinks that the boys have taken his laptop, he is remembering the issue of the shoes. Or he knows that I go to his room to check that his possessions are out of sight on the day that the carpeting firm comes. So he realises that I have the laptop. He is wondering if I will open it. I bet on him to believe that I won't look at anything at all. He's that proud of me, the banker's daughter. He has never asked me what I know about IBCD, whether I have ever mentioned any of the inner facts I possess to anyone else. He has never considered me a weakness in the armour he wears to protect himself from even the thought of everything that might be done to him. Am I changing? In these last few hours, have I started to change? I feel like I've been tying knots in a length of string sitting on the floor inside a small room for two years and now the string has been yanked away from me and the walls have vanished, the floor is starting to slope and I won't hold on to my place for much longer.

I remember a different time that I was close to secrets. I was twelve and Baba took me and my mother with him to a gathering of senior IBCD people chaired by Sherpao himself. It was in the Villa d'Este on Lake Como. The purpose of the gathering was to make a decision about the future of IBCD. Sherpao had started the bank with money from a small number of Arab investors. He was not certain when he pitched the idea of the bank to them that a new bank like his could make money; but he was certain about the wider mission of such a bank. Every week Sherpao wrote a circular to all bank employees, even when they were all within hailing distance, enclosed in the first small rooms he rented in the City of London. The circulars carried in digest form on the last page a summary of major transactions and new hires. The larger portion of their content was a letter from Sherpao. 'Our mission,' he wrote in one of many such missives, 'is to alter the circulation of money to the benefit of our clients and, beyond that, to alter the means by which money circulates to the benefit of the towns that we have come from and the legend of the ancestors that we remember in our prayers.' Or, as another letter put it, 'We don't make high fives when a deal is struck, not in this bank, we don't raise our hands in victory because we keep in mind all the grasping hands that we don't see.'

By the time of the Como meeting, IBCD had a dilemma. Contrary to Sherpao's early doubts, it was making a lot of money. The bank was a success and the original investors wanted to inject more capital. Others wanted in as well, many more powerful individuals from the Arab world. Yet, if this new money came in, then the returns for the investors would have to keep growing, and the alternative mission that was the prime mission as far as Sherpao was concerned could no longer be accorded the same importance. If

IBCD took more money, it would have to make more money too. If it didn't take the money, then the future was uncertain. That was the choice. And Sherpao came to Como to ask IBCD what it wanted to do.

I had breakfast with Sherpao while we were at Como. I woke early, unusually for that time, and came out on the patio by the water. Sherpao was already there. He saw me and called me over to join him. I didn't expect anyone else to be around given how late my parents had returned after what was to be an extravagant evening of dinners, drinks and dancing. I was wearing a T-shirt and jogging bottoms. Sherpao was wearing a light blue suit and a crisp white shirt with red stripes. I was embarrassed to sit at his table but he stood up and smiled so broadly at me as he beckoned me over that it was impossible not to follow his instructions. There was a moment of breeze as I sat down, the air cooled by the sulky water of the lake, and it made me shiver. Sherpao asked me if I wanted his jacket. He had already half taken it off before he asked, so I let him place it over my shoulders. It felt smooth and crisp, like dried slices of mango. He asked me if I knew what the gathering was about, 'the essential purpose of our communion', he called it. I shrugged my shoulders because I was shy about saying yes.

Sherpao seemed to understand. 'Every business that I started,' he said, 'became more political than what my enjoyment wanted.' Then he told me a story that I had never heard from Baba or my uncles.

Sherpao's father had owned a small shop. When business was best, it contained four sacks, two of rice and two of flour, from which his father made sales measured using different sizes of old cooking-oil tins. Sometimes he carried sugar sold from a small plastic bucket as well, but sugar was risky because it was prone to infestation. There was soap for sale, hair oil, cigarettes, chewing gum and, during the fiercest summer days, he would buy a block of ice and sell glasses of crushed ice flavoured with syrup. The shop was in a poor part of town but a few local people had recently gone to work on oil installations and construction projects in the Gulf. With the money they could remit back to Pakistan, they wanted to build and furnish new homes. They needed someone to manage that work and to look after the homes after they were finished. Sherpao's father was trusted in the streets around the shop and soon there were a dozen homes to which he held the keys. Sherpao helped, and soon he found ways to increase the returns from what he immediately understood was a business opportunity. The houses were filling up with consumer goods bought by the Gulf-earned money. There were fridges. So Sherpao spoke to the local medical store and, for a small fee, arranged to store new medicines for them that they couldn't stock before because they didn't have refrigeration. There was an illicit side to the business as well. There were card-players who needed a place to gamble in peace, which Sherpao provided. There were couples who needed privacy that family homes and Islamic mores made it difficult to find. Sherpao helped them out, set an LP playing for them in the house where the owner had recently bought a music centre. Before long Sherpao could buy meat for the family table and toys for his younger brothers and sisters. But his business was not sustainable. There was no way of knowing when the mosque might come crashing down on him as a sponsor of immorality. And sooner or later one of the Gulfies would arrive home unexpectedly and Sherpao would be rumbled, with consequences for his family's livelihood and reputation. The business, as he had told me in the preface to his story, had become more political than he wanted. So he disposed of it.

He had known for a long time that, above the tailor's shop in the arcade next to the college, there was a brothel. Sherpao had never seen any of the girls that worked here. Nor had he seen the gangsters who were supposed to watch over them. But it seemed to him that, if he wanted a buyer for his business, then the buyer may be one of those men. He could charge clients more for the use of one of the nice beds in the houses. He could use the houses to store the cigarettes that people said were stolen by the same gang that ran the brothel. With this proposition, Sherpao walked up the stairs next to the tailor's house and got himself an appointment. Within three days, he had met the head of the local mafia, negotiated a price for copies of the keys that he held, and acquired the rights to sell alcohol procured by the same gang from under the counter in his father's store.

Sherpao told me that this long-ago decision he had made alone, without the knowledge or help of anyone else. But the decision he had come to the Villa d'Este to make, though similar in that it concerned the future of a business that he had begun, had to be made in a completely different way. As I think about it again now, it was a challenging confession for him to make to me. I was the daughter of his then chief executive. Yet he told me that he would rather make the decision about the future course of IBCD alone, without the help of any of the people he had brought all the way to an expensive hotel, including my father. When he finished his story, he went quiet for a long time and buttered a piece of toast, then covered it in marmalade. He offered it to me and I shook my head. He ate slowly. While he did, I told him that my parents had fallen out recently but that last night from listening to their voices with each other it had felt like they were getting close again. Perhaps I told him this to impress him that I knew about such things, that he had been right not to think of me as a child and to tell me what he had. I don't know. Perhaps I told him just because it was on my mind and we were on a patio by a lake with no one else around and he was kindly and it felt fine to tell him. Anyway, he listened and he didn't comment on my story, just as I hadn't commented on his.

I spent the rest of that day in a wonderful mood, thinking about Sherpao as a boy, thinking about how I would rise early the next morning as well and have breakfast with him again. There was no one else my age on the bank trip with us. Ghalib had been due to come with his father. Then Yani discovered that he had been in a fight at his boarding school with a younger boy, he had hurt that boy and taunted him in the days after he hurt him. Yani had grounded Ghalib for three months. That evening my mother fell as she was coming down the large central staircase to drinks before dinner. The sun had not set by that point in the afternoon, but it was receding. The hall had become dull. Some of the lights were on, not others; in that gloaming, she lost her footing, just in front of me. I watched her fall, down a full flight of stairs. She banged her head, though not badly; the serious damage was to her right hand, which was caught underneath her body as she slid. I remember the hand, as she lay at the bottom of the stairs, flopped over to one side, and her looking on, appalled but calm, as if her own hand was a giant bug inside a glass case. My father and I went in the car with her to the hospital to have the wrist set in plaster. I said to my father, as we were waiting in the corridor outside the doctor's room, that I could look after my mother, he ought to go back and participate in the discussions at the hotel. He looked at me with surprise for a moment, then he touched my hair and told me not to worry about that.

We went back to the hotel in the early hours of the morning. I fell asleep in the car and was carried up to my room. I didn't wake on the next day until noon. It was one of the last days and, in the end, I didn't have a second breakfast with Sherpao. He ate alone I imagine every morning and the decision about the future of IBCD was indeed made, while I kept my mother company. IBCD decided, in that villa by the lake, that profit wasn't its only motive, it must keep doing the other work for what Sherpao had described in his circular as 'the towns where they had come from' and that therefore they must refuse the new money and the new business plan that would have to come with it. Even Uncle Terry argued it that way, though he was teased for it by my father, that he was doing the bidding of his sentimental Pakistani wife when he ought to be using the cool clear logic of his Bank of England upbringing. In any case IBCD remained special, not like the other banks, and that created another spike upwards in the ambitions of my father and my uncles. After Como, they didn't have any other doubts, at least not until the very end when the bank started to break. They did exactly what they themselves thought was right, and they never were shaken from it. And still it seems that is how they are, even though, just as much as the decision made at Como allowed the bank to continue to be the bank that Sherpao, Baba and the others had wanted, it was the decision that eventually led to the fall as well. The Arab investors they turned down by the lake came back to hunt IBCD a few years later. And Sherpao himself, he did as he had suggested he might when he spoke to me at breakfast: he left. Sherpao stopped having a daily role in the bank just a few months later; Baba became the true true boss, everything started with him, everything led back to him.

The waiter lays out the tea service while I ask him questions about his family. His son teaches him English. He practises with me. When he has finished, he leaves and I realise that I'm disappointed that we couldn't talk for longer. Everyone other than me has work to do. I'm not even the client, that's Baba. I look up and don't see him yet. I imagine him briefly in my suite, searching for his laptop. He will come down here, I think, and ask me to return it. He always starts by asking me something. He's used to asking me, and I'm used to doing what he asks. I don't know yet what I'm going to say to him when the confrontation occurs. I had the same feeling after my mother died and Baba had to be led away from the mosque by Uncle Yani because he wanted to wash my mother's body himself rather than leave the women to do it. 'She belongs to me,' he shouted, 'not to your cult of women.' I was scared to speak to Baba afterwards. I had touched his wife's body after him, ended his pre-eminence in all things to do with her. 'You should have left with me,' he told me in front of the guests at the funeral reception. Then he pulled me close to him and whispered hoarsely in my ear: 'Never tell me about it.'

I am remembering that whisper when he kisses my cheek and sits down next to me. He was delivering a threat when he spoke to me like that. How often does he do that? 'I ordered Earl Grey,' I tell him.

'You know?' he says. 'I haven't tasted any other tea since 1986.'

'What else have you not done since 1986?'

'I haven't mowed a lawn since 1986,' he replies.

'I don't believe you've ever mowed a lawn.' He lifts his eyebrows, like he is about to tell me a story about those earlier days, those days before my memory begins. Instead he pours himself a cup of tea.

'I invited Ghalib along,' he says. 'He's only here until tonight. I feel he's lonely whenever he's not pitching. He lives for pitching deals. If you haven't ordered, you should wait until he gets here and ask him to pitch you a tea from the menu. Do you want tea?' I shake my head. I pick up a magazine and read the titles of the articles from the contents page.

'Dull,' remarks Baba. 'I looked at it this morning.'

'Can I take a different view?' I ask him.

50

He laughs. 'You have your own mind,' he says.

'Well, perhaps not so much,' I say. 'You're here. And I'm here. We're in this mindless suspension together.'

He sits in silence with me while I turn pages. Eventually I throw the magazine onto the table. 'Is it Rami's garden?' I ask him. He makes a rasping noise through his closed lips.

'I should assume,' he says after a pause, 'we're talking about an item that you've seen on my computer.'

'In fact it is Rami's garden,' I tell him. 'I know it is.'

'Rami has nothing to do with it,' he says.

'Decapitation,' I remark, 'isn't to everyone's taste I suppose.' Baba shrugs his shoulders. 'No,' I tell him, 'no, don't shrug your shoulders. Speak.'

'I'm not discussing it, Hanna,' he says. 'You are not to become involved in this.'

'Well obviously,' I reply. 'This is serious. Why would I be involved in something that is serious?'

'Stop it,' he says. 'We're not going to pursue it.'

'I haven't pursued anything since 1983, Baba. That's when I was born. Don't you want me to pursue this? It would be good for me.' He looks at me for a long moment.

'You're right,' he says. 'This *is* serious. Let's talk about it in private.'

'Baba,' I say to him plainly. 'I want to know what's going on.'

'Let's drink our tea,' he says.

'I don't have any tea,' I reply. 'Baba,' I add, more gently, 'you can't keep me out of this.'

'Can't keep you out of what?' says a man's voice close to me. I look to my right and Ghalib is standing behind me, looking at Baba. He is holding a wheel in his hands. I panic briefly, and scan the conversation I've just had with Baba. What did Ghalib learn by overhearing it? Baba wasn't saying much. Then hopefully I wonder if Baba was stalling because he saw Ghalib on the approach.

'Why are you holding a bicycle wheel?' says Baba. Ghalib glances at the wheel in his hands, like he had forgotten he was holding it.

'I was taking a walk through the hotel,' says Ghalib, 'and there are some fucking weird things on the walls. There always are in hotels. But a bicycle wheel is pretty special. I've never seen a bicycle wheel on a hotel wall before. Have you noticed this before?' he asks, spinning the wheel and then dropping it onto the sofa, next to me.

'Take it back,' I tell him.

'That's the other thing,' says Ghalib. 'I took it. Like, easily. It wasn't particularly secured to the wall. And over there,' he says, pointing to the wall next to the reception desk, 'there's a sword. I could pull that off the wall as well. And would they say anything? I don't think they will. I don't think they will say anything if I take that sword off the wall as well.'

'It's a five star hotel,' says Baba. 'They don't stop you from doing anything. That's the point.' He reaches forward, takes a sugar cube from the tea service and throws it at Ghalib. 'You have to stop yourself. I could throw these sugar cubes at you one by one, and when the bowl is empty, they will bring me another one so that I can keep doing it.'

'Do you think so?' says Ghalib. 'Keep going. Let's find out.' He vaults over the back of the sofa and lands next to me. He fishes out the bicycle wheel from behind him and places it on the table.

'Take back the wheel,' I tell him again.

'They'll come and get it,' he says. 'We're fighting sugar cubes here. I have to stay.' With a huge grin, Baba picks up another sugar cube and throws it at Ghalib. It strikes him on his raised right arm. 'What can't he keep you out of?' Ghalib asks again.

Baba shakes his head. 'Tell me,' he says. 'Why are you buying equity in the company you told us about last night? From what you said, they need a two-year loan. Get them a loan and take a banker's fee now. Why do you want to wait two years for your money?'

'We like equity stakes,' says Ghalib. 'It gives us something to do. There's board meetings and strategy sessions.'

'So you don't trust the chief executive?' says Baba. 'What an excellent basis for investment.'

'Whatever,' says Ghalib. 'We're a private equity fund. Equity is what we do. We're not a bank.'

'No,' says Baba, 'but I thought the general plan was to make money. You could make sure you make money, whatever you want to call yourself.'

'Do you want a strategy session?' says Ghalib. 'Shall I get my partners and my father on a conference call?'

'Did you get your father's advice on this?' asks Baba.

'Of course I fucking didn't,' replies Ghalib. 'As far as I remember,' he continues, pointing at Baba, 'I didn't ask for your advice either.'

'He's changing the subject,' I tell Ghalib, standing up, pointing at Baba too. 'He doesn't really care if you buy equity or not.' I wonder if there's anything I could do at this point that would make Baba come after me. I could throw something at him, pull my shoes off and chew on them.

'Hanna, you have to return the laptop,' he says.

I shake my head and walk away. I glance at the sword by the reception desk and think about pulling it off the wall myself, while Baba and Ghalib are still watching me. Then I imagine holding it and I think immediately of the photograph, whether it was a sword that produced its subject. I feel a sudden sharp dart of nausea. I cover my mouth and walk to the stairs. When I reach the stairs, I stop. I don't want to be in my room. I don't want to be by the swimming pool. I want to leave here, to leave the hotel. I walk back, past the reception desk again, shaking my head when I see the sword. I succeed in not looking over to the area where Baba and Ghalib are sitting. I walk out of the doors of the hotel, into the street that I thought just a few hours ago had been bombed. The doorman nods at me and I wave for a taxi, the driver of which will speak in Arabic to me, because they always do, and I will explain, as I always do, that I don't speak Arabic. I'll ask him in English to go to a boutique or a café. They're not adequate destinations, but I hardly know any place else in this city. Baba has turned me into a more limited creature than I was. And yet I was happy with my options until today. Or I had lost track of happiness. I was just here, that's all, in Beirut, because that's where I had to be, that's where we had to be.

CHAPTER 4

The roads in Beirut aren't straight. There are multiple gravities in this city that pull them one way then the other. Sometimes they stop abruptly, as if going further would expose a secret. Their sides are broken into by shops, restaurants, other roads entering on unlikely vectors. I lose places of interest in Beirut all the time. I think I know where they are, then the road does something surprising and my geography is cast into disarray. The only route I can drive adamantly myself in this city leads out of it: it's the highway that I take into the hills to go and look at the long flat valley on the other side. And I've hardly used it, perhaps three times in total I've driven more than half an hour out of Beirut. The first time there was a mist up on that road and, while I was caught in it, it was the perfect opposite of looking at the sea, which is what I must do from my hotel room every day. I stared into the lights of the car in front of me and I felt calm. I suppose it was because my immediate destiny was settled in those moments: to follow the car in front of me, that's all I could do. When the sky is clear up there though, the hills are as full of secrets as the city, roads leading off in untold directions, half-filled villages with shuttered windows and cloth posters of men in gabardine suits, half-completed buildings with metal rods sticking out of the tops of concrete pillars. Each time, as I've been returning, I've struggled to find our hotel. Instead I find houses where there didn't seem to be any, Porsches shooting suddenly out of their driveways; I find apartment buildings with unlit lobbies and shining tops. Once I ended up in the area by the sea called the Quarantine. There were rows of warehouses, each bearing a large sign, yet I couldn't see any of the entrances or entranceways. I was afraid that I would suddenly come across a posse of armed guards. I parked and called the hotel to send a car to find me. I played the radio until it came to stop myself from feeling afraid.

While the taxi takes me to the boutique I can imagine that Baba and Ghalib are still talking over tea, the same way they were last night over dinner, Baba asking questions about business, Ghalib eliding the details he doesn't want to provide, trying instead to persuade Baba to tell stories about old deals, mention people that Ghalib might want to meet. A lot of times stuff happens within networks. In fact there's a network in action in the institution of the fund itself. Ghalib started it with my cousin Mudassar and my former boyfriend Alain about four or five years ago. They called it GMA, a simple collation of their initials.

Mudassar and Alain were at the same university as me. They were both reading business administration, while I was studying art. I had been set on going there for a long time and I think Mudassar opted for it because he couldn't be bothered finding out about the alternatives. It was London and that was good enough. It was Mudassar who introduced me to Alain. Ghalib was in the US but he came to visit me in London and through me he got to know the other two. I think I attached myself to Alain because he gave me the most to do. Despite being brought up in Paris, he knew nothing about art when we met and it was a task for me to teach him. At the same time, he had a conceptually romantic view of business. He talked about demand curves and supply chains and value propositions, not deals, not trades. He would give me mini economics lessons and I would tell him, drawing on conversations I had heard Baba and my uncles have, about the filthy insides of the companies he idealised. It sounds transactional, but then I've never had that lightning-bolt hit from a man that loosens the emotions. Nevertheless, I did stay with Alain for the whole of my first year in university. I used him for as long as that – to experiment with intimacy and to have a sort of base camp for the nights and weekends while I tried to figure out a way to function in the art set. And I guess he used me too, not least for the insight I gave him into Baba and my uncles and their bank. When I dumped him he didn't even seem that sad.

I ended it because of how he had changed. I realised that, by that point, he talked as casually about business and money as the other men I knew, and he had acquired a *commerçant*'s interest in art. He talked of falling and rising prices, percentage returns on investment. That type of interest in art was worse to me than no interest at all. I stopped seeing him, yet I know that the change in him was my own fault as well. I helped to bind him to the men that he chose to imitate.

The trio of Alain, Mudassar and Ghalib was a strong one as soon as it formed. Even when I stopped seeing Alain, it continued with no negative effect. Still I was surprised when he joined up with the other two in forming the fund. Yes, he had become their friend, but his family wasn't wealthy and I imagined he would take a safe job in a safe bank somewhere when he graduated. The money for their fund came mostly from Yani, who had to kick in I suppose to support Ghalib, his son. Mudassar's dad, Bilal, put in a little as well, overriding Habib's concerns on this occasion. They didn't ask me for money when they started up. Baba gave me my own money to manage when I started university at eighteen. I must have spoken to Alain a lot during our year together about the money; I was proud of this independence that Baba had given me. Though I've done nothing with it of course. I didn't invest it with Alain and the others or anywhere else. It stays in the same bank where Baba put it. Actually, thinking of G, M and A, I think none of them had the guts to ask me after the response they got from Baba himself. Baba turned them down and he was quite fierce with them when he said no. They were using money from their families, or at least two of them were, but Baba believes you need to start from the mud, like he did, or you never make anything that is worth having.

Baba says he had nothing when he came to London. He left Pakistan shortly after his father died in an accident at the cement factory where he worked. He had no idea what he would do when he arrived in London, but he had ambition all the same. He had shiny black hair that looks like it's daubed on with paint in old photographs. My mother used to have one or two of those photographs. They disappeared after she died, presumably into Baba's possession. He wore white shirts buttoned to the collar. While he looked for work, he stayed with his older brother who had made the move westwards several years previously.

Baba met Sherpao at a mosque on a Friday, though neither of them was there to pray. Baba had been in the UK for almost four months by then and he didn't have a job. In order to earn some money, he had started doing accounts and tax returns for a few Pakistanis who had their own businesses. There was a desk in the office at the mosque and a printing calculator, and they were mostly spare on a Friday. So Baba went to the mosque a couple of hours before Friday prayer each week and crunched through the work. Sherpao had come in to talk to the imam about the mortgage on the mosque. There was some trouble with it and Sherpao planned to fix it by buying the building and letting the mosque use the ground floor for no charge. Baba remembers that Sherpao was sitting in the office when he arrived, dressed in a brown suit, brown shoes of the exact same shade, white shirt, a red bowtie, and long hair pulled back to a tail. Legs crossed, he was holding a pencil in one hand and writing in the air. He continued after Baba came in; didn't nod to him, or say anything. Baba took his cue from this and, without a word, sat down, set out his papers. Baba says they spent ten minutes like this, Sherpao writing in the air, Baba tapping numbers. (When I was twelve, Sherpao told me the same story at an IBCD Eid dinner in front of my parents and, as he had it, the mutual engross-ment was thirty minutes long, Baba getting a great noise out of the calculator and Sherpao drafting what became a clause in a contract for the financing of an oilfield purchase by the Sultan of Qatar.)

Their reveries were broken by the entry of the imam. The imam shook Sherpao's hand and sat down in an armchair by the window to receive the banker's largesse. It was only when he was interrupted in this way that Sherpao seemed to notice my father. Without yet speaking to the imam, Sherpao stood up and looked over Baba's shoulder at the work he had been doing. Baba didn't know that Sherpao was standing over him and continued working until he reached the end of a calculation. Then he looked up.

'You've stopped,' said Sherpao. 'What will you do now?'

'I'm going to check the numbers,' said Baba.

'They're correct,' said Sherpao.

'I'd prefer to check,' said Baba. He picked up the stack of papers he had been working through and began to make the same calculation again.

I don't know if the imam ever got the deal for the mosque. What both Sherpao and Baba have told me is that Sherpao waited until my father had run through the calculation a second time, then took him for lunch and offered him a job. IBCD was brand new then. Baba was employee number sixteen. He turned up for work at a rented floor in a scruffy building on Threadneedle Street that was then IBCD's world headquarters (Needlepoint, Sherpao used to call it). There were two armchairs directly opposite the lifts where he came out, providing a reception area, skirted by a narrow corridor leading to the offices. There was no name in lights, no art in those original offices. Between the armchairs there were three palms in pots; presumably they were all fresh and green when they were brought in but they didn't stay that way, they wilted and dried and they were never changed. They were moved into the toilets on Fridays, to clear the area for Friday prayer, as it was the only space in the offices large enough for the staff to pray together along with the Muslim staff from other banks close by who had been invited, each and every one by Sherpao himself, to join in. Even in that humble beginning office, Sherpao wanted IBCD to lead.

Three of the rooms in that original set-up were filled with desks, laid out as if for a game of dominoes, covered with stacks of papers. Each room contained a safe, tall as a man, the most imposing piece of furniture by far, but the ramshackle-ness of the early operation was such that the safes weren't closed on timers and there were evenings when people would forget to lock them. IBCD could have been robbed very simply in those days but few people knew that those rooms in a crummy building contained a bank. Needlepoint was threadbare, Uncle Yani used to joke.

When Baba turned up at Needlepoint on that first day, no one knew what he was supposed to do, not even the man who had been told that Baba was going to work for him. But that didn't bother Baba. He was toured around the offices and all the other men said salaam. He was told that the fourth room, the conference room as it was called, was the space the boss, when he was around, used as his base. So, as soon as he was left to his own devices, Baba took an empty desk and dragged it out into the corridor and put it outside the conference room. Next he took the door off the store cupboard that was next to the conference room and, with the help of a couple of other men, who obviously assumed that he was acting on instructions from Sherpao, cleared out an entire safe, moved it into the cupboard, then sat down behind the adjacent desk.

When Sherpao came in the next day and saw the new arrangements, he was delighted. He had found in Baba a personality as forceful as his own. He went to the threshold of each of the three rooms with desks, with Baba at his side, and declared: 'Gents, this man with me, Mateen, will be my eyes, my ears and my right hand.' It's a statement that Sherpao recalled to a lot of people while he was the chairman of the bank. It suited him. He liked it to be known that he had excellent instincts and total confidence in acting on them. As for Baba, by what he did that first day, he made sure that he had a special place in the bank. And he seemed to decide at the same time that there was to be no connection between what he had been before and what he wanted to be. I've never met Baba's mother or his brother or anyone else from his family. When I ask him about his childhood, he says he doesn't remember anything. Baba eradicated the past when he walked into IBCD and up-rated the present, began already as a clerk to live like a successful and long-established financier. The future was all that there could be. And I was born into this new world that he had made.

When Sherpao left the bank, Baba had even more space for his new world. Sherpao left because, as he told Yani one night, 'the right hand has become a right fist.' My father's style was clashing with Sherpao's own. They shared the same ideals for the bank, to be more than a bank, to be a developer of businesses and nations. But Sherpao wanted to do it gently, to convince the wider world of the virtues and achievements of the bank almost by stealth, to grow gradually, organically. I think this is what made him nervous at Como, that it was too big a decision all at once, and it was made by everyone and with so much confidence. Baba loved that of course, to have such clarity and no dissent. So he charged ahead and he manoeuvred and bullied and preened. When the Nigerian government was deciding whether to take financing from IBCD or the World Bank, Baba gave a press conference to explain the differences between the two offers. He took the World Bank's own criteria for financial assistance and argued that the IBCD offer was better on every one. When one of the world's biggest mining companies made a takeover bid for an expanding Indian firm, Baba called the largest shareholders of the bidding company and a couple of newspaper editors and told them that the financing plan was moronic. IBCD had nothing to do with the deal; Baba's calls were made purely to play the part of the prodigal upstart. And he chose how to play that part without any reference to Sherpao. The founder didn't even get a chance to offer his counsel. After Sherpao left, strangely Baba talked to him about business more often than when he had been the chairman. It was as if all along Baba had in part been behaving like he did in order to get rid of Sherpao. He wanted him around as an adviser, no more, and that is what he achieved.

Sherpao himself thought that he would be able to choose who succeeded him. I've heard from Ghalib that Sherpao dropped a lot of hints to Yani that he might have preferred him to take over rather than Baba. But Sherpao and Yani were outflanked. Baba was typical Baba as soon as Sherpao suggested that he might move on. Before any formal process could be set in motion for appointing Sherpao's successor, Baba organised a press conference and prevailed on Sherpao's secretary to set a thirty-minute board meeting immediately before it to which he took a draft press release, including a valedictory statement from Sherpao endorsing Baba as the new and absolute leader of IBCD. No one wanted to take Baba on full frontal in the meeting and that was what he relied on. By the end of the day, websites and nameplates had all been changed. Baba had already been the chief executive and now he was the chairman of the board as well. Yani remained what he was, a vice-president for operations.

In coming to Beirut, I think Baba made a further break from the previous episodes in his life. He talks infrequently about my mother here, never about IBCD, unless it's in the news and I shove the coverage in front of him. It's as if that London

66

life has nothing to do with life today in Beirut. Sometimes I feel myself getting lost across the boundaries between the different episodes. Baba encouraged me early on when we got here to make false statements about who we were, if people asked, if I couldn't avoid saying something, if they didn't already know. Often, as I told it, we were just holidaymakers; to other questioners I said that Baba was a curator of a private collection and we were here to buy objects. I kept three or four stories going concurrently for several days at times. I had moments when I felt I was floating between the different accounts, and could awkwardly land in the wrong one, not the one that I had told previously to the person I was speaking to, or not the one I needed to inhabit myself when I was alone. This profusion of lies was supposed to provide safety, that's what Baba said, and I went along with it, but he was much more expert than me in keeping it up. I heard him give false answers to other hotel guests very easily. He never got confused between the different versions he was giving to different people. It should have struck me: if there are stories for other people, is there a story for me as well?

The taxi stops outside the boutique for which I had asked. I pay the driver and get out. I stand in front of the building, but I don't go in. I go into the bar next door to it. Within an hour I drink two long vodkas, then come outside and hail another taxi. This time I ask the driver to take me to Centrale, an old Beirut house that has been revamped into a bar and restaurant since the end of the war. For me it's the best place to have a last drink. It's always packed, so much so that moving through the crowd requires physical endurance and that makes it hard for melancholy to intrude. As soon as I get back to the hotel after Centrale, I will take a sleeping tablet and by that route pass into another day.

The taxi is slow, caught in a tide of cars. 'So many people,' I say.

'That's right,' says the taxi driver emphatically, as if I'd said just what he was about to say himself. 'Here it is like this all the time,' he says. 'It's like there is a party and every person in the city is invited.' I watch the cars while he speaks. I see a driver talk on a mobile phone, downloading her missions for the night: get to Gemmayze, the strip where all the hippest bars are at; park in the last spot on the street; smoke a cigarette; shove into Dragonfly. I feel jealous for a second or two. 'Everybody goes out at night here,' he adds.

'Everybody,' I reply softly. 'Sisters, couples.' What he's describing is striking for me as well. I grew up on dinners with adults and a glass of sparkling water at drinks receptions, moving from group to group one step behind my parents. Going out in Beirut is different. The bars are the society here. Families go out to bars. Couples go out to bars.

'How long you live here?' asks the taxi driver.

'Two years,' I reply honestly.

'You are happy here?' he says.

'Happy?'

'You like it?'

'Exceptionally,' I tell him.

'Beirut is the exception to everything,' he says. I nod. He is right. Beirut is a zone of abnormality, that's why Baba and I are here, that's why royal and rich Arabs from all across the Middle East come here. I asked Baba to come to the Beirut National Museum with me last week. My question didn't compute with him easily, like I'd shown him a red piece of fruit and called it a banana. He doesn't think about Beirut as part of a nation, he thinks about it as an exception, a free zone, a sleight of hand.

Soon we stop outside Centrale. The bar area is narrow and usually crowded; it's easy not to be noticed as a singleton. It's in the attic and accessed by a lift that goes up from a corner of the dining room. As I walk past the diners I think of Baba having dinner alone tonight. For a moment I feel sorry and then I stop myself. A few hours of solitude won't damage him. He ran a bank. He escaped his pursuers. Recently it's possible he sat at a garden table while a man was killed in front of him. My absence, a disappointment before dinner, doesn't compare, I don't compare, to any of that.

In front of me, while I wait for the lift to the bar, there is a large painting of trees in lieu of a window that provides a view. I've seen the painting before, I believe, in a book or a catalogue. My memory for paintings ought to be more whole. I only remember what I like, I don't remember like a businesswoman. Uncle Yani by contrast remembers relentlessly. Even after he stopped dealing in art himself and became a banker, he retained the information, always the name of the painter, the name of the painting, the price at which it was sold, even the estimate if he had seen it pre-auction. I think about when I started dealing in art after I graduated from university, the enthusiasm that he had for what I was starting, how much he tried to teach me. To the extent that I embedded any professionalism at all in how I did it, I learned the habit from him. And I was lucky to have him. I had already discovered that I couldn't make art. Compared to someone like Pen, I felt that I wasn't smart enough to become a critic either. And it wasn't just about being smart. I couldn't draw people to gather around me when I was talking about art in the way that she could. So dealing seemed like the only option left and Yani helped me to believe that it wasn't just an insurance option, that it could be better than that for me. He gave me all his old auction catalogues. He sent me links to articles I should read. He bought me a subscription to the artnet website. Even the idea of focusing on art from Pakistan, that came from him.

A long time before that I gave Yani his name.

His real name is Ghassan, a name that, as a child, I simply couldn't say. So I latched on to the word that he used in every sentence, 'yani', which is like an Arabic version of 'you know'. After I started calling him Yani, the name caught on, to the extent that it was the name used in newspaper reports and magazine articles after IBCD collapsed. I remember there was a point when he tried to be Ghassan again. He had writing paper printed with the name Ghassan and refused to answer you if you addressed him as Yani. But it only lasted a few weeks. Baba told him to stop being such a pain. The bank's counterparties know you as Yani, he told him, that's who you have to be.

Yani met my father near the beginning. Baba had set himself up behind the desk in the corridor close to Sherpao's conference suite; Yani and his grandfather walked past that desk about nine months later. Yani's family were Iraqi Shia from Basra, though his line of the family had been out of there for some time, forced to leave due to an escalating vendetta between their family and another one. They set up far away, in Aberdeen, where a family friend had gone before them. Yani's great-grandfather was the primary emigrant, a mechanic who sought work in quarries. He was good at it and moved into management and then began to buy into neighbourhood shops in the Greater Aberdeen area. There weren't many people with foreign about them in northern Scotland at that time, so it brought the great-grandfather a lot of attention: typically the sort he had to ward off by standing tall and being willing to throw the first punch, but one sample of attention was more welcome. She was named Rose, red-haired, soft-voiced, certain that her life in that cold, wet corner of the world ought to be more interesting than that of her friends. Rose and Yani's great-grandfather were married within a year. Yani told me their story on the boat one night when he and I stayed up smoking cigarettes.

Yani's grandfather emerged in that Mesopo-Hibernian alliance, the first son, the second child. He worked Saturdays and school holidays in the shops from around the age of nine upwards. He left school at fifteen and took over one of the shops. The great-grandfather wasn't going to let that last for long. He wasn't a stand-still sort of person. He wasn't going to have a stand-still sort of family business. So he gave the grandfather a loan and told him to see what he could do with it. The grandfather bought out a fish and chip shop, smashed through to the empty unit next door, expanded, took on two or three more within the next few years. In tandem, the great and the grand built the network up to seventeen commercial premises that they ran directly, thirteen more that they leased; they took on petrol stations so that there was much more cash running through; soon they owned flats, then a hotel, then more. Keep going like that for two decades and a half and eventually you have enough money to come and speak to a discreet sort of bank about it. Helpful that it's Shia like you, helpful that it extends its hand before it asks the questions 'we are obliged to ask'. 'I can stop writing at any time, you just tell me when you need me to stop.' 'You can show me your passport if you like, but I am not required to see your passport.' Those were much wilder days in banking and that was the sort of conversation that Uncle Yani's grandfather came to London to have with Altaf Sherpao.

But Yani had different aspirations. He worked Saturdays and school holidays in the business like his grandfather and father had done. He spent a summer vacation wallpapering in a row of houses his grandfather had bought up cheaply from the council. He never gave anyone cause to say that he had strayed from the family's work ethic. However, then he came to the end of school and made a choice that none of them had made before: he went to university, he went to London. He started on a law course, practical son in a practical line of succession. He didn't immediately stray to the history of art – it took him a further six months to have the courage to make that switch and a further six before he told his paternal line about it.

Even though Yani wasn't in the business full-time, he spent a lot of time with his grandfather. Yani was the cleverest grandson, different, but not disloyal. So Yani came with his grandfather to IBCD and the grandfather on the one hand and

Sherpao on the other prodded Uncle Yani and my father towards one another, as if they were eight year olds. Go and spend some time together, they were told at the end of the meeting, we think you will get on.

They are about the same age, Baba and Uncle Yani. Uncle Terry is a good bit older, but Baba and Uncle Yani were born three months apart, in 1956. They're both Shia. Neither is religious, but being Shia matters. Shia are a minority in every Islamic country apart from Iran, in every Islamic emigrant community as well, including in Aberdeen and London. But they've always been a minority, long enough to be proud about it, proud enough to be sure about it. Close to the beginning of their friendship, Baba and Uncle Yani were both arrested one night. They were out in Wembley to eat Pakistani food. Baba had parked his car in a car park he didn't know was used to sell drugs and it happened to be under police watch that night. Baba and Uncle Yani returned to the car late on, and they were rushed by three or four police officers each. They were taken into separate cells in a police station. After a few hours of rough treatment, a higher officer came in and told each of them that the other had given way, that they had found drugs in the car and that Baba had pinned it on Yani and Yani had pinned it on Baba. Baba and Uncle Yani laughed at the man. Even though they hadn't known each other for long. Even though it was Baba's car and Uncle Yani

74

had no idea what might be in it. Even though Uncle Yani had a briefcase with him and Baba didn't know what was in that. They laughed at the man. It got Baba a smack in the mouth, Yani a blow to the stomach I think. And the way they told the story afterwards, it was always that perhaps one of them might have dealt in drugs, that wasn't the nub of the joke, the unbelievable part of it was that one of them would tell a lie about the other one to escape the consequences of the crime. Shia boys didn't live like that, Shia boys held things up on their shoulders.

Despite the bond between them Uncle Yani didn't join IBCD until later. First, he tried to deal in art in London. The modern masters scene in London is laden with high names and wild accretions of wealth. Yet Uncle Yani insisted in trying to prise off a piece of it. He set up in a small office, turned up at everything where he could get past the door, and tried to help people buy the paintings that he loved. Business was not good. Hardly anyone came to his office. He went to see paintings, took notes, went to houses from time to time to talk about his notes, and that was the limit of it for a long time. During his first six months out of college, he came closest on a Kandinsky clone for the owner of the restaurant on the same street as his office, but the vendor chucked in the deal after two weeks of dithering, decided to hold on to the painting.

The meeting he came to with his grandfather at

Needlepoint changed everything for him. At first things went well. Sherpao introduced him to a Saudi family who had bought a large flat in central London. Saudi homes are usually decorated with framed calligraphies, colourful renderings of important Quranic verses. But this family had business links in France and Germany, as well as in England, so they wanted some European art as well. Thanks to Sherpao's careless acclaim for Uncle Yani, they asked him to help them decide what to buy. It was a major opening for him. The family wanted five pieces and they had an indicative budget of five hundred thousand pounds.

The father of the family delegated most of the looking to his eldest daughter, Nayla. Uncle Yani spent about two days a week with her for two months. I remember he told me that she tied her hair in a ponytail every five minutes, drawing it out of its previous bind, using both her hands to pull it together in a tight bunch, then enclosing it in a plastic band. She smiled while she was doing it, as if to distract him from watching her hands. And she rarely smiled otherwise. She was enthusiastic though about buying art for her family, never hesitated when Uncle Yani asked her out to a gallery or a show. She was serious about her task, and game for listening to Uncle Yani describe and contextualise the paintings that they viewed together. She played her role better than Uncle Yani played his. She was his first serious client. There was a lack of daring in him about pushing on from an appreciative conversation about a piece to convincing her to buy it. He didn't want to be direct, but he didn't know the hints that he was supposed to use either. Nayla, equally inexperienced as a buyer, assumed that the transactional inertia was due to some fault on her part. So, two months later, she started bringing her younger sister, Mona, on the trips. Mona was more impetuous. Mona asked Yani to tell her the price of things. Mona, unlike her older sister, was unmarried.

With the introduction of Mona, the tempo changed. They bought five paintings in a fortnight, then went beyond the original remit, bought six, bought seven, bought eight, every one by Paul Klee, an artist that Uncle Yani, he told me once, hadn't thought much about until the sisters picked him out. This in itself was exciting for him. That advising on art didn't mean he had to be a static repository of expertise, perform as a stern arbiter of conversations about what's likeable, rather than a participant who can himself be changed by the experience, learn a new painting, admire it, love it. More obviously, the Klee flush was good for business. Rumours about their spree were shared among galleries and the auction houses. Each of the paintings stopped over in Uncle Yani's office before heading into one of the houses of the family. Some other buyers came to see him. But what was fateful in the end was Yani's introduction to Mona.

During their visits, Mona clambered over the particulars of Uncle Yani's life, quizzing him whenever they weren't in a hushed gallery. She had spent all of her childhood and adolescence in Saudi Arabia, so Yani, this former art student, more exotic than any Arab she had met before, with a pure Scottish great-grandmother, who shared a house with two women artists and a singer, she wanted his interest, access to the life he led. She came to their meetings dressed in a way that caused her no grief at home, then went to the toilets to change into a short skirt or dress, bared more of her neck. Her sister didn't do anything about it because, I think, she trusted Yani not to react, she trusted him to notice that Mona was a young girl trying to grow up, not to think badly of her for doing it in front of him, and not to be confused by her attention.

I don't know what Uncle Yani did or didn't do. No one has talked about it because of what happened next. A friend of Nayla's family saw the group of Nayla, Mona and Yani at a sale. She passed word back to Nayla's parents about what she saw. By coincidence, Nayla and Mona arrived home late that day, later than they had said, having gone shopping after they left Yani. In the same period, a business partner of the father, seeing one of the new Klee acquisitions, told the father that Klee was Jewish, something that Yani had never mentioned, even though he could have assumed that the father, like many Saudis, was hostile to Jews. Actually Klee may not have been Jewish, but the damage was done. The father felt that he had been doubly fooled, both his honour and his wallet had been got, his family and his faith, all besmirched. The father invited Yani out to Saudi to visit the family. Yani went; he was probably flattered, excited, charmed, looked forward to more business with them. He was met from the airport by two men. They took him away for a week. They took off his right hand.

Baba looked after him when he came back. Uncle Yani called Baba and Baba took him into his house. Yani's grandfather wanted to fight. It was more than the violence and the impairment that provoked him. He also saw, in the removal of his grandson's hand, the latest insult against the Shia by the fascist Sunni kingdom of the Sauds. But Yani wasn't in the same state at all. Yani disassembled his art-dealing office. He threw away his more colourful clothes. He stayed indoors. He contracted a flu that became a chest infection and then bronchitis. Throughout, Baba brought him food, forced him to take vitamins, snapped at him when he broke down crying. After three months, with Baba's encouragement, at Sherpao's insistence, Yani joined IBCD.

I order another vodka drink at the bar. I haven't been drunk since the last time that Ghalib was in Beirut. We went dancing with his client and the client's girlfriend. The girlfriend was Canadian. She had massive breasts I remember. I asked her late in the night if I could touch them. She smiled and told me 'of course'. After I had touched them, she clapped her hands and laughed. I hope I remember her for that posture of openness, not merely the size of her breasts. Though perhaps her body compelled her to show a certain kind of candour. It's like Uncle Yani. He doesn't have the choice to be discreet about his hand, and that part of his personal history. He doesn't have a hand. Everyone notices.

I walk along the bar to suggest that I'm in the midst of something, looking for my friends or leaving. I settle in a busy spot where many small groups share boundaries and no one has to claim me, each can assume that I belong to one of the others. I stand and sip my drink. I close my eyes from time to time and nod my head to the music. Otherwise I watch people and my overriding impression of them is that their choices are lighter than mine. For them this day will pass and they will never think of it again. And they are here as themselves, not as someone's child, not as a cipher to a historical event. If they are recognised, it's a pleasant thing to happen, not an encumbrance, not something that has to be managed. They will drink and then they will sleep in their own beds tonight.

I put my glass on the counter, close my eyes and listen to the music again. I think about a conversation I had with Ghalib when he was here last time about when he first found out why his father didn't have one of his hands. He was fourteen when Yani told him, too old to find out about it mildly, as Ghalib put it. His response was to join a martial arts class and buy a knife from one of the school janitors, which he carried everywhere with him for over a year, until Yani found it and cut him on the arm with it, to demonstrate to him that it was more dangerous to carry a knife than not to carry one. Ghalib showed me the scar from the cut. Yani had made him wait thirty minutes with just his hand over it before he called a private doctor to come over to the house and stitch it up.

When I open my eyes, my glass has gone. I watch a bar tender carry it away and place it upside down in a rack. The music is too loud for him to hear if I make a comment. I raise my hand to order a new drink. While I wait, a hand reaches my shoulder. I turn and find Ghalib.

'Your father said I would find you here,' he says. I look back at him until he flinches.

'Baba is always spot on,' I reply. 'Do you want a drink?'

He shakes his head. 'What's going on with him and you?' he says.

'Don't worry about it,' I reply. I have the attention of a bar tender now. 'Two vodka soda,' I tell him.

'It seems tense.'

'We like tense,' I reply. I watch the bar tender set our drinks down on the bar. I pay him. I pick up a glass and hand it to Ghalib. He takes his hand off my shoulder to receive the glass.

'Hanna, I need to talk to you,' says Ghalib. 'I have news. Habib called me.'

I close my eyes again and listen to the music.

'Hanna,' he says, irritation in his voice.

'Go on,' I say.

'Habib called.'

'And?'

'There's a big issue.'

'Right.'

'Open your fucking eyes,' he says.

'Okay, I will,' I reply. I turn to him. I drop my arms to my sides. 'What did Habib say?'

'You want to hear it here?' he asks.

'You came here to tell me,' I reply.

'Yes,' he says. 'I suppose I did. Habib called. Mudassar has had an accident. He was in his jeep.'

'Tonight?' I ask.

'Tonight,' he says.

'It's bad?'

'Habib says it's bad.'

'He said that specifically?' I ask.

'Yes,' replies Ghalib. He reaches for my shoulder with his hand. I let him hold me and then I turn away from him and finish my drink.

CHAPTER 5

I lead Ghalib down the stairs from the bar to the garden. I sit down among the smokers. Ghalib stands and fidgets with leaves on the low-hanging branches of the trees. 'I'm sorry,' I tell him. 'I had to get out of that noise.' He nods.

'I should fly tomorrow morning,' he says. 'Though this obviously messes up the Beirut deal. I'll go and see the guy tonight. Maybe we can still have a shot at it in a couple of weeks' time.'

'How badly hurt is he?' I ask.

'You know Habib,' he says. 'He was calculatedly vague. He just said to come. To tell you.'

'To tell me?'

'Sure,' he replies. 'You're family,' he adds quickly. But he knows and I know that there might have been a different implication to Habib's remark. Mudassar is the same age as me, and people have often thought that we are lovers. There are already several inter-cousin marriages in my mother's extended family. 'They're circling the wagons,' I remember Baba said when we were attending the last one at Ma's house. Ma is how my grandmother likes us all to call her. All the family weddings take

83

place at her house, across the massive lawn. Uncle Yani was with us and he burst out laughing and he and Baba kept telling small jokes to each other throughout the ceremony.

I watch Ghalib as he glances at every person in the garden in turn. He reminds me of Alain at a fashion party in London that Baba sent me to with IBCD tickets after my mother's death, to force me out of mourning he said. Alain watched the models and the actresses and the dancers and from time to time he slipped his hand into mine, as if to suggest that surely I must forgive him for looking given where we were. This idle avarice, I suppose Mudassar shows it too. I've been in a car with him dozens of times. I remember him glancing over at other cars when stopped in traffic, trying to grab the gaze of any pretty woman who looked back at him. He has always had large cars, cars that do attract attention, gifts from his father, Bilal, to him that Habib was unable to block. He drives them carelessly, he drinks and then he drives. One holiday when I was staying at Ma's house in Lahore with my mother, he tried to drive in when the front gate was only half open. He hit it and the noise woke everyone up. I watched from my window as Ma came out and gave him a playful clip around the ears and then he took her in a bear hug and she laughed and laughed. Ma was a big fan of the theory that Mudassar and I would get together one day. But I'm not anything like as close to her as Mudassar. The last time I spoke to her was after my mother died. She rang me to say that she wasn't going to come, that she was too old to travel, too old to travel for this, she added. She wept and then she paused and I remember thinking that she wanted me to weep with her, at the same time, to hear me mourn her daughter. I put the phone down on her. Other family came. Mudassar came. Bilal came. I caught them drinking large measures of whisky from Baba's drinks cabinet even before the funeral was over.

But Mudassar was better than this once, at least to me. He was my first guest when I moved into my parents' flat in London after graduation. I had resisted moving there for several months. I could too easily picture my mother by the window, perhaps spotting a bird in one of the trees in the square outside and calling Baba over; and he might have stood behind her, with his arms wrapped around her. In the kitchen, Baba might have dropped an egg on the floor while he tried to make breakfast for my mother at the weekend; my mother might have watched him from the doorway, rubbing the sleep from her eyes, as he cleaned it up. After a large dinner, they might have sat in the smaller lounge, shoes kicked off, in separate armchairs, comparing notes on their guests. I haven't loved as they loved, and that flat was their first together. It came before the house in Pakistan, the chalet in the Alps, the duplex in New York, the new build in the English Cotswold hills, the boat. It was their first. Eventually, as they kept pressing me to move into it, I had to give in. There was no way that I could explain to them the reason why I didn't want to live there.

Baba came over on the evening that I moved and he brought with him a team from Christie's who removed the left-behind tapestry from the wall. It was Baba's gesture to help me make the flat my own. I hadn't asked him to do it. He didn't even want the tapestry in their new house, he was putting it into storage. 'This is your first wall,' he told me. 'Do whatever you want with it.' Looking around the flat at all their other pictures he added, 'Hopefully we can soon give you some more walls to use as well.' He forgot about that last part of what he said. The tapestry was the only piece that ever came off the walls, which otherwise remained as he and my mother had left them. And it was about a year before I put anything even in that one space that they had given me. I left it empty because I thought I would enjoy it, it might help that there was a part of the flat that had nothing of theirs, and was pure potential. Then I began to resent it, to think that this was all the space I had. I told Mudassar the story of the wall when he came to stay. He told me to sign it. He hunted around in his briefcase and found me a marker pen. He gave it to me and I used it to put my name in the bottom right-hand corner. Then he drew three noughts and cross grids on the wall. We played and he let me win each game.

The door to the restaurant opens and the noise from inside stirs me. 'You said you need to go,' I remind Ghalib, standing up.

'I'll drop you at the hotel,' he says. He leads me to the street and the voiturier finds us a taxi. 'Saint-Michel hotel,' Ghalib tells the driver, 'then Saifi Village.' They banter about the price and Ghalib settles easily. The voiturier is standing behind Ghalib waiting for his tip but Ghalib doesn't notice him. I step forward and slip a banknote into the voiturier's hand.

'The price should be less than this,' I tell Ghalib, getting into the taxi beside him. I speak in Urdu, knowing that Ghalib picked up some of it hanging around with Mudassar.

'It's fine,' he replies firmly in English. I remain quiet as the taxi driver leads us through the jam of people dropping off their cars to go into the nearby bars. Ghalib drums his fingers on the window and I wonder if he is thinking of his friend or of the deal they had been trying to make. I notice his watch and I remember that he, Mudassar and Alain bought identical Patek Philippe watches when they finished raising their fund. For a while they took photographs of their three arms together with the three watches in different places, wherever they travelled. They made an album of the photos and sent it around by email.

As the driver turns onto the larger arterial road, I lean forward and remark: 'Saifi Village is closer. Go there before the Saint-Michel.' The taxi driver half-turns towards me and offers a thumbs up.

'I said that I was going to drop you,' says Ghalib.

'Saifi is just there,' I reply. 'It's stupid to go to the Saint-Michel and then come back.'

Ghalib shakes his head.

'Fine,' he says. Then a moment later, he adds: 'You haven't said if you're coming with me to Lahore.'

'It's not as easy as that,' I reply.

'Mudassar had an accident,' he says. 'I think it's remarkably easy.' I shake my head and turn away to look out of the window. 'What?' he adds. 'You have to stay here and keep your father out of trouble. Is that it?'

'Is that what I do?'

'Mudassar is your fucking cousin,' continues Ghalib. I ignore him until the taxi turns into Saifi Village.

'This is Saifi,' I tell him. 'Where do you want?'

Ghalib gets out without saying goodbye and leaves his door open as he walks away. I reach for the handle and close it and tell the driver to take me on to the hotel. It's a short drive. As the taxi turns onto the road that will lead straight to the hotel, I ask him to take a detour.

'What you mean?' he says.

'Drive around,' I tell him. 'Fifteen minutes.'

'What you mean around?' he says. I hand him five dollars to help explain that I will pay him extra for the diversion. 'No, it is more than this,' he says.

'We agree price. Why you pay only five dollars?' I give up and hand him the rest of the money, leave him in peace to drive me to the hotel and drop me off.

Staring out of the window, I review what I said to Ghalib in the bar. Still nothing about the photograph. I wonder what I have more of: disbelief that the photograph exists; doubt as to what it means; trust for Baba; distrust for Ghalib; fear for what has happened to Mudassar. Each of these feelings is in me and I can keep them in a vaporous state while this taxi is moving, but how much longer. I need to make some decisions. Yet all my instincts are buried. I haven't received news for two years. I haven't moved for two years. Now a lot is changing at once. I'm set to the wrong speed for this. Or perhaps if I had been hit before, hurt before, then I could comprehend better the violence I've seen in the photograph and confront Baba about it, much more obviously indignant, much more obviously moved; or, if my mother was alive, connecting me more firmly to her family, where Mudassar comes from, then I could be impelled to go to him, not have to deliberate and choose, then I could act, not improvise. As Ghalib said, he is my cousin. There are photographs of us when we were babies eating together. I've run screaming around Ma's house with him playing hide-and-seek.

The taxi stops at the hotel. As I get out of the taxi, it looks as if there's a commotion inside. I walk past two large black cars and a black van, each with small flags mounted at the back. I guess that a royal family from someplace in the Gulf is arriving. It's not an uncommon event. Often Baba and I sit and watch them parading in, with their bodyguards and advisers and their own domestic servants. It's a game for Baba and me to spot who has the royal substance; it's not easy when all the men are dressed the same and all the women concealed. It's like trying to spot the nucleus of an atom, which part it is that exerts a force on the others, and it's hard to tell when they all move in sync. There are three of their guards at the door of the hotel. I try to walk past them casually but they stop me and quiz me about my reason for wanting to enter. 'I live here,' I tell them. 'I've lived here for two years. Ask inside.' One of the hotel doormen sees me and comes to the entrance. He confirms that I'm a guest but the bodyguards won't rely on him, the door is theirs tonight, not his. They ask to see my room key, inspect it and eventually they let me in. Immediately I'm stuck again though. All the lifts are in use with luggage being sent upstairs. A concierge sees me and shrugs his shoulders and smiles. I'll have to wait and watch the arrival with everyone else, until it is complete. I look around the lobby and find Baba. He has a newspaper across his lap and a glass of wine on the small table beside him. He is already looking at me. I wave weakly and walk over to him. 'You're still drinking,' I say. 'You never drink after dinner.'

'Don't worry about it,' he says. 'I haven't been drunk since 2002.' He picks up his wine glass and sips from it. My mother died in 2002. I sit down in the chair next to him.

'Did he find you?' he says.

'Could you tell which country they're from?' I ask him, pointing to a rocking horse being led towards the lifts by a man like all the others from the entourage in white and golden Arab dress. Baba shakes his head.

'Qatar?' he says. 'What's your guess?' I am about to give one, then I slump forward, thrust my hands onto my knees to provide a limit.

'I dropped Ghalib off on the way here. He's gone to see the guy he wants to tie up the deal with. He's leaving in the morning. Do you know how bad it is, the accident?'

'He's in a critical condition,' says Baba. 'Habib didn't want to make a prediction as to how he'll get on. I've organised a plane to take you to Lahore. You can leave first thing tomorrow morning. Ghalib too.' I realise while he is talking that I didn't wholly believe what Ghalib had told me about Mudassar until now, until Baba repeated it.

'I haven't travelled for two years,' I reply.

'That's right,' he says. Then he adds gently: 'I assumed you would want to go.'

'Of course,' I reply loosely, emphatically. 'Well I should go, yes, I think I should. Is he going to die? Is that what they think?' Baba shrugs his shoulders.

'I had hoped,' he says, 'that we would have dinner tonight and then watch the royal arrival and talk, without Ghalib being around.'

'I had to get out,' I tell him.

'That's fine,' he says. 'And now you have to go to your cousin. Go, and you should stay for as long as you like. It's your decision.'

'Unless I'm arrested,' I say. 'Then it isn't my decision.'

'You'll be okay,' he says. For some reason I start nodding. I have no idea of whether I will be okay or not. Perhaps I am agreeing with something else.

'Why are you sending me away?' I ask him.

'I'm not sending you away,' he says. 'You're going to see your cousin. To be honest,' he continues, 'I thought the first time you'd leave would be for your grandmother's funeral. But instead it's this.'

'It's a really bad time to leave,' I say.

'You've been here two years,' he replies. 'If you stay any longer, you might stay for ever.'

'But isn't that what you meant to happen when you came to get me in London?' I ask him. 'What did you have in your mind? That I would settle you in and then I would leave?'

'I don't think it matters,' he says. 'It's already a long time ago. Take this chance. Get out.' I sit upright again in the chair and put my hand on Baba's leg.

'What's going on, Baba?' I ask him. 'Why are you sending me away?' He frowns and takes a sip of wine.

'I've tried to do my best,' he says.

'What do you mean? Your best about what?'

'Without your mother, despite my old culture, I've tried to do my best,' he says. 'I've never suggested you should get married to someone I know. I've never put any limits on you.'

'It wouldn't have come easily to you to do those things,' I reply.

'Nevertheless,' he says.

'It sounds like you're disappointed,' I tell him. 'Perhaps I haven't used the freedom you gave me in sufficiently interesting ways?'

'That's not what I think,' he says. 'But you're not tied to me. That's my point. You have to go to your cousin now. You might choose to stay there after what you saw today on my laptop.'

'Really?' I ask right away. He glances at me very briefly and then turns away to watch the continuing royal arrival, lifts his hands and holds the tips of his fingers against the sides of his mouth and joins the thumbs under his chin. That's it. That's the end of the conversation. That's what he wants. I know these small moves he makes. They may be inadvertent on his part, yet I can read them. We both watch a large dressing table with a marble top disappear into the lifts. I stand up and block his view.

'I won't do anything stupid,' I tell him. 'But I need to know.'

He doesn't respond or move. There he is: this is my Baba. And this is why I don't ask him things. This is why I wait to be told. I'm not a teenager any more; I can't shout at him, try to break him with girlish intimidation. There were only two or three times that I did that anyway, like when I could see that my mother was sick, had been sick for weeks, and neither he nor she would tell me what it meant. Even after that tantrum, he didn't tell me right away, he made me wait a full day and a full night; I had to be told, I couldn't ask. I walk away from him now and take the stairs up to my room while the lifts transfer the royal household to the only suites that are a notch above ours. It has suddenly come. I am leaving Beirut. I am un-escaping. I had anticipated this departure in the same way as Baba. To the extent that I had imagined it, I thought it would come for a funeral, like he said, but not Ma's funeral, and certainly not Mudassar's funeral; I had thought I would leave with Baba's body to bury him next to my mother. Instead it is this.

I go into my room and straight to the hiding place for the laptop. I am grateful to find that it is still there. I can't leave it here while I am away. No one else must find this machine. I call house-keeping and ask for Annette. Sometimes she eats dinner at the hotel with the kitchen staff to save money at home. After some discussion in the background, Annette comes on the line. 'Can I ask you for a short visit?' I say.

'Of course,' she replies.

I wait close to the door until she knocks on it. I try to hand her the laptop as soon as she is inside.

'Please take this to Baba,' I tell her.

'Are you sure?' she says, not yet taking it from me.

'It belongs to him,' I reply.

'Yes, I saw in the morning,' she says. 'I tidied up room with him, then he took this computer, this, and put on desk. He said you will take when you come to the room.'

'This computer? He wanted me to take it?'

'Yes, it is new,' she says. 'I have not seen before.'

'I don't think it's new,' I reply, clinging to some chance of having a say against her. She knew that Baba wanted me to take the computer. She was complicit in this play by Baba to shock me, to change me – to do what?

'Is everything all right?' asks Annette.

'I don't know,' I reply, shrugging my shoulders. 'Really I don't know. My cousin is in hospital,' I add, remembering suddenly.

'Your cousin?'

'In Pakistan,' I tell her. 'He had a car accident. I'm going to see him.'

'That's terrible,' she says.

'He might be okay,' I reply.

'Now I shouldn't ask you,' she says.

'Ask me what?'

'Now I shouldn't ask you,' she repeats.

'You can ask me,' I tell her. 'It's okay. What do

you want to ask me?' She shakes her head, but then she speaks anyway.

'The carpet is no different,' she says.

'What do you mean?' I ask her.

'He showed me before,' she says. 'The new carpet is purple. But I look tonight and the carpet is no different. It's the same carpet as before.'

'But so what?' I tell her. 'Purple was a pretty bad idea. He changed his mind.'

'Yes,' she says, nodding more certainly. 'You're right. He changed his mind.'

'Purple was a pretty bad idea.'

'Yes,' she says, smiling now. 'Do you want I take the computer?'

I hand it to her and she holds it across her arms like she is carrying an object into a temple. 'Goodnight, Annette,' I tell her. 'See you when I come back, in two or three days probably.'

'Goodnight,' she replies.

I turn from the door and withdraw far into the suite, opening the storage cupboard where I have an empty weekend bag. I place it on the bed and sit down next to it. After a few minutes, I stand up and walk out of the room. For the second time in the day, I rush towards Baba. I want to see the carpet. I want to ask him to open the laptop in front of me. This can be quite quick. He can make it quite quick. It's just one photograph. It won't take long to explain it. He wanted me to see it. He wanted to tell me about it. Then the news about Mudassar came. I have to tell him to ignore that. I have to remake his original plan. I knock on his door. I wait with my ear against it. I knock again. 'Baba,' I call, but not loudly. I can't do it loudly. If I do it loudly, I feel that I will burst into tears. 'Baba,' I call. Three times more, but there is no answer.

LAHORE

CHAPTER 1

I watch the right wing of the plane rise through the window by my seat. I'm dismayed to see it, it means that we're descending, this middle time – between Beirut and Lahore, Baba and Ma, exile and a vigil – is ending. The plane trip has been short. Somehow I expected that it would take many hours, and a night, and at least one interruption, before I could depart the place where I have been for two years and find myself somewhere else. I press my forehead. I feel like there is a too-large ball of cotton behind it, gathered up tightly and tied with a piece of rough twine. I poured a large measure of vodka into a glass as soon as I got on the plane and took it down quickly. Its blast has disappeared now. 'Ten minutes to Lahore,' yells the pilot through the open cockpit door. 'We're back to our scheduled time. Never mind that bureaucratic nonsense.' We were held on the runway at Beirut airport. The officials thought there was an anomaly in the pilot's paperwork. I watched them from the window talking to him, waiting for one of them to turn towards me and point me out to the others. I had already taken the vodka. I worked through the idea that Baba had sent them, that he had changed his mind and I wasn't to go anywhere.

The pilot brings us down softly. The wheels of the plane squawk twice and then adopt a rolling rhythm. 'Welcome to Lahore,' says Ghalib, sitting down next to me. He yawns. When we got on the plane, we watched an episode of a cartoon on the television screen. Then he went to the back and slept across two seats. His shirt is creased around the neck, like someone had grabbed hold of him there while he was sleeping. 'You didn't sleep?' he says to me. I shake my head. I woke up this morning in a panic and went downstairs to see if Baba was in the breakfast room. It was too early; the room hadn't opened yet. I went back to my room and showered, dressed, went downstairs again and saw Baba sitting at a table with his typical breakfast. But I didn't go to him. I had made a fool of myself on the roof yesterday. I had gone to him last night, long after I knew he would be in bed and mewed uselessly at his door. I didn't want to go to him a third time in a state of panic for him to disregard me. I sat down out of his sight in the lobby. Just before Ghalib was due to come by, I checked on Baba once more. The table had been cleared. He had a cup of tea in front of him, no doubt brewed by the method that he had taught the hotel staff to use when we arrived at the Saint-Michel, in a pot over a gas ring, with cardamom pods as well as tea leaves, adding milk after a few minutes, then waiting until it rises to the brim before lifting the pot off the heat. I didn't say goodbye to him. When Ghalib came, I took his arm and he led me to the taxi that was going to take us to the airport.

'I'll do papers, shall I?' says Ghalib, when the plane has come to a stop. 'I fly in and out of here a lot. Let's not show them your face, just in case,' he adds. I take my British passport and Pakistan identity card out of my bag and give them to Ghalib. He laughs. 'No, that's my point,' he says. 'Stay off the grid. Keep these in your bag.' He opens my passport. 'Hideous photograph, by the way,' he says. I take the two documents back from him and put them in my bag like he said. 'Wait here,' he concludes.

He opens the door of the plane himself and jumps out. Like me, he has been travelling in these small private planes for all time. Baba and I flew on a plane like this one when we left London. We went to Jersey and then took another plane on to Monaco. I watch the pilot emerge from the cockpit. He crouches down next to me. 'Anything to drink, madame?' he asks. I shake my head. He smiles and returns to the cockpit. I can see him now, scribbling in a notebook. After a minute, he notices that I am watching him and looks up. 'You're okay, madame?' he says.

'Sure,' I tell him, but he keeps looking back at me. I feel a quick shake of disquiet. The trouble with a man like this is that he would listen intently

103

if I spoke to him now about Baba, the photograph, my cousin's accident. And he would listen equally intently if I spoke to him about restaurant standards in Beirut or the shopping I might do in Lahore. He is one of the super-service people that I have known all my life: someone paid very well by my father not to be actively curious and, by the same rules, to listen when I want to talk, though not to react to anything he is told. He is a sheet thrown over my head. He is a long roll of that plastic wrap that has pockets of air in it. I pick up my bag and look through it needlessly. He goes back to doing his note-work. My bag is almost empty. I couldn't focus on packing last night and not even this morning. Twice I stood over my bag for a while and did nothing. At the last minute, I put in some underwear, some make-up, my travel documents and a book. There are always clothes for me in Ma's house, Asian clothes, *shalwar kameez* gathered two or three a time during the summers that I stayed there with my mother, each time when my aunt, Mudassar's mother, lost patience with how out of fashion I was on the *shalwar kameez* front and took me forcibly to the market. They are in a cupboard filled with old clothes. Some of them belong to other visitors, other girls from the extended family or even their mothers, some of them belong to Ma's sister, who died about twenty years ago; my mother's old clothes are not among them, I think those are in Ma's own room. Ma's house is a large building in the Defence cantonment. It looks like the last remaining part of an old fort, or like a page from an architect's study of a fort. Inside there is a surprising combination of rooms filled with light from large windows, air conditioners smashed into the walls next to them set to the maximum level in a battle against the heat, and dark rooms with heavy, over-long curtains that trail on the floor and large cupboards that spit mothballs when you open them. Baba told me that Ma moved into the house in 1959. It wasn't built for her, and she immediately knocked down walls and re-sized rooms. Baba says that she didn't involve an architect and the work was cheaply done. 1959 was before Habib had joined the family. Nowadays Habib would take care of a piece of building work but in 1959 Ma handled it, or Bilal did, and so they have to live with large cracks in many of the walls and ceilings, where the structure of the building has moved and is still moving. From time to time, certain rooms in the house are cordoned off, when the cracks become as large as a fist, and workmen fill them in with plaster. In my imagination though, the cracks make the house seem more permanent, like it's hewn from a mountain, not built, and although it moves, it moves like everything moves, according to the earth's tectonic plates.

I watch the pilot put his headset on and nod slowly until he takes it off again. He writes another few words in his notebook and then closes it. He gets up from his seat and walks towards me. 'I suppose there's someone waiting for me outside,' I say to him. He nods. This is his limit now. After I've gone, he will sit in a seat with his legs up on the next one and call his wife or his mother. Then he'll eat lunch somewhere around the airport, perhaps buy a present for his child. This evening or tomorrow he will take a call from me and learn that we are going back. Then he will return to the plane, review the stock of drinks in the fridge and check the plane's instruments so that he can take off as soon as I say so.

The air outside is warm and the sky is overcast as I step through the plane door. There are streaks of grey and streaks of orange in the sky. I come down the steps of the plane and a black jeep parked a hundred metres away pokes forward to indicate interest. It has darkened windows and the registration plate looks temporary. It crosses my mind that Baba may be having me kidnapped. It's not so extreme to predict that, having fouled up on his keeping of secrets, he would now disappear me. I watch the window on the passenger's side slide downwards until I can see a head protruding from the area of the back seats into the space between the front seats. A hand moves into sight as well, making gestures. Then it disappears and the head eases back, revealing the driver to me. His posture is familiar, his head back against the seat, one arm stretched straight out before him and gripping the wheel at the top. On that arm there's a familiar watch, the same watch that I saw on Ghalib's arm last night in the taxi in Beirut. He is wearing a silky blue shirt and darker blue trousers. Though I can't see them, I know that beneath there will be black suede boots. It's the uniform that Alain adopted within weeks of arriving at university in London. He shifted between blue and grey, added a coat when it was cold, replaced the suede boots with leather ones when it was raining. I open the door of the jeep. 'Good morning,' I tell him. 'Is there news?'

'You should get in,' he says, without looking towards me. He's wearing dark glasses. He wore those whenever he was hungover. I do as he suggests and climb up into the passenger's seat. He sets off as soon as I close my door.

'I think this mean I'm going to a funeral,' I say.

'Since about three hours ago,' says Ghalib, from the back seat.

My first thought is that I should go back to the plane. I came here to see someone who had a serious accident, not someone who is dead. There's no need for me to go to the funeral; Mudassar's entire family will be there, Ghalib and Alain will be there, his friends and his business partners. I would mourn him with just as much feeling in Beirut. But I know that I can't go right back. Baba sent me. Ma is expecting me.

We don't talk very much inside the jeep. I remember these ambiences from after my mother died. Sitting with visitors meaningfully in silence, nibbling from time to time on taste-free conversation topics, someone remembering aloud something that my mother had said one time, and that statement turning for a few minutes into a window on her immortal soul. I hated that all, and also the hugs; I was hugged by everyone who came, even though it couldn't possibly be a good idea to remind me of physical affection. I wanted people to sit in place and say nothing, make it very clear to me how my life would be different now that my mother – a talker, a hugger, my mother – was dead.

We stop briefly in traffic and Alain says: 'The car is a bad wreck.'

'Who has the insurance?' says Ghalib.

'I think we do,' says Alain, 'the firm.' I turn and watch Ghalib nod his head.

'What happens to the firm?' I ask them.

'The firm is dead,' says Alain.

'Long live the firm,' adds Ghalib, snorting.

'You won't continue?' I ask them.

'Continue what?' says Ghalib. I turn and look at him again. He stares out of the window.

'What about the Lebanese deal?' I ask him. He doesn't reply.

'Insurance won't pay out,' he says eventually, to Alain.

'Yes, I thought so,' says Alain.

'Why not?' I ask them.

There's no answer and Alain drives us in silence through the entrance to the Defence cantonment. The gate stands the same. The houses in this old part of the cantonment won't ever change I think. Mudassar and I used to ride through these streets on our bikes in the evenings when the sun had dropped. We made guesses about who lived in each of the houses: politicians, television stars, cricket players. If a gatekeeper waved to us, we stopped and asked him questions. When I was last here, Mudassar lived in a room on the first floor of Ma's house. Though he had an office in one of the new commercial areas, he preferred to live in Defence rather than in a new apartment building. As for Ma herself, I don't think she has left the cantonment since her husband died. The gravity of the place is that strong. I used to criticise Mudassar for staying here, but in London I lived in my parents' flat, now I live in a hotel – range is not something that I've achieved in my life either.

The last time that I saw Mudassar it was also here in Defence. We met at a coffee shop. He had a small flask with whisky in it, which he mixed into his coffee. He was going out to a concert that evening and he told me that he couldn't drink quickly, so he had to start early, or he would have a completely different buzz to the others going with him. I don't readily remember anything else that he said. I have nothing for the salon conversation that I am about to join at the house. My best-fixed memory of him is from when I was twelve. My mother and I stayed in Ma's house for a week while Baba was on a business trip to Peshawar. It was July. Mudassar was there. We

109

were inside from 10am to 6pm due to the heat and he and I spent a lot of that time in the formal lounge alone, where no one ventured during the day, lying on cushions on the giant rug that covered the floor, playing cards. I've never been that interested in playing cards and I didn't realise what he and I were doing until the fourth day, when the evening had begun to cool and everyone moved outside to sit in the garden. I took a shower and changed. I was combing my hair by the bathroom window and I saw him sitting outside through the glass. So I went outside as well, comb in hand, and sat down in a chair in front of him, combing my hair slowly. I didn't say anything to him. He didn't say anything to me. He kept looking at me and I kept looking at him as we listened to the adults talking. The next day in the lounge, we set our cushions down a little closer together than before. After a few hands, when it was my turn to shuffle, Mudassar moved his legs so that they were touching mine. I shuffled the cards for a long time, sitting still, as he brushed his right leg slowly across mine. Then I dealt and he stopped, until it was the end of the game, when he touched his legs against mine again.

Later that day, before the evening meal, I went to find him in his room and asked him to close the button around the neck at the back of the *kameez* that I had put on. He did it carefully and then he pressed my shoulders for a few moments. I was pleased. It was something that a man would do. We all went out to dinner that evening. We walked after dinner through a market street. I wanted to walk closer to him, away from my mother, and hold his hand, but I wasn't bold enough to do it. Later on, he knocked on the door of the room where I was sleeping. He knocked so faintly that I wasn't sure that he had knocked. By the time I got up and opened the door, he had left. I saw him at the opposite end of the corridor, his back to me, walking away. I saw that the door of his father's study was ajar. It must have deterred him I thought. And I went back to bed thinking what I would have done if he'd come into my room.

'How did it happen?' I ask inside the jeep. 'The accident.' Alain shakes his head.

'Forget it,' says Ghalib.

'Tell me.'

'Police officer told me that there was a mechanical failure,' says Alain.

'Habib must have had a word with him right away,' replies Ghalib. 'Did the police officer describe the precise details of the mechanical failure?'

'He did not,' says Alain.

'Why would Habib need to have a word with him?' I ask.

'To keep the family name in decent shape,' says Ghalib. 'That's his job, right? I was going to say to keep the family name clean and pure, but it's long since been too late for that. Don't say a word to Ma,' he adds.

'About what?' I reply.

'They were very close,' he says. 'She thought he was the sun god or something. This will make the adoration much worse. She'll talk about him for months to everyone.'

Alain slows the jeep down as we approach a barrier set across the road. There are two police officers standing next to it. One of them knocks on the window. Alain slides it open. 'I went past an hour ago, you idiot,' he says.

'Security,' says the police officer simply. He peers through the open window at me.

'Her family is paying you to be here,' remarks Ghalib. 'Habib, who paid you to be here, works for her grandmother.'

'Our instructions are to stop every vehicle, sir,' replies the police officer. He steps back and waves to his colleague who moves the barrier to one side. Alain accelerates sharply through the gap.

'Fucking idiots,' says Ghalib. 'Right, are we ready for this?'

'Sure,' I reply.

'Everyone will be looking at you in particular,' he says.

'Yes, I know, I've been away for a long time.'

'Plus they think you and Mudassar were an item,' adds Alain.

We drive through the gate of the house. Alain's window is still open and I smell through it curry and rice. I feel hungry, and resent it. The convention is that every guest at a funeral should be fed

112

afterwards, I understand that, but the smell of the food propels my base senses out ahead of my deeper feelings. There are mounds of white flowers placed regularly in three lines across the lawn. I get out of the jeep and stand leaning against it. 'Are you okay?' says Alain.

'I'm fine,' I reply. 'They move fast, don't they?' I point to a group of men putting up a bouquet of white flowers on each end of the gate.

'Habib,' replies Ghalib, simply.

I nod. I should have guessed it myself. Habib is hard-working, clear-headed, especially at times like these. Baba told me after the fact that Habib had offered to make the arrangements for my mother's funeral as well, but Baba had refused. Baba didn't want any arrangements. He didn't even call anyone to say that my mother had died. He certainly didn't buy flowers. It was as if he thought there was something indeterminate about her death and, if he held his nerve for long enough, it might turn out that she wasn't dead after all, that she might come back to him in secret. It was the staff of the house that spread the news when Baba was refusing to do it. They called Ma, they called my mother's key friends in London. When I realised that they were filling the gap left by Baba's inaction, I felt embarrassed. I decided to take charge. I gathered all the staff of the house together and asked them what they thought had to be done. Their list overwhelmed me and I retreated to my father's study, left them to get on with it.

'We should go to the hospital,' says Alain. 'Come with?' he says to Ghalib. 'Can I leave you here?' he says to me.

'I'd like to see him,' I reply.

'Ma will expect you to be here,' says Ghalib. 'The women are here. The hospital is close by. We'll be back quickly. Go and see Ma.'

'Is that all right?' adds Alain.

I nod blankly this time and stand away from the jeep. I watch Alain and Ghalib get back in and drive out. I walk through the gate and towards the house, remembering that Mudassar used to say when we were kids that the house looked like Pac-Man. I kissed Mudassar once. It was just after university. He came back to London to visit me. We went out on a picnic. He was wearing an IBCD T-shirt, printed in Ukrainian with one of their favourite slogans, 'We Grow When You Grow'. We drank champagne. We took a taxi back to my flat. We were looking out of opposite windows. I grabbed his wrist and pulled him close and kissed his mouth. He kissed me back for a few seconds, then he stopped and I fell back into my seat. For the rest of the journey it felt like there was a large dumb fly inside the cab battering itself against a pane of glass. 'Do you want to come upstairs?' I asked him sarcastically, when we got back to my flat. His things were there and he did come up, and he sat in the chair in the hallway where I usually sat to remove my shoes and told me about his new girlfriend.

I wander around the house looking for the verandah outside Ma's private lounge. I remember sitting with her once as a girl while it rained and she smoked. She offered me her old-style unfiltered cigarette. The smoke made me cough even as I held it in my hand. She laughed as I handed it back to her without putting it to my mouth. She called me 'little bird' then and it's what she has always called me. I spoke to her a year ago. I persuaded Baba to give the reception at the Saint-Michel a list of people who could be connected by phone to either my room or his. I called Ma and Ghalib and told them that, if they ever needed to reach us, they must ask for us using a code that Baba devised. Ma was overexcited to hear from me. 'Little bird,' she exclaimed, 'fly home to me. My heart is cold. Your mother left me. Then you.' I couldn't stay on the phone with her for long, not least because Baba was sitting next to me making ghoulish faces trying to make me laugh. He thinks she's crazy, though whenever I've seen them together, he has been impeccably civil to her, in that improbable way that kings in films are civil to each other just before their armies go to war.

I stop at the glass door behind which Ma sits during the day. I knock on it and a young girl, perhaps fourteen, opens it and stares at me. There is a large ring through her nose and her hair is dyed with henna. We stare at each other. 'Do you want to see Ma?' she says in Punjabi.

'Speak Urdu, child,' shouts Ma from behind her. The girl moves aside to allow me to pass.

'My name is Hanna,' I tell her.

'Who is it?' yells Ma again. I enter the room. Ma is sitting on a large cushion on the floor. She opens her arms when she sees me. 'Come press yourself against my chest, little bird,' she proclaims. I figure I have no choice. I kneel and let her embrace me. She smells of aniseed and roasted peanuts. She kisses the side of my face repeatedly. 'You have come back to me,' she says. The young girl sits down behind her and starts working on Ma's hair with a large comb.

'Ma, how are you?' I ask. She waves my question away with a motion of both hands.

'I'll think about that after he is buried,' she says. She reaches out with her right hand and grips my chin. 'Is he nice to you?' she asks.

'He's my father,' I tell her.

'Years and years,' she says. 'It's been years since I saw you.'

'How are you, Ma?' I repeat, dumbly. She lets go of my chin and pulls me down to sit next to her by my hand, forcing me to press my head against her shoulder.

'At first,' she says, 'the men will pray. That is the first thing. My little bird,' she continues, 'after they have prayed, they will leave here and bury your dear cousin. Then they will come back and they will come and greet us with their women and we have to give them the chance to express their grief

116

to us. Have you seen this before?' she asks. I nod. I've seen it here, at her house, for her brother-in-law's funeral. Her husband had died a long time before I was born. His brother was a rival to her in running the family's affairs and she held the funeral for him here, grandly, with hundreds of guests, as if to extinguish all memories of how they had fought. She lets go of my chin. 'Good,' she says. 'We will be together to receive them then – me, his mother, his sister. Hanna, my little bird,' she says, 'should you be in this line with us?'

I almost laugh nervously, but I am able to stop myself and issue a positive grunt instead. She kisses me on the forehead.

'Continue,' she says to the girl with the comb. 'Do you recognise her?' she asks me, reaching back with her left hand and grabbing the girl's chin. I shake my head. 'Isn't there a resemblance to your uncle Bilal?'

'Is there?' I reply. Mudassar has a sister, whom I know, but I have never seen this girl before.

'Believe me,' says Ma, raising her eyebrows, 'there is a resemblance.' She laughs and pulls the girl towards her and kisses her face. 'But only you and I should ever notice it,' she adds.

I sit silently and watch as the girl combs Ma's hair. Ma's hands keep moving across her lap, fidgeting with the hem of her *kameez*. They are the same restless movements that my mother would make. I imagine that inside Ma's worn and weathered hands, there are my mother's hands and inside those, there are mine. 'My little bird,' she announces again, 'you will stay with me a few days now, won't you?'

'Of course,' I tell her. I don't yet know what I will do but I don't want to have a discussion about it now.

'You should rest,' she says. 'The housekeeper made up a room for you. It's going to be a long day.'

'Can I see his room?' I ask her. She shakes her head emphatically.

'We don't play with the belongings of the dead,' she says. 'He has gone to Allah and that is all the knowledge we have.' I wait and consider arguing. I want to see something of his, before the funeral begins. I want it to draw out of me one more specific memory before his dead body becomes my overwhelming impression of him. 'Go and rest,' says Ma again. She puts a hand on my shoulder and pushes me.

I do as she says, stand up and leave the room. Outside in the corridor a maid picks me up like she's been watching a conveyor belt, waiting for me to pop out.

'I'm Hanna,' I tell her. She nods and guides me to a bedroom on the first floor. Once the maid has gone, I sit down on the bed and call Baba's mobile phone. 'Where are you?' he asks.

'I'm in Lahore,' I answer in a puzzled voice. 'That's where you sent me.'

'I didn't hear from you,' he says.

'The pilot called you,' I reply. 'You heard from him, didn't you?'

'You've seen your grandmother?' he asks.

'Yes,' I tell him.

'How is she?' he says.

'Her hands look like mum's hands,' I say. 'Did you ever notice that?' He makes a small growling noise and doesn't answer. I didn't mean to say this to him.

'Is there news about your cousin?' he asks.

'He's dead,' I reply, dropping the critical word as steadily as I can, as if it's one of those games where the buzzer goes off if you touch the wire with the hoop.

'So it was bad,' he says, 'the accident.'

'No, it was a good accident,' I tell him. 'He was unlucky, that's all, to be the one person who dies in a good accident.'

'Where are you staying?' he says, ignoring my stupid remark.

'At her house,' I say. 'Ma keeps calling me her little bird, so I'm in the nest I suppose.'

'Are you okay?' he says.

'What about you, Baba?' I ask him. 'Where are you?'

'I'm in my room,' he says.

'The room with the unchanged carpet?' I ask.

'What are you getting at?' he says.

'Why didn't you change the carpet?' I ask.

'I was going to put in a purple carpet,' he says. 'Didn't I recover my sanity just in time?'

119

'Baba,' I tell him, 'I have to go.' It's a lie. And I don't end the call immediately. I hang on listening for him to say something else. He hangs on waiting for me to say something else. 'This is useless,' I tell him. And then I do hang up.

I lie back on the bed and close my eyes, but sit up again quickly. If I fall asleep, I think that I might sleep for hours and not wake up until after the funeral is complete. Events will move quickly now. Islamic funerals take place within hours of the death. Right now Bilal, Mudassar's father, might be washing his body and draping it in a white sheet, with Ghalib and Alain looking on. I wander out of the bedroom and search for the lounge in which Mudassar and I played cards many summers ago. The door is locked; probably on Habib's instructions, to manage the risk to the privacy of the family from the funeral guests who will arrive shortly. I go into the garden and watch a team of men laying white ribbon across the lawn. Later the men will line up along the strips of ribbon to pray. I hear voices raised outside the front gate and walk over to have a look. A large truck is parked outside with a battered black jeep mounted on top of it. My first thought is that Alain and Ghalib have now been in an accident as well. They were travelling in a jeep. But then I see Ghalib standing among the men shouting at the driver of the truck. It's Mudassar's jeep I realise up on the truck, it's the site, it's where he died. Its wreck looks like a bird, an ugly and mangled bird that would be shooed away instantly. As I look at it, I think that his head at the very end might have rested on the steering wheel, perhaps with a similar expression to the head in the photograph on my father's laptop. 'For fuck's sake,' exclaims Ghalib, coming towards me, 'I don't know why they thought to bring it here. Get fucking rid of it,' he shouts, turning again. The argument between the men of the house and the truck driver continues behind him. I wonder if the truck driver will take it away now and dump it somewhere. He will drive to an empty lot in a new housing development and unlatch it, let it tumble to the ground and leave it there. 'Did you see Ma?' Ghalib asks me.

'Yes,' I say. 'Is the body on its way from the hospital?'

'Do you want a drink?' he asks. 'I know where Bilal has his secret stash.'

I follow him through the garden into the house. I wonder if I can breed familiarity with the house again, by walking to and fro like this, restore the past few years, not be out of place after all, slip my hand into Mudassar's hand. But it is Ghalib ahead of me, not Mudassar. Mudassar and he were close. I even remember feeling jealous of how close they were. A few months after I had broken up with Alain, when IBCD opened a new headquarters in Decca, I invited Mudassar to come with Baba and me to the party. Bangladesh had become an important territory for the bank. Though there were no senior Bengalis in IBCD, focusing on Bangladesh fitted the bank's conception of itself. 'Not the World Bank, but the Third World Bank' as Sherpao put it often in his monthly newsletter. The new headquarters included a large library with a deep collection to which all the teaching staff from the city's academic institutions were given access for free. There was a lecture theatre where the bank held an annual symposium on the economic prospects of Bangladesh, inviting the celebrities of international finance from Washington, New York and London. The Decca opening was a big party, noisy and long. Mudassar bought marijuana from a new teller and he and I slipped away to smoke it in his hotel room. When I woke up the next morning, I remember that he had already showered. He was walking around the room with a small towel around his waist, talking to Ghalib on the phone about a trip they were going to take together. I made coffee and he thanked me with just a gesture while he continued talking to Ghalib.

I watch Ghalib pour a glass of whisky and pause with the bottle above a second glass. I shake my head. 'Come on,' he says, pouring the second glass regardless. He hands it to me. 'Join in,' he says. 'We're all here living beyond our limits.'

'What do you mean?' I ask. He turns and looks at a photograph on the wall while he drinks. He turns to me and points at it.

'Is that your mother?' he says.

'I have absolutely no idea,' I tell him, deadpan, without looking. He shrugs his shoulders.

'Mudassar had money in with us,' he says. 'His share of the family money. Habib is going to yank it away.'

'Do you know for sure?' I ask him.

'Of course he will,' Ghalib replies.

'That's a pity,' I reply.

'No, it's worse than that,' he says. 'We don't have the money.'

'What do you mean?' I say again.

'We don't have it,' he says. 'It's not there any more. We've invested it.'

'Well, maybe it's a good investment,' I tell him. 'You could convince Habib.'

'Oh, fuck off,' he says.

'Why?' I reply quickly.

'Well, that's not the end of it, is it?' he says.

'What else?' I ask him.

'Some sketchy Lahore family second son that Mudassar used to take drugs with,' he replies. 'Put in a sum that I never believed actually belonged to him. I think he stole it from his family. Turned up to see us with a suitcase full of cash. But Mudassar wanted it in. They were good buddies. They were probably together last night before Mudassar got into his jeep. His guy has already called me today to ask for the money back.'

'Same story?' I ask. 'The money has been invested?' He glares at me and then takes a step towards me.

'I know what you think of me,' he says. 'And what your father thinks of me.'

'I was asking a serious question,' I reply.

'I might surprise you,' he says. 'I might very well surprise you.'

'It sounds like an awful situation,' I tell him.

'Especially when your best friend has just died,' he replies. He puts down his emptied glass and looks at mine. 'You don't want it?' he says. He comes forward and takes it from me, drains it in a couple of gulps.

'Are you okay?' I ask him.

'Aren't you listening?' he says. 'I am basically fucked. You know what it's like?' he continues. 'To owe people such large sums of money? You have no idea. Already on the phone today, the tone was getting heavy, like they know we don't have the money, like they know they're going to be putting the pressure on before it comes back to them.'

'You'll have to tell them to wait,' I say.

'How long will they wait?' replies Ghalib. 'Five days? Fifteen? So what? What happens after that?'

He pours more whisky and takes a glass with him as he paces the length of the room. Through the open door, I watch a maid walk down the corridor towards us. 'What is it?' I ask her, before she reaches the threshold.

'I'm sorry, madam,' she replies. 'The body is here.'

'Right,' says Ghalib behind me, slamming the

glass down on a hard surface. He walks quickly past the maid and me. We follow him.

The funeral lasts ten minutes. I gather with the women behind the house. We listen in silence as the imam guides the men through the prayer on the other side of the house on the front lawn. Then the imam speaks in Arabic. I flinch every time he uses Mudassar's name, as I imagine him glancing towards the body wrapped in the shroud before him. The imam stops speaking. We hear people start to move and then the women start to talk. I watch Ma drop onto a cushion on the floor. 'My Mudassar,' she exclaims. 'My beloved boy.' Mudassar's mother and a couple of other women crouch down with her and take her in their arms. The men now will take Mudassar's body to the graveyard. Women don't go. Now that the funeral is over, shortly someone will stop me and ask me questions about Baba, about me, about how long I am staying here. I wander towards the trees that shield Ma's house from the house behind it. I remember my mother told me that she had hidden objects around the trees when she lived in this house as a young girl. They weren't of any value, she said, but putting them in the ground was the way she could get them away from the brigade of maids and cousins and make them exclusively hers. Somehow I don't want to find them; I just want to see the marks where she dug the holes, but evidently they're not there now, so many years later. I put my hand on one of the tree trunks and actually I want it to trap my hand, prevent me from running towards the front lawn as I now want to do in order to glimpse the body wrapped in the shroud. I am useless here. I could do something out in front. I could help to carry him. But there are dozens of men there now. It would suffice even if I could go to the graveyard and take a fistful of the grass that grows on his burial plot. But women don't go to the graveyard either. I take out my mobile phone and call Baba.

'The funeral prayer is finished,' I tell him without preamble when he picks up.

'Hello,' he says.

'The imam was to the point,' I continue. 'I think he does a lot of these.'

'Is your cousin buried?' asks Baba.

'Matter of time,' I say. 'My cousin looks good in white.'

'I haven't worn white since 1978,' says Baba.

'What are you doing?' I ask him.

'It's soon lunchtime,' he says.

'The pots are bubbling here as well,' I tell him. 'Funerals are a hungry affair.'

'Be careful,' he says. 'Ma might be listening to you.'

'Ma's not listening to anyone,' I reply. 'I haven't made up my mind about when I'm coming back,' I add.

'Private planes are convenient, aren't they?' he says.

'I'll call you back,' I say, then hang up the phone.

I turn away from the trees and find Ma in the crowd of women. The men will be returning soon. Then the commiserations will take place. I kneel next to Ma and speak softly, close to her ear. 'I am only his cousin,' I tell her. 'I won't stand next to you and Auntie but I am happy that I can be with you today.' She pauses a moment while she takes this in. Then she puts her hand on my forehead and presses. Her lips are moving softly. She is saying a prayer for me. She raises her hand and then kisses the place where it was. She wanted to let me stand in the line of Mudassar's direct family if that was the right thing to do. I wonder if she is relieved that I didn't force her to place me there. There would be the comment that this would attract, her grandson sleeping with a ruined girl, the daughter of a deceitful man who vanished in shame. Perhaps she has blessed me for having outdone her offer of kindness with one of my own. Though equally I wonder if she has said a prayer for me because she is sorry that I was not Mudassar's lover; perhaps she has asked Allah to give me a better capability to love.

I do as I told her. When the men come back and they unite with their women relatives to speak to Ma and Mudassar's mother and sister, I stand away with the others. It's fully an hour before everyone has had a turn to commiserate with the women. Then the food is brought out and people disperse across the garden. I disappear into the room they've given me and this time I do fall asleep.

CHAPTER 2

I wake up in the dark. I've dreamed and I believe it was a dream that woke me. Two men trying to grapple me into a car, yes, that's it, it was a dream of the almost-violence in London that happened to me at night in an unfamiliar part of the city. I dreamed that, after I got away from them and reached my flat, I undressed in my bathroom and found bruises on my skin. The bruises looked like words. I think I read the first of them and that's what woke me, but I don't know on this side of sleep what the word was. I feel there is a hastily constructed wall in my head that obstructs my recollection of the dream and that the foundations of this wall rest on my jaw. My mother used to feel this pressure on her jaw when she woke up. Her jaw hurt in the morning because she was tense during the night and clenched her teeth. She had always to eat a soft breakfast. When she tried to eat toasted bread, she made little yelping sounds due to the pain.

I get out of bed and go to the bathroom looking for sleeping tablets, but then I remember that I didn't bring my sleeping tablets from Beirut. I rest my forehead against the cool surface of the bathroom mirror for a moment. Without my sleeping tablets, there is little or no prospect that I will fall asleep again promptly. But I don't want to spend the rest of the night awake, not in this house, not this night. Somewhere in the house there must be sleeping tablets. I leave the room to look around in the kitchen. I don't put on shoes and cross the floor stepping with my toes. Noiseless like this, I remember Mudassar coming to my room that night in this same house, the culmination of that flirtatious day. I imagine how accurately we might have kissed that night, trying it out, mouth matching perfectly onto mouth, not convinced that this kissing concept happened in real life, testing it with care.

As I approach the kitchen, I notice that there is a light on inside. I glimpse through the doorway the cook over the stove scrubbing. She isn't looking at it. She is staring at the wall in front of her. She detects that I am behind her and turns around. 'Salaam,' I tell her. 'I couldn't sleep.' She isn't startled that I am there. She nods and takes a step away from the stove. I can see that it is completely clean already.

'Long day,' she says in English. I didn't realise that I had spoken to her in English.

'Everyone is sleeping,' I continue, in Urdu now. 'You should rest.'

'Thank you, miss,' she says. 'I'm sleepless. I can't

stop thinking about the accident.' She turns away from me as soon as she has said this, as if she's made a mistake and hopes that I won't notice. I realise suddenly that of course she has known Mudassar probably for all of his life. I wonder how many special breakfasts she made for him over that stove, whatever he wanted, mushed his food when he was a baby, compelled him when an adult to eat something in the evening before he went out with his friends. 'You must be very sad,' she says to me, still facing away. Her voice is hard, but not aggressive. I want to step forward and take her hands in mine. It is unfair. Probably she spent more time with Mudassar than his mother or Ma, certainly more than me, yet she feels that she has to defer to our grief, because we are family, and she is only a woman who works in the house. Ma will speak to her, I suppose. I imagine that Ma will recognise her grief. Or perhaps not. I remember Baba saying that my mother's family have no curiosity for asking questions, not about themselves, especially not about other people. 'They used all their curiosity three generations ago,' he remarked about her family in front of my mother. 'When they made their money, they used all the intelligence they'll ever have.' My mother didn't reply. She just smiled, that was all.

'I'm going to take a walk in the garden,' I tell the cook. 'Would you like to join me?' She shakes her head emphatically. She's right. My offer was dumb. 'Please go to bed,' I tell her. 'If he felt any pain, it's finished now.' I don't know where this pronouncement comes from. I didn't imagine that I thought like this. Now I'm afraid that she might reply, try to expose the shallow edges of my grief, pull ahead of me in her memory of Mudassar. I leave the kitchen quickly.

I stride out towards the heart of the lawn. The air is invigorating. I feel it sweep around my face. I pull up my hair and expose the back of my neck. Then I notice that there is some rain in the air as well. Soon it might fall harder. It will tamp down the earth above Mudassar's grave and dribble through to soak the shroud in which he's buried. I never watched him shower. Suddenly I think of that: his body under the spray, his arms in motion, applying soap, rubbing it off. The morning after I slept with him, while he was talking to Ghalib on the phone, after his shower, he must have suspected that I was watching him at one point. He grinned at me lying on the bed, and I pretended quickly that I was asleep. I didn't want to talk; I wanted to watch him for a little while longer. Now I'm glad that I fixed my lie to Ma earlier, before she put me in the line-up. I am spinning and I should keep my arms by my sides or I will hit other people.

I shelter from the rain under a group of trees. I look up into the branches and spy for birds' nests but it's difficult because the moonlight is dim and there are few lights on in the house.

Alongside one of the trunks on the ground there is a paper bowl, discarded from the meal after the funeral with food still inside it. By the morning the bowl might be empty and the paper torn by beaks. I am revolted by the idea of the flesh in the bowl, the pieces of meat from the curry being carried off and consumed by the ants, the birds, the mice, whatever quotidian wildlife have the run of this garden at night. There is other flesh in the ground tonight. The same creatures can burrow through cloth just as well as they can tear through paper. I would like to pick up the bowl and dispose of it inside the house but I am afraid of handling it. I turn away from it and stand with a shoulder against the tree trunk. I wait for a heave from my stomach but it doesn't come. Looking up, I hear a car arriving outside the house gate. I watch the guard open the gate and the car move carefully down the driveway. The driver's door opens and in the light from inside the car I watch Habib get out and pass across to the other side. He opens the door and drags out with both his hands another man. They walk towards the house. Habib advances and opens with a key a door into what I think is a private lounge, like Ma's lounge but on the opposite side of the house. Habib props the door open and then holds the other man's collar in his hand to pull him inside. I come out from under the trees and approach with an arm raised above my head as a greeting. Habib sees me as he emerges again

133

from the house to close the door. 'Is that my uncle Bilal?' I ask him.

'Miss Hanna,' he declares with a smile.

'It's nice to see you, Habib,' I reply. The last time I saw him was in a betting shop in London with Baba a few months before the collapse of IBCD. Baba took me along with him to meet Habib. It was the day of the Grand National, the only time that Baba ever bet on anything, and he liked to do it with Habib, who is an expert on horse racing. Baba told me on the way that Habib could live off the money he makes from betting on horse racing. He could quit his work for my mother's family at any time. 'Looking after your mother's family is by this stage a habit for him,' Baba said. I think now of one of the stories that Baba likes to tell about Habib. About five years ago, a never-married aunt from my mother's family died leaving a large house here in Lahore. The furniture and textiles were divided up among grand-nieces and grand-nephews, but no one was interested in the carpets. Many of them were worn, all of them were cast in pale colours, so they were sent to auction, other than two which Ma gifted to Habib by way of a beneficent after-thought, a thank you for all the work he did to organise the aunt's affairs in life and after death. The family's disregard for the carpets was such that they didn't pay attention to the auctioneer's letter with his estimates for the sale. They were vast. It turned out that the never-married aunt had bought rare Mughal-era carpets which, after some light repairs by the auctioneer, attracted massive interest. There was a newspaper article about the sale, which Baba copied and sent anonymously to each of the family homes by post to underline to them, as he put it to me, 'the drought of refinement in their souls'. Habib saw the article too, and now knowing the value of the carpets he had been given – they were worth six or seven hundred thousand rupees each – he offered them back to Ma, but she felt that she couldn't take them of course, and she had to tell Habib to keep them to save face. Baba was delighted when Habib told him about this. I think Baba admires in Habib both his patience and his luck (for if Habib had been a patient loser, Baba wouldn't have drawn him close; he likes Habib's luck as much as his patience).

'Flight was okay?' asks Habib, turning the key to lock the door through which he thrust Bilal a few moments ago.

'Flight was fine,' I tell him. 'Has Bilal been drinking a lot tonight?' Habib shakes his head and puts a hand on the door again, as if Bilal might be about to force it from the other side and he has to protect me from my uncle's depravity. Bilal is a drunk. He has been for years. I remember waking up on another night in this house and he was sitting outside my bedroom on a chair drinking a glass of milk, his eyes blood-shot. I asked him if he was all right. He stared

135

back at me as if he couldn't understand what I was saying.

'Not tonight, I asked him,' says Habib. 'One night I thought he could be sober.'

'He's addicted,' I reply simply.

'Your cousin was going the same way,' says Habib. 'I am sorry to say this. I sent his jeep back to the house today in case Bilal might see it and realise what he has done. He led his son down the path that led to that battered jeep.'

'I don't know if he saw it,' I say.

'No, he didn't,' Habib replies. 'He was already in a bar.'

'I saw it.'

'I'm sorry,' says Habib. 'I hadn't planned for you to see it.'

'No, that's okay,' I say. 'I think I had to see it. I had to see something.'

'He asked for a new one every six months,' says Habib. 'A new jeep,' he adds, pointing towards the driveway. 'Every time he got one, the first thing he did was to take his father out for an evening of drinking.'

'The work of the firm didn't distract him?' I ask. Habib shakes his head.

'Every few days,' he says, 'he drove to a clinic that your father set up. I was trying to make him the manager. Write the orders, organise the bills. He wasn't interested in that either.'

'Nevertheless he kept going to the clinic?' I suggest. Habib smiles.

'Other reasons,' he says. I stare into his eyes and he looks away. I notice that he is still wearing a tie. I wonder what he will do tonight now that everyone that he looks after is behind closed doors. 'How is your father?' he asks.

'Baba is dedicated to being Baba,' I reply. Habib laughs.

'When do you go back to Beirut?' he asks.

'I have little or no idea,' I tell him. He nods sympathetically. I wonder if, like Ma, he thinks that Mudassar and I have been lovers.

'I'm going to London in two days,' he declares. 'Your aunt wants to go to the house there as soon as possible, get away from all of this. I'll probably start refurbishing it to give her a diversion.' I feel that he is on the brink of laughing about what he has just said, but he doesn't. I do it in his place. 'I should say goodnight,' he says warily.

'Of course,' I say, 'it must have been a long day for you.' He shakes his head mildly. 'And a sad one?' I add, in a more challenging tone. It's not right to put that to him and I regret it immediately. He doesn't respond.

'If you come to London,' he says, 'come and visit us in your aunt's house. Or in my office,' he adds, with a sudden smile. 'You could call it that. You saw it once with your father on the day of the Grand National. Do you remember?'

'Of course I remember,' I reply. 'Forty televisions. Green chairs. It was great.' He smiles again, waves to me and walks towards his car.

I watch him drive out of the gate and then I go back to my bedroom. I lie down, my face on the pillow, and will myself to sleep. After a long attempt, I get up and sit in the window looking out at the trees. All the neighbourhood is dark. As I look from one large villa to the next, I wonder if within each household there's a figure like Habib, that each of these bespoke landmark homes is in a strange way like a ruse, a genius act of misdirection by all of the Habibs, to convince us that inside these homes there live great families, whereas in reality they are full of drunks like Bilal and sentimental old women like Ma, rich but careless, potentially powerful but with no grasp at all on the future. I begin to sing quietly under my breath. My eyes have become heavier when I notice a tall rectangle of light opening in reflection in the window. I see a figure that I recognise. I turn to him and watch him standing in the doorway. It's Alain. 'Do you want to have a drink?' he says. 'Ghalib says the house is littered with half-full whisky bottles.'

'Is half a bottle enough?' I reply. I get up from the window and join him in the doorway. I glance each way along the corridor. There is no one around. I take hold of Alain's arm and pull it upwards until I can read the time on his watch. It's after midnight.

'Come with me,' he says. 'It's not too late to have a drink, is it?' I sigh. I don't want to have a drink but somehow I am glad to find him here. I take his hand, pull him inside the room and close the door.

I fall asleep after him and the night passes in two further instalments. Each time I wake with ill-defined dreams, dreams that seem still to be making themselves, dreams that I'm trying to dream too early. Ultimately, I get out of bed, get dressed and go out into the corridor. I call Baba and there's no answer on his mobile phone. I suppose I am checking once again that he is still in place. Annette's story of the carpet has spooked me, and her suggestion that Baba left the laptop out for me to find on purpose. I calculate the time that it is in Beirut and realise that Baba will be asleep, it's the middle of his night. I return to the bedroom and take up the seat in the windowsill again. When the sky begins to lighten outside, I wake Alain. He grins at me and kisses my mouth. 'Are you in trouble?' I ask him.

'I won't tell anyone about last night if you don't,' he replies.

'That's not what I mean,' I tell him. 'Ghalib told me that the firm is struggling for cash.' Alain nods his head.

'Yes, we are,' he says.

'Is it bad?' I ask.

'It's very bad,' he says. 'Why do you want to know?'

'I'm just asking,' I reply.

'Yes, I thought that's all it is,' he says.

'What do you mean?' I ask.

'Never mind,' he says. He runs his hands through his hair. 'Should I have been more in touch with you the last two years?' he says.

'Not particularly. I've been okay.'

'I emailed you a few times.'

'I didn't reply.'

'No,' he says. 'You never did.'

'Last night was just last night,' I tell him. 'You know that, don't you?' He clears his throat.

'You slept with me because you were overcome with grief for your dead cousin? Something like that?'

I shrug my shoulders. He stands up and searches for his underwear. As he picks it up, I notice that his hands are shaking.

'Are you cold?' I ask him, pointing to his hands.

'It's September in Lahore,' he says. 'It's still basically the summer. I'm not cold.' After a moment he adds: 'You know, you haven't changed.'

'What does that mean?' I reply.

'Somehow you are surprisingly good at getting what you want,' he says.

'Ha,' I respond. 'That's ridiculous.'

'Really?' he says, still mildly. 'What happened between us at the end? What was that?'

'That was a long time ago.'

'You were finished with me. Just like that. Just like this morning.'

'I don't think that I've ever been mean to you.'

'No, I agree,' he says. 'You're not mean. You're

careless. You miss things. You really do miss them. There's no artifice. There's no intention.'

'You're being vague,' I tell him. 'Anyway you have to go before other people start waking up.'

'Mudassar was like this as well,' he says. 'There were things we just couldn't make him understand. You're not stupid, either of you. But there's something about this family that makes people careless. Perhaps you've had money for too long.'

'This isn't really my family,' I tell him. Alain laughs.

'Sure it is.'

'I was kind to you bringing you in here last night,' I reply. 'Now you're overstaying your welcome.'

'Kind? You were lonely.'

'Me? I was lonely? You were the one who turned up at my door with your erection in your hand.'

'That's me,' he says quietly. 'Can't get paid. Can't get laid. My stepmother is American. That's what she says about me.' He leans over and picks his shirt up from the floor. I turn away until he has finished getting dressed. 'So this morning I'm disgusting,' he comments. 'That's great.'

'Just leave,' I tell him.

'I'm going,' he says. 'Goodbye.'

I don't reply. I sit waiting until he has left the room. He leaves the door open when he goes. I get up and roughly make up the bed and then leave the room as well. I don't want to stay in there alone with the thought that I have used Alain again, just like I used to do. The fact that I did that: does it make me like Ma? Does it make me like Baba?

I find women in the kitchen. Ma is there, a maid, and the cook that I met last night. I stand by a counter on one side watching them. I remember a dinner with Baba, Uncle Yani and Uncle Terry on a boat on the Thames in London. My mother was there and an Indonesian businessman and his wife who were making a deal with IBCD. All night my mother talked to the wife and the men talked about the deal. I was there because Uncle Yani via Baba had asked me to come. He told Baba he wanted to plan visits to galleries with me because he had been away from London for two months and thought I could help him reconnect. But he didn't talk to me during the dinner. He kissed me on the cheek to say goodnight at the end and still didn't mention a word of the scheme that he had told Baba about. I remember that I called Alain as soon as I was in a taxi on my own, asked him to come and visit me – and he came. Like last night, I took charge of him when I was feeling powerless. I told Pen about the guilt I felt about calling Alain that night after the boat trip. She knew Alain, knew the whole set. But I had never spoken to anyone properly about my relationship with Alain, not even her, and that day it poured out of me. When I had finished talking, I remember she blew a curl of hair out of her eyes and said: 'Wow. You really aren't in love with him.' She was right, but it was also quite a shocking thing to hear for me. In what I said, I had tried hard to suggest that there was more ambivalence in my feelings. But she saw straight through me. She didn't let me hold the middle ground.

'Aha, there you are, my little bird,' says Ma, dispelling my thoughts. The maid says salaam. The cook doesn't turn to look at me.

'I'm sorry that I went missing yesterday,' I reply. Ma shakes her head.

'I'm happy that you're here,' she says. 'That is more than enough for me.' She turns to the maid and points to a pile of plates. The woman takes a plate and fills it with food from different pots under Ma's instructions. She hands the plate to me when it is complete.

'Eat,' says Ma.

'I'm not hungry,' I reply.

'Don't be silly,' she says. 'Not eating doesn't take you any closer to the dead.' She picks up a piece of roti from her own plate and scoops up some yoghurt with it to show me that she means it. She waits until I take the plate prepared for me before putting the morsel in her mouth. I remain standing, eating slowly, looking from one woman to the other. They talk about the new pickles in a large jar that has just emerged from storage. I watch Ma eat another mouthful of food. She notices that I am watching her. 'Go outside, sit and eat,' she says to me, pleasantly, and points to the chairs on the verandah outside the kitchen. I walk out with the plate she gave me. Outside I find Ghalib and the pilot from my plane.

'Madame,' says the pilot, standing up, 'good morning.'

'Please, sit down,' I say. 'Hi, Ghalib,' I add. He waves at me while continuing to eat with his other hand.

'Thank you, madame,' says the pilot. 'I must go. Please tell them thank you for the food.'

'You're very welcome to stay,' I tell him.

'Call me when you are ready, madame,' he adds. 'The plane is all fine.'

'Okay,' I reply. 'Thank you.'

After he has gone, I take another pastry from my plate and nibble at the corners. I set the plate down on a table next to me. Ghalib is watching me. 'How long are you staying?' he says.

'I don't know,' I tell him. I remember that Alain asked me the same question last night after we had sex.

'You didn't bring many clothes,' he says.

'Do you know where Alain is?' I ask him.

'He had some errands,' replies Ghalib. 'Why?'

'Why was the pilot over here?' I ask.

'I told him to come and eat his meals here,' replies Ghalib.

'Have you met him before?' I ask. Ghalib shakes his head.

'Reema told me that you have lots of clothes here from years before,' he says. Reema is Mudassar's sister.

'Where is Reema?' I ask him. 'Is she up?'

'Did you bring a computer with you?' he says.

'Why?'

'I don't want to use Mudassar's computer,' he says. 'It's upsetting. Where is yours?'

'I didn't bring one,' I tell him.

'Your father was talking to you about a computer when we had tea together in Beirut,' he says.

'I packed really light,' I reply.

'Yeah,' he says. 'But you did have a full case with you. Reema told me that you have clothes here from years ago, so what else was in the case?'

'What else do you think was in the case?' I ask him.

'Hey,' he says. 'Never mind. Do you fancy a trip?'

'Where?' I reply. He has turned away, to watch two servants who are walking around the grounds with refuse sacks. 'I had dinner with Reema when she came to England to study,' I tell him, when he turns back. I remember that I took her to a pub to eat. She spoke too softly to be heard in the noisy room. On the walk back to my place, she told me about a trip she took with Mudassar and Mudassar's girlfriend, rhapsodising about how beautiful and intelligent the latter was. 'Is she still based there?'

'She didn't finish her course,' he replies. 'Didn't like it. Came back to Lahore to study here. The wild west isn't for everyone. Listen,' he says, 'I was going to make a trip to Mudassar's office at the clinic. Habib used to send him up there. Amputees and sad cases like that. I think your dad set it up.'

'Habib told me about it,' I reply.

'Oh, you saw him,' he says.

'Briefly.'

'Did he say anything about me?' he says. I shake my head. 'Okay,' he says. 'Well, do you want to go to this office? You know what Habib is like. He'll have it cleared out by the end of the day. We should go and rescue Mudassar's stuff.'

I cross the lawn with Ghalib and get into the jeep. As soon as we set off, he places a call to Alain on the in-car phone system that I can hear.

'Bud,' he says, 'we're on our way. That's me and H.'

'You're leaving now?' says Alain. I notice that his English is less accented now than when I met him. It's not fair of me, but it means I like his voice less than I used to do. It mattered to me that he bore always the strong musk of another place. It was like a promise that I might ask him to keep in the future, to extract me from where I already was.

'We've left,' says Ghalib.

'See you there,' says Alain. '*A tout.*'

Once the call is over, Ghalib puts on music. Then he immediately puts it off again. 'Are you thirsty?' he says. 'Let's stop for a Pepsi.' He pulls over next to a shop on the side of the road. The owner is sitting underneath a half-raised shutter while a young boy brings out empty drinks crates

146

and puts them upside down in front of the shop for customers to sit on. Ghalib taps on the steering wheel with his closed fist.

'I'm not desperate for a Pepsi,' I say.

'What about a Sprite?' he replies and laughs.

I open my door and turn halfway to sit with my feet on the side-runner. I watch an open van drive past loaded with large containers of water. There is a young boy sitting amid the containers studying a sheet of paper on a clipboard. I can't explain it much better than this, except that it's a comfort that I would be able to read the sheet of paper that he is looking at. I'm not at home, I'm not comfortable, yet more is in focus than in Beirut. 'So Habib didn't say anything about us?' asks Ghalib. 'Or about the money from the family that's in the fund?' I don't reply. Another car pulls up next to us and a man asks me directions. I point him to the man sitting outside the drinks shop. I move again to sit straight in the seat. The young boy from the shop brings Ghalib a drink.

'How far is this place?' I ask Ghalib.

'It's a short drive,' he says. 'Did your father never tell you about it? The place is like a clinic and a resting place for people who have lost their arms or their legs. Your father set it up. They do amputations and replacements and help people with rehabilitation. Is that what it's called?' he asks me. 'Rehabilitation. Recovery, you know? Learning to walk again, learning to grip things with the new hand that they've fitted you.' Ghalib pauses and taps his fist on the steering wheel.

'Baba did it alone?' I ask him.

'You mean: was Yani involved?' he says.

'Was he?'

'Because he's an amputee? That's why you're asking?'

'Usually they did stuff like this together.'

'Usually they did.' Ghalib snorts and turns away.

'How did Mudassar get involved?'

'Habib made him do it.'

We sit in silence for a while. 'How long are you staying?' Ghalib says eventually.

'I have no idea,' I reply.

'Two or three days?' he says. 'A week?'

'I need to speak to Ma about it,' I tell him.

'Yeah, okay,' he says. 'Your phone is buzzing.'

I pick up the phone and answer the call.

'Warm like a vegetable purée,' says Baba right away.

'I'm sorry?' I reply.

'It's a warm day,' he says. 'Humid too. Pea purée, I'd say.'

'Right,' I say.

'What are you doing?' he asks.

'I'm going to see a clinic that you fund,' I reply.

'Oh yes?'

'It's near here,' I tell him.

'I'm aware of it,' he says. 'Anyway, that's not why I'm calling. I need to know what you're doing.'

'Doing about what?'

'I realise your cousin's funeral was only yesterday and your mind may be on other things,' he says, 'but are you coming back? I would like to know.'

'And that's why you called?' I ask.

'Personally I think it's a good idea for you to stay out there for a while,' he says.

'Why's that?'

'Ma's your family too,' he says. 'I've been monopolising you.'

'Baba, I don't get it,' I tell him. 'What do you want?' There is a long silence.

'I don't know,' he says.

'You want me to look after you?' I ask.

'I don't need that,' he says.

'You want me to go swimming with you then,' I reply. 'Is that it? You want me to sit across the table from you at dinner, well-dressed, looking slim, though only at dinner, certainly not at breakfast.'

'Hanna,' he says, 'have you considered that I made a mistake two years ago? In a moment of weakness, at a time of extreme stress, I asked you to come with me and I shouldn't have done that. I regret that I did.'

'Great,' I reply.

'I have always wanted for you to be free,' he continues. 'Free in ways that I was not when I was your age. I had to create a free state for myself. I wanted to make sure you had it all along. I have never asked you about marriage. If your mother ever suggested the name of a boy that we should introduce you to, I refused to discuss it. I wanted you to be free. What Asian father is as happy as me in giving that freedom?'

'That might not be freedom,' I reply. 'That might be disinterest. You want to call me free because you don't care what I do? That doesn't sound right.'

'Hanna,' he says, his voice falling. 'It's getting dangerous here. Let me say as much as that.'

'That's not enough,' I tell him. 'Tell me what that picture is.'

'Not over the phone,' he says.

'There's always a reason not to tell me,' I reply.

'Just not over the phone,' he says.

'Right, so in that case,' I tell him, 'I will be coming back.' I press the red button on my phone and end the call.

'My fucking dad,' I say, as I put the phone away.

'Intense,' says Ghalib.

I shake my head. 'Is it far away?' I ask. 'The clinic?'

'No, it's close,' he says. He throws his empty Pepsi bottle out of the window and restarts the car.

Soon we are on an empty road, clearly new. There are channels for grass or plants alongside, but there hasn't been time for anything to grow. Ghalib is driving more quickly than back in Defence. We pass an incipient commercial area, probably the market of the new residential colony that is being

150

created on all sides. There are piles of bricks and mounds of sand. Men with sand on their faces are working at tasks that I can't understand the purpose of from watching them. There's a woman in a black shuttlecock burqa carrying a small child in her arms, like an architectural find being carried off to a place of safe keeping. The child is wearing a long shirt with a dark orange stain on it. He glances at the car as we pass but misses my stare. I realise that the windows of the car are tinted. I could stop breathing or suddenly cough blood onto the glass and no one would see. We pass through the area under construction within minutes and we are back on a new, empty road.

'It's right up here,' says Ghalib. I look up and he is pointing towards a gate a short distance off the road. Behind the gate, there is a long driveway and a large, short-stacked house. There is no formal exit from the road here but he slows down and drives over the verge across a track where others have clearly been before us. We stop outside the gate. There is a white-washed gatehouse. Ghalib opens his window. 'Hurry up,' he shouts, and a man comes out of the gatehouse dressed in a light-brown uniform. There is a gun on his hip. He rubs at his eyes, as if he has been sleeping, but his posture is erect. He looks over the car, peers into the car at me through Ghalib's window. 'You've seen me before,' says Ghalib. 'Remember? I came here with Mudassar. I've come to clear his office.' The guard doesn't respond. Ghalib, shaking his head, fetches his wallet from a pocket and removes a banknote from it. He shakes the guard's hand through the open window and then the guard nods. He goes back into the gatehouse and comes out a few seconds later. He pushes a button in a panel on the side of the gatehouse and the gate opens. Ghalib drives through it and speeds up as we mount the driveway. 'Well, here you are,' he says, looking at me again after a long while. He points to a large plaque mounted next to the front door of the main building. It says: THIS BUILDING AND INSTITUTION IS DEDICATED TO A DEAR FRIEND AND BROTHER, YANI.

'You said they didn't do it together,' I say to Ghalib.

'No, they didn't. Your father paid for everything. Guess when?'

'I don't know.'

'Right after he took over the presidency of the bank.'

'He was saying sorry?' My tone is incredulous.

'Don't be silly,' replies Ghalib. 'He was saying: fuck you. He was saying: you're a fucking cripple. I get the presidency of the bank. You get this.' I make a noise blowing out air through my mouth and shake my head.

'My fucking dad.'

'Got it in one.'

We get out of the car and walk up to the building. Ghalib asks me to wait in the entrance hall. I watch him go through a door into an office. He opens a small fridge sitting on the floor and takes out two bottles of water. 'Take this,' he says, handing me one of the bottles. 'You must be thirsty by now.' I take it gratefully and drink a long slug of water. He watches me do it and then does the same himself. 'Come on,' he says. We return to the outside and go around the side of the building. There are trees planted on both sides of the walkway, miniature for now. There's a thin water pipe for irrigation installed along the paving. It's been put in carefully. There are small lights embedded in the ground.

'It's going to turn into a really pretty place,' I remark.

'Oh yeah,' replies Ghalib. 'They're particular, your father and Habib. No doubt about that. You have to wonder though,' he says, 'where the money for a place like this keeps coming from.'

'IBCD created foundations for the charitable work,' I reply.

'Right,' says Ghalib, laughing. 'Foundations.'

We turn the corner and go under an arch into a large paved courtyard. We enter at the front and there are more rooms at the back. At the centre of the courtyard, there is a garden and a fountain. Underneath a verandah, there is a group of men. One of them is in a wheelchair. A number of them are in wheelchairs, I then realise, not only the one. There is a pair of men in wheelchairs playing backgammon, facing each other side-on, their chairs

153

pointed in opposite directions. There's a man in a wheelchair making a phone call using a phone installed onto the back wall of the house. Ghalib walks towards them and I follow. 'Don't introduce me,' I say quietly. He hears me and nods, stops walking. I look back towards the garden in the middle of the courtyard and I can see now two men sitting on the grass. One of them is lying flat on the ground on his back; he has neither of his legs. The other man is sitting up, leaning on a short crutch; he doesn't have a right arm. I look more closely at him and notice that there are scars on his face. In fact, the scars are where his right eye should be.

'Do you think I should take over from Mudassar in helping out here?' says Ghalib. 'I could ask your father. He could pay me a salary.'

'If he wanted you to do it, he would have asked you before,' I reply. Ghalib goes very still and looks at me.

'Right,' he says. 'Well, in any case, it's a super-depressing place. I don't think I would want to do it. Do you want to meet the doctors?' he asks.

'They have a clinic right here?' I say.

'Sure,' he says. 'That's the point. I mean, none of these people had proper amputations and stuff till they came here. They were just carrying around dead limbs, you know, and bits of limbs.' He shakes his head. 'Some of it's fallout from suicide attacks,' he says, 'a lot of it's from up north, where the Taliban are fighting the army.

Some of these guys are ex-soldiers. Some of them are just unlucky.' I try to nod several times while he's talking. It's important for me to focus a little bit on having this conversation or, having seen these amputees, I will stand here thinking of the man whose head was in the photograph, whether his body was chopped up afterwards, or before. There's a spinning motion starting inside my head.

'Are there women here?' I ask, looking around the courtyard. I can't see any but I wonder about the second part of the building at the back. Ghalib follows where I'm looking.

'Women are in that one,' he says, pointing. I see that there are balconies at some of the windows on the second storey. 'Do you want to go?' he says.

'I don't want to visit them,' I tell him. I notice that the women have the curtains drawn so that the men cannot see them. They can't use the balconies, I suppose, except at night perhaps, after the men have gone to bed. If there are women, their children will be here as well. I hope the children come out into the courtyard sometimes. Ghalib stands still in the middle of the courtyard, at a seeming loss. I'm not moving either, just looking around me. One of the men in the garden calls to Ghalib, beckons him to come over. Ghalib shakes his head. 'Do they know who you are?' I ask him.

'They've seen me before,' says Ghalib. 'They'll be curious about you. Plus they might want to beg money,' he adds, after a pause, looking towards the group of men under the verandah. I take a last look towards the building where the women are.

'Can we go?' I say. I start walking back the way we came before Ghalib replies. He follows me right away.

'I'm going to look in Mudassar's office,' he says, as we return to the front entrance.

'Oh yes,' I reply, remembering. He leads me into the room.

There is the small fridge, a simple desk and some bare shelves on the wall facing me. There is a television suspended on a wall bracket. Ghalib goes in behind the desk and stands for a moment with a hand on his forehead. Unaccountably, I want to go around the desk and take him in my arms. I realise suddenly that he may be as lost as I am. And it's worse for him: it's not just what his father might be up to with mine, it's not just Mudassar, it's the issue of the money, his business slipping away from him. 'I can't imagine Mudassar sitting behind this desk,' I say. 'Can you?' Ghalib shakes his head as he looks around the room, as if appraising it again in order to answer my question.

'I guess he was never here for a long time,' he says. 'There's a TV though,' he adds.

'I don't see a remote control,' I say.

'Give me a chance,' he says. He takes a set of keys from his pocket and tries them in each drawer of the desk in turn. There is a knock on the office door and we both watch Alain come inside. He is wearing an elegant light blue shirt with the sleeves rolled up past his elbows and blue trousers. His feet are bare inside blue sandals. 'Here it is,' declares Ghalib, hidden behind the desk. He stands up, holding a packet.

'What's that?' I ask him. He tosses it up in the air and catches it. It's a square plastic bag packed with powder.

'Heroin,' says Ghalib. 'With any luck, high quality, near 100 per cent heroin.' I watch him tuck one side of the bag into his trousers and pull his T-shirt across the rest.

'What else is there?' I ask lightly. 'An elephant tusk?'

'There's a handgun,' says Ghalib. 'But I have less use for that.' He closes each of the drawers and locks them. I wonder if he's joking. He puts the keys in an ashtray sitting on top of the desk.

'Just one bag,' says Alain.

'Just one,' says Ghalib. 'But it might be pure. A lot of the men in here are from the west near Afghanistan. Their visitors bring in the best stuff. Mudassar made a good connection here.'

'It's too little,' says Alain.

'We're not going to sell it,' says Ghalib. 'We don't have the first idea of how to shift heroin. This will be a gift to Mudassar's friend. It might buy us another two weeks.'

'That's not much,' says Alain.

'Well, we can go back to the police and ask them

if they found Mudassar's watch in the wreckage,'
says Ghalib. 'Do you fancy doing that? We can take
our dead friend's watch and give that to the guy as
a gift as well. There's maybe another week in that.'

'If the watch survived, the police will have sold
it by now,' replies Alain.

'Well, you talk to her then,' says Ghalib, pointing
at me. 'You fucked her. You talk to her. She absolutely hasn't realised that she can help us yet. And
I'm not begging her. You can do that.' He walks
out from behind the desk and goes towards the
door, shaking his head.

'Where are you going?' I ask him.

'They have a lunch here,' he says, without stop-
ping. 'Rice and then rice pudding. *Prix fixe*.' When
he has left the room, I turn to Alain.

'You need me to help you?' I ask him.

'We have some financial problems. Ghalib told
you about them.'

'He says Habib will want the money back that
Mudassar had invested in the firm and there's
some other guy.'

'Yes,' he replies, 'and the other guy hangs out
with some nasty people.'

There's a pause. He looks at me.

'Well?' he says.

'Well what?'

'Will you help us?'

'I don't know anything about your fund,' I reply.
'I don't invest my own money. It's in a bank in
London.'

'You could make us a loan.'

'A loan? It doesn't sound like you'd ever be able to pay it back.'

'So make it a gift. This isn't easy to say, you know?' He turns away from me and then bangs his hand down on the table.

'You've screwed up, haven't you?' I ask. 'You're in a lot of debt?'

'Shut up,' says Alain.

'Was Mudassar drinking too much because he was stressed about the fund?' It's a mean question, an unthinking question. I regret asking it as soon as the words have left my mouth. Alain turns and rushes towards me. He puts his hand on my shoulder and squeezes hard. I pull away from his grip. He doesn't let me go and pushes me back against the desk. He grabs a fistful of the cloth of my *shalwar kameez* around the waist. 'Let me go,' I shout.

'I could make your life very difficult for you,' he says. I can feel him growing as he presses against my crotch. I jag my fingernails into the back of his hand until his grip releases me. Then I hurl my elbow into his chest.

'Stop it,' I tell him. I walk to the door.

'I have journalist friends,' he says. 'Your story, your deceit – they would like it.'

'What deceit are you talking about?'

'You know what I'm talking about. The paintings.'

I have my hand on the door knob. It drops to my side.

'We need a million dollars,' he says behind me. I turn to him.

'That's it,' I reply. 'All this nonsense and you're only down one million.'

'See,' he says. 'It's easy for you. You're rich. You can give us the money.'

'You're pathetic,' I tell him. 'What a pathetic little business.' I stride out of the door. Ghalib is standing behind it.

'Drive me to the PC,' I tell him. 'Right now.'

'You have a lunch at the PC?' he says. The PC is the Pearl Continental hotel, where Baba stayed if he was with my mother and me in Lahore. He never stayed at Ma's house. The PC came to me immediately as the place to where I can flee.

I walk past Alain and go and stand next to the jeep. I watch Ghalib and Alain have a conversation. I can't hear them. Alain goes back inside the office. Ghalib walks over to the jeep. 'We're desperate,' he says, when we're in our seats. 'People do silly things when they're desperate.' I don't reply. 'He's sorry if he hurt you,' he adds. 'We're both under a lot of stress.' I still say nothing. Eventually Ghalib starts the car. It's a long drive and I look fixedly out of the window on my side. Ghalib doesn't speak either. By the Pearl, he stops before the security barrier. 'Can you get out here?' he says. 'I don't want to get searched.' I collect my bag and open the door. 'I'll come over tonight,' he says. 'Maybe we can speak more reasonably.' I leave the jeep without replying. Three formal smiles later, I have a key to a room. I refuse any assistance in finding where I need to go. As soon as I'm inside the room, I lie face down on the bed.

CHAPTER 3

I am ruined for houses and homes. Ever since I left my flat when Baba came to get me, then, installed in the Saint-Michel, watching on television news a crew of police officers standing around my parents' house, it is hotels, not private residences, that I associate with safety, refuge, quiet. I have come to the PC after just one day and one night in Ma's house, no more than twenty-four hours. I've fled her house, though it doesn't feel like I've thrown off any ropes, it's quite different, it's rather that I've come to the PC to be tied up with the ropes of the hotel, like Odysseus in the story when he asks the sailors to tie him to the mast of his boat. I need a period under restraint to find out what I'm doing. Baba is getting jumpy on the phone. Ghalib and Alain are making threats. I need to orientate myself. I think that starts by finding out about the photograph. Is Baba the villain? Or is he in danger himself? I can go running back to Beirut to get away from Ghalib and Alain, but is it the right place to go?

I believe that I can recognise the face of the man if I see it again. My first step is to find out who he is. As soon as I arrived here, I called downstairs and asked them to get me a laptop. They brought me a hotel computer, but I sent them away to buy one from a shop. They could search a hotel laptop after I return it and find out what I've been looking at. While I wait for the box-fresh laptop I lie on the bed and convulse with shame. I don't know if Alain would do it, I don't know if anyone would show any interest, but if he wants to, he can carry out his threat and reveal my secret. I confessed to him when I made my little fraud. He was the only one I told. We weren't together at the time, though we still slept together occasionally. On a Sunday morning, I told him.

The name of the artist that I messed around with is Sudhir Patwardhan. The person who bought the forgery I created is called Mustafa. I sold it to him in Dubai. Mustafa owns a car show-room. He wanted to fit the walls with pictures. I had helped his cousin buy two pictures in Karachi. She convinced him to see me. I went to him with a selection of pictures, including *The City*, a picture by Patwardhan. It features two men: one of them, in a white shirt, is facing away as he stands on a railway platform looking at a train full of people – his expression is invisible to us; the other man is in a grey shirt, facing towards us, drinking tea that he has poured from his cup into the saucer. He could be at the train station or he could be somewhere else. The composition of the painting is ambiguous. His eyes are closed.

I didn't expect Mustafa to pick out this painting as it had nothing to do with either cars or luxury. He loved it. In fact he asked for two more pictures by the same artist. He told me that the glittering thing for him about *The City* was that, if someone who walked into his showroom recognised the scenes in the picture, if someone had once lived simply like that and since risen, then Mustafa will have shown, by putting the picture in his showroom, that he understood that person. That person would buy a car straight away, said Mustafa. Perhaps it was a business decision then, but I think it was something else as well. Perhaps he recognised the scenes in his own life. Perhaps he saw his father or his son in the picture. I can remember him very clearly, this man whom I tricked. He was well-dressed, wistful, kind to me. He had bad balance, due to a problem with the fluid in his inner ear. He walked with both arms halfway extended, always braced in case he stumbled. He had built up a medium-sized property business in Karachi, from not very much to start with I think – his family wasn't wealthy. He took over the Dubai car show-room from an Englishman who had been caught with drugs in his luggage and put in prison. Mustafa claimed to have no taste in art, he told me so at the beginning, buy whatever you want was his instruction to me. But I believed that no one really thinks that in the end, not when they're spending money, so I had brought him some pictures to look at, including *The City*. It was the first one he chose.

Mustafa never spoke to me about what I did to him. I didn't try to call him either after the fact. He never publicised what happened. He could have ruined me, quite easily. All he did was to write me an email when he found out. He told me that I had treated him like a fool and that he didn't understand that, because he hadn't mistreated me or squeezed down my fee. I had done it to him, he said, because he didn't know anything about art. I remember the phrase he used. He said that he was only a 'middle-class person' and that I had made him feel embarrassed about it.

It wasn't what I had been thinking at all, but it's true that I wouldn't have tried what I did with an experienced collector. Mustafa had asked me for two more pictures by Patwardhan. I was excited by that, I liked *The City* a lot myself. The problem I encountered in trying to meet his ask is that Patwardhan is a practising doctor, a radiologist, so he doesn't paint lots of canvases. Whatever I did find for sale couldn't be placed alongside *The City*, it was different in outlook and style. Time was pressing. Mustafa wanted the pictures as soon as possible. He trusted me to find them quickly. I couldn't visit Patwardhan and commission them. It would take too long. I even told gallery owners that I would pay a premium for anything suitable by Patwardhan that they could find for me. I was ready to pay more from my own funds than I was going to ask from Mustafa.

But still nothing came out. So I did something venal and wrong and ridiculous. I knew a young artist who admired Patwardhan too. He wanted to make some money. Patwardhan was hardly that famous, so the risk was low. The work was for a car showroom, not a gallery. So I asked the new painter to make me two paintings that could hang alongside *The City*, one to feature the man in the white shirt, to hang to the left of the painting, and the other to feature the man in the grey shirt, to hang to the right. Within three weeks, I had them. I sent them to Mustafa in the showroom. I was too scared to take them to Dubai myself. I should have gone. If I had, I might have struck sense just in time. I stayed in London. I think I smoked two packs of cigarettes, sitting in my flat window, on the day of delivery. Mustafa rang me that evening. He was delighted. He sent me a photograph of the three pictures hanging together high on the wall, with him and all his salesmen standing underneath them.

I felt giddy after he called me and I saw that photograph. I sent the artist who had produced the additional paintings some extra money, as if to share the shame the better. It was much worse because of Mustafa's delight. He told people who asked about the paintings all about me and I got clients through this. I was back in Dubai within a month talking to two new prospective buyers, both introduced to me by Mustafa. He told me to come to the showroom to visit him but I made excuses.

I went back to London and moved on to other things. Whenever I thought of it though, of the possibility of being discovered, I felt ill, like there were air bubbles forming inside my veins. Months went by, and perhaps I began to relax a little bit. I was found out in the end when Mustafa wrote to Sudhir Patwardhan at his radiology clinic in Thane, near Bombay, enclosing a photograph of the three paintings together, proclaiming his adoration and his gratitude. Patwardhan wrote back, charmed by Mustafa's enthusiasm I expect, but wanting to explain to him as well that a mistake had been made. That was when Mustafa emailed me as he did. He took down the two fake paintings and returned them to me. He kept *The City*.

What would happen if the story came out? I would feel embarrassed, but in Beirut there aren't many people who can embarrass me. I have no close friends, no colleagues in that city. I would have to tell Baba beforehand. But somehow, now that I've seen the photograph on his laptop, that feels easier than it has ever done before. No, I think worse than embarrassment there's the chance that the people pursuing my father would use it as a lever in the attempt to get him. I have committed fraud. I passed something off as being of a higher value than it was. Baba asked me, while we were leaving London, if I had ever been questioned by the police before. I said no. He suggested some possibilities: perhaps I had used drugs, perhaps I had been holding on to them for a friend, perhaps

I had a car accident and left the scene. I kept saying no. I didn't confess. Baba was worried that in time the police might discover that they had a way to put pressure on me, and hope that I might relieve that pressure by telling them something about Baba. It's shame that I'm feeling more than fear. I lied to Baba. I made him feel more safe than he is. And I suppose the shame also comes from the realisation that I would like to keep lying, or do whatever else I need to do to keep my fraud a secret. I have the money that Baba put aside for me. Could I really just give Alain and Ghalib one million dollars?

A knock sounds on my door. There's a man around my age standing outside with a box. 'Madam,' he says, 'this is the laptop you wanted. I will come in and set it up for you.'

'No,' I reply. I hold out my hands and it takes him a moment to understand that I want the box from him here in the doorway.

'I set it up,' he says. 'It's my pleasure.'

'Just give it to me,' I tell him. I take it and close the door without signing anything. I set down the box and go back to the phone. 'I want a woman,' I say down the line when the receptionist picks up the other end. 'Anytime that you're sending someone to my room, I want a woman.' I put the phone down before receiving an answer.

I sit down on the bed with the box. I swear aloud when the sticky tape on the ends doesn't come off with my nails. I am overwrought. By the time that I have opened the box, taking scissors from the bathroom to cut the tape, strewing the packaging across the bed, I am crying. I feel ashamed. I feel angry, at Baba, Ghalib and Alain. From time to time, I remember the touch of his penis on the skin around my vagina before he came inside me last night. I shudder, then I see that I am clenching my fists and I try to think of something else. I even feel angry at Ma, like she should have protected me from all of this, if I am her little bird, then this is what she should do. But all that she asks me, all that anyone here asks me, is how long I will be staying. I'm right to be in a hotel. The life I've made, I belong in a hotel. At the same time I have fear as well. I imagine Alain going further in intimidating me. Between the two of them, Ghalib and he could have locked me in that office and done much more. And what if Alain does tell the world about the fake Patwardhans? I imagine sitting at tea with Baba in the Saint-Michel, police officers from Dubai coming in to find me, a Brit with them, an American. They would already have interviewed Mustafa, they would have found the artist who made the forgery for me, they would have made a net to take me away in and they would give Baba a choice. The Brit or the American would be the one to articulate it. Either Baba could go with them or I could. It would be for Baba to choose.

I sit in a chair by the window and watch two men laying out garden furniture. Perhaps it doesn't matter now. Perhaps Baba has made a far worse mistake. I open the laptop and set it up. I didn't recognise the man in the photograph on Baba's machine. But it's still possible that he was an IBCD man, that Baba was meant to recognise him, it could be that the photograph was sent to Baba as a threat: we got him, next it's you. I begin searching for pictures of men who were formerly in the senior team at IBCD. I knew many of them, but not every one. I ignore a knock on the door. Later there is a phone call. I watch the telephone until it stops ringing, then go back to looking at the screen of the computer. I scan through the websites that purport to tell the secret story of IBCD. I survey professional networking sites. Hardly anyone mentions IBCD itself in their own profile, but I know the names of its fronts and subsidiaries, and some people use those more obscure names rather than leave a gap in their career history. I remember names from conversations between Baba and my uncles, Sherpao, Yani or Terry; I picture the seating plans for dinner, mounted on easels outside the dining room, when the worldwide senior team was together at Como, where I had breakfast with Sherpao; I search against all of the names that I can recall. Though I hesitate over a couple of photographs, within two hours I think I have ruled out that the man in the photograph on Baba's laptop is someone who held a senior position in the bank. But there are other possibilities. He might never have held a public role in the bank.

He could have been a private fixer who worked for Baba and now doesn't turn up on my searches because he lived incognito, funded by a lifetime grant from Baba. He could be a former driver or bodyguard. I knew several of those people, but possibly not all of them. I could ask Habib for help, he's here in Lahore, he might have met some of the shadow men of IBCD, he might recognise the man in the photograph, but I don't have the photograph with me now.

There is the other scenario as well. Baba didn't stop me from coming to Lahore; in fact he made it easy. It may be that he isn't under threat, rather my absence makes it simpler for him to complete something the start of which is depicted in the photograph. Ghalib may be right in what he said when he came to Beirut: Baba has the look that he gets when he is executing something that he has planned. He may not be finished yet. There may be more awfulness to come.

Looking at the websites about IBCD takes me back to what happened after Como – and the day that Baba told me about it. The websites have never got it right, but they pass close to it sometimes in their speculation and theory-making. I've read that the bank was about to declare massive losses just before it fell; or that it made strange trades in the frantic few days before the collapse – in fact, that's a matter of public record now, it certainly did – or even that the bank was always kept afloat by CIA money and they started using a different bank and that was it.

Three months after we arrived in Beirut, beyond the period when we confined ourselves to our separate rooms, after the first investigators, state and newspaper, had gone, Baba asked me to go out with him on a boat into the Bay of Jounieh, north of Beirut, and, after he had swum, he said, 'Do you know why our bank collapsed?' He had a towel around his shoulders. I had set down two glasses of water in front of him. I shook my head. I had never asked him directly. I had assumed he wouldn't tell me. Or that he would tell me a lie. 'In fact,' he said, before drinking the first glass of water, 'you were there when the ruination began.'

The downfall of IBCD, he revealed, was the decision made in the Villa d'Este on Lake Como, where I had breakfast with Sherpao, where my mother fell down the stairs. The bankers had gathered on Lake Como, Baba explained, to make a decision about an offer that had been made to them by a group of financiers from the Gulf. I already knew about that. 'Sherpao told me,' I reminded him. Baba shook his head. 'Blow it open,' he said. 'That's what they wanted us to do: blow it open. We were going to be the world's biggest bank, not just the world's biggest Arab bank. But there were conditions,' he said. The Arab investors wanted IBCD to move money around for them, to support what they called 'Islamic causes'. 'Education, they said, money for schools

172

and books,' Baba remembered. 'Of course there would have been plenty of that. You have to say the Sunni religious freaks don't forget about the books. So there would be some education. But there was going to be money for other causes as well, to establish training camps, to induce government officials to look the other way, to buy military intelligence, and of course arms.' Baba explained that the proposition was that all of this additional funding would be done under the cover of a new Islamic banking operation to be run through IBCD. There would be a massive incentive payment for the bank and the investment to expand the banking infrastructure that IBCD was establishing in key countries. 'We went to Como to talk about it,' Baba said. 'Did we buy into this or did we say no.'

'You said no,' I replied.

'IBCD said no,' he repeated, 'though only Sherpao, me and a handful of others knew what the deal really meant. The issue was put to everyone else solely on the financials, and obviously we had to talk about what it meant for the kind of bank we were, big and clunky, or agile and mean. It was a huge relief that everyone was with us. We said no to the Gulfies.'

'Everyone said no?' I asked him.

'Not immediately,' he said. 'There was discussion. But we reached a common decision. It was how Sherpao and I wanted it done, by discussion, so that everyone was going to stand behind it.

There were three or four hold-outs, but only three or four, and I handed them cheques and told them to find other jobs.'

'Who told the Gulfies?' I asked, using his phrase. I remember he laughed when he heard me say it.

'I did,' he said. 'It was the sort of conversation I couldn't allow Sherpao to have. He was the figurehead, he couldn't give the big no.'

'Did Yani go with you?'

'Of course not. I did it alone. Sherpao hesitated at one point and thought Yani should do it in place of me. He thought I would be too triumphalist about it. But that's what we needed. Actually I did it while Sherpao and Yani were still talking about it.'

After Baba broke the news, the investors took away the money they had already put into the bank. It was about £500 million but the bank was growing at the time and it coped. In fact, it kept expanding, kept trading up, kept buying other firms and businesses. 'Then,' Baba told me, on his second glass of water, 'the Arabs came back. They made their offer again. Saddam had been removed from Iraq. There was a struggle for the spoils. We had a great network in Iraq, in Kurdistan too, agents where we didn't have branches. So they offered us the same partnership. But we felt we were in the position of strength then. We refused right away. I,' Baba said, 'convinced Sherpao that we didn't even have to put it to the board. I went back and to the same faces said no for a second time.'

Sherpao and Baba assumed that, upon this second refusal, there would be no further consequences for them. These people had, after all, removed their money already. But that's not how it went. As soon as Baba had been to see them, they started sending letters in fact to the board members of IBCD and in each there was a photograph of the IBCD headquarters with the letters of the bank's name hanging off the building precariously, about to fall to the street. More widely, the would-be investors started to spread rumours about IBCD, to say that it was working with the Americans, that there was a Mossad agent on the board, that the Shia bosses of the bank were creating trouble across the Sunni Muslim world. They used every bit of influence they had with the governments, sovereign wealth funds and major families from the region to convince them to pull their money out of IBCD as well. The revenge strategy culminated in seven major investors giving notice to IBCD on the same day. 'It was plainly premeditated,' Baba said, 'but we couldn't complain, which they were relying on of course.'

IBCD didn't want to shake the confidence that the markets had in it by resisting the demands. Equally they had done enterprising things with some of their capital and they couldn't afford to give the regulators a hint that there was a problem. So they paid out the claims. 'We could do it,' Baba said, proudly. 'We were doing well. We squeezed every single cash facility that we had for every penny of cash, we leveraged till we were dizzy, but we paid them all. We made it. Financial historians ought to record what we did in those few weeks to make those payments, professors ought to teach it in business school.' He paused and stared at the sea then; I remember it. 'But within the same week they hit us with a second wave,' he said. 'And that was it. We had done the first call as discreetly as possible, kept our cash-raising fairly quiet. We had to, or the predators in the market would have been onto our positions. It was a great piece of banking. I'm proud of what we did on the first wave. But we couldn't do it again. We had used every mechanism available to us, called on every source of credit we had. When the second call was due, we fell.'

Baba stopped talking then and we sat in silence for a short while watching the water. I checked in my mind what he had said against what I had read about the fall of the bank. Some of the better journalism had already described, within days of the fall, that IBCD had been unusually active on the capital markets in the previous few weeks and that liquidity had been the issue on its last day. Baba had told me before that IBCD suffered because it was Shia, that the story of the bank could be added to the ongoing story of injustice faced by the Shia. After he had spoken, after the silence, I followed up with question after question. I felt that he might never speak about it again. I had to take the chance, fill myself up with the best understanding of why I was in Beirut, not any more in London. He answered my questions softly, evenly. Then, he stopped. 'More later,' he said. And this wasn't a lie. He didn't stop talking about it. He confided in me once and it didn't scare him. So he kept doing it. He told me in more detail about the meeting with the consortium on the second occasion that he refused their money, the threats that they made. Yet Baba didn't credit them at the time, didn't report them back even to Sherpao. 'On we go,' he said to Sherpao when he came back from the meeting.

I know the names of the people who were in the consortium that brought down IBCD. In his retellings, Baba gave me all the names. Despite everything, I think he admired what they had done as well. I'm sure that, if he was on their side, he would have been ruthless too. Nevertheless they killed his bank. Baba was in sole charge by the end. Sherpao had already gone. I remember how disconsolate Baba was when he came to find me in my flat to tell me that IBCD had fallen. And they didn't only kill his bank, they ended the life he had: the travel, the objects, the thrill of leading a massive and successful organisation. I think I have to envisage that Baba is capable of a terrible revenge. I have to search for images of the men who brought down IBCD.

I remember that I heard a noise at the door of my room while I was occupied earlier over the computer. I get up from the chair by the window and find on the floor a hotel envelope that has been slipped under the door. 'Message from Ghalib Chalabi,' it says. 'Ma wants to see you. I haven't told her where you are.' I believe the handwriting is Ghalib's own. On reading it, I realise that I do have to tell Ma that I am here. If Ghalib tells her, she will force him to come here and try to bring me back. When that fails, she will commission Habib to do it. I go down to the front desk and order a taxi.

The taxi driver takes an overlong route but I don't complain; I'm happy for the time it gives me to look at the surroundings in the pretty light of the later afternoon. I'm in no rush to see Ma, no rush to go back to the hotel after seeing her and make my next set of macabre searches. I begin to remember places I've been in Lahore to visit artists or collectors. In Defence itself, not far from Ma's house, there was a collector called Ahmed who taped everything I said when I reported back to him about pictures that I had seen for him. He switched off the recorder once, when he asked me to dinner after a meeting from which his wife was absent. I told him no and that was pretty much the end of the business he wanted to do with me. In the older parts of the city, there's a restaurant on a roof that doesn't have a kitchen. It brings in food from the carts on the streets nearby. The house was or still is a brothel. There are paintings of the women on the stairs that lead to the roof. There I met a man who buys girls from poor villagers like the gangsters do; he paints them, then lets them go. He said that his art was honest about the exploitation by the artist of other people. The prices that he set for his work varied according to the prices that he had paid for the girls depicted in them. I think Pakistani art is more or less still like this. I read about it from Beirut. There's an at times quite extreme anxiety inherent in it. Its presence is long-standing. There is a large painting in Ma's house of her great-grandfather wearing a colonial uniform. Baba told me that he was never part of any colonial organisation. So the uniform was procured for the painting, as if the only person at that time who could be depicted in a painting was a man with a colonial connection and, even in a private setting, where Ma's grandfather had paid the painter, he wouldn't ask the painter to undertake the activity of making art unless he was more than a subaltern.

The police barrier on Ma's street is still in place but there's only one officer on it now. I think to myself that Habib is saving money where he can. 'Ma is my grandmother,' I tell the police officer. 'I don't have this car on my sheet,' he replies. He is old, fifty at least. His beard has turned from black to mostly grey. I realise that it's not fair to argue with him. After all I don't pay him; I don't set his instructions. I get out of the taxi and settle the fare with the driver. I tell the police officer my name and wait while he calls the house. 'Please welcome,' he says to me in English after he finishes the call. I walk to the house and notice Ghalib's jeep in the driveway. Within the gates of Ma's house, I wave to a servant polishing the knobs on the doors. He seems to recognise me and smiles. I walk directly towards Ma's room on the other side of the house. I walk past Uncle Bilal's door where I met Habib last night. Bilal has been an alcoholic for a long time. I recall my mother furious with Baba after a dinner in London ten years ago where Baba had refused to drink, daring Bilal to keep going even though he the host wasn't drinking, and of course Bilal had.

I find Ma on her verandah speaking to the same young girl she introduced yesterday and another woman, older than me, perhaps forty. I saw her at the funeral. I don't know who she is. 'Little bird, come here,' yells Ma.

'Salaam,' I tell her when I present myself at the threshold of the verandah. I smile in turn at the others as well and repeat 'Salaam'. Ma watches me with a look of surprise, as if it's an affront to her that I am giving my attention to anyone else. She beckons me to come closer. She grips my arm when I do.

'This is my granddaughter,' she says to the other woman. 'The sole daughter of my sole daughter. She doesn't live in Lahore.'

'I haven't seen you before,' says the other

woman. 'You arrived today?' she asks me. Ma shakes her head.

'She came immediately for her cousin's funeral,' she says. 'So promptly, no one could equal this. No lunch?' she asks me.

'I went out,' I reply.

'I thought you were in your room all day,' says Ma. She pushes a strand of hair away from my face.

'No, I went out,' I tell her again.

'Did you have errands to do for your father?' she asks. 'He buys *shalwar kameez* in Lahore, doesn't he? Not that he wears it often.'

'Ghalib took me out,' I reply.

'He's a nice boy,' she says. 'So devastated that his friend is dead. Broken. Poor broken boy.'

'Are you doing all right, Ma?' I ask her.

'It will pass,' she says, grandly. 'Don't go out for dinner,' she adds. 'Dinner we'll eat here together.' She releases my arm and turns her attention back to the woman that I don't recognise. 'One hundred acres?' she says. The woman nods and resumes some account that she had been giving before I arrived. I stand and listen for a minute, then turn away. I walk over to a chair and sit down. I watch the young girl. She is sleepy. Her eyes close and her head nestles into one side of the chair. Her feet are painted all over in henna. One of them jolts suddenly then curls up off the ground.

I stand up and make for the door and Ma doesn't comment. I leave the verandah and walk the long way around the house to the front door. Perhaps it doesn't matter if I stay here or in the hotel. If I show Ma my face once or twice a day, that may be all she requires. Ma is at the core of her own drama, she sees me only from a great distance. I go to the room where I slept last night and take some clothes from my old wardrobe. There's an open door to my left. I walk through it in order to look around, in case it's the lounge where I spent the summer with Mudassar when we were kids. A lot of the rooms in this house are similar. It's disconcerting that I can't place my memories from this house. I don't know which is the room where my mother used to sleep when we came here during vacations, where I used to go in the middle of the night to check that she was still there, to subdue my fear that I had been abandoned in this strange old house. I wonder if, by my next trip, I will forget the room in which I slept with Alain last night. It's quite possible.

In the larger room next to mine, I find a framed document on the wall in front of me. I haven't seen it before. I walk up to it and try to read the Urdu. The handwriting makes it hard for me. I find an inscription on the bottom edge of the frame. The document is the written draft of a speech by Ma's grandfather given when he was contesting a seat in the first-ever parliamentary election held in Pakistan. I know that he lost. Habib told me about it. He didn't stand in the area where he owned land, he had masses of land

and could have won there. He let his brother take that seat. Instead he stood in the city and lost to a man who had factories locally. Habib said that Ma's grandfather could have won if he campaigned in the areas where the factory workers lived but he accepted that the factory workers ought to vote for his rival, their factory owner. He couldn't see his way to upsetting that social order. I wonder why he gave his speech at all.

Returning to the bedroom, I pick out four outfits and some underwear. I place them inside my bag and put it on my shoulder. I hear a sound in the corridor and instinctively step behind the open door where I can't be seen. Somehow it is illicit to be leaving here, not to be sleeping in the room Ma told me to sleep in. A person pauses in the doorway and after a few seconds moves on. I wait for the sound of the footsteps to pass a few metres along the corridor, then I stand in the doorway and peer. It's Bilal. He is wearing a loose shirt and trousers that stop on his calves. I consider whether he has taken the trousers from his son's wardrobe. Mudassar was short, probably shorter than Bilal. He is pressing his right shoulder with his left hand as he walks. I watch him and then I follow him. He is passing through the house towards the area that Ma inhabits. He stops and throws an arm towards the wall but he doesn't reach and I think that he is about to fall, then he plants both his hands on his knees. I hear him sigh while he's down in that position. Habib suggested last night that the drinking is as bad as it's ever been. I saw for myself last night I suppose but it is different to see it here, inside the house, during the day, without Habib to hold him. I would go and help him but he's looking for me and first I want to know why. Soon he sets off again.

As I continue to follow him, I remember that Mudassar didn't discuss his father a lot. When Bilal came to London, Alain went drinking with him, to look after him. Mudassar couldn't bear to do it himself. It was good of Alain to do that. Though it seems that here in Lahore, Mudassar had become the carer, the supporting drinker, the son-advocate. I don't know how an addiction to alcohol works. Baba is a controlled drinker. He can take it or leave it. But perhaps that's no accomplishment. If Baba drank, he might not have done some other things.

I have passed into a part of the house that I have never seen. The corridor is narrow. Unlike the parts of the house that I know, there are no console tables bearing vases or statuettes. There are small tapestries on the walls. I watch Bilal knock on a door and pass through it when it is opened from the other side. The door remains open and I hear Ma's voice. 'It's in the cupboard,' she says. 'Pour me a small one,' says Bilal. There must be a maid inside with them, or the young girl that I met yesterday.

'Sit down, Bilal' says Ma. I walk slowly towards the door. 'Doesn't she look pretty in these clothes?'

I hear her say. I don't hear Bilal say anything in reply. I guess that Ma is talking about the young girl, Bilal's daughter from some affair, as she intimated to me yesterday. 'Go to him,' says Ma, addressing I think the same person.

'Where's the other one?' replies Bilal. 'She's not in her room.'

'She said salaam,' says Ma. 'She's in the house.'

'When is she leaving?' says Bilal. 'Stay there,' he adds in a different voice, talking to the young girl I guess.

'God knows,' replies Ma. I am standing in the doorway now. I see Ma, sitting on cushions on the floor, picking at the rough skin on her feet. Another step forward and I can see Bilal. He is sitting on a chair with his legs wide apart; the young girl is standing between his legs facing outwards.

'What do you want to say to me?' I declare. No one moves for a few seconds. Then Bilal pushes the head of the young girl and she leaves him to stand by the window onto the garden. Ma sighs and beckons for me to come to her. 'I'm here,' I tell her, without moving. 'What do you want to say to me?' I watch Bilal clear his throat and fold his arms. He looks across at Ma, smiling.

'Your uncle requires your help,' says Ma. Bilal laughs.

'You silly old coward,' he says.

'Then tell her yourself,' says Ma.

'She wants money from you,' says Bilal, still looking at Ma, not at me. 'From her little bird, she wants money.'

'It's not for me,' replies Ma. 'It's for Mudassar.'

'Why does Mudassar need money?' I ask her. 'Now, after he's dead, why does he need money?'

'He had debts,' says Ma. 'He had large debts and this house was resting its hopes on his future income. He was a smart boy, he wanted to do everything, pay his debts, rebuild this house, but now he's gone.' I watch Bilal shaking his head while Ma is talking.

'Why didn't your father come to my son's funeral?' Bilal asks. 'He's a fugitive but he thinks he's better than us?'

'Perhaps he is,' I reply.

'Perhaps he is,' repeats Bilal, snorting.

'Whatever he is,' I add, 'he's not here. It's just me. You're talking to me.'

'Hanna, this will wait,' says Ma.

'How much do you need?' I ask her.

'My little bird,' she replies, 'there's no rush to talk about this.'

'How much do you need?' I repeat.

'Perhaps Habib should be here when we talk about this,' she says.

'Did you write down a number?' I ask her. 'Did you make a little account?' Bilal laughs again. When I turn to look at him, I see that there is a glass on the table next to him and it is empty. 'Do you want another one?' I ask him.

186

'Of course I do,' he replies with an ugly smile, baring his teeth.

'Well, does someone have a number that they want to state?' I ask. 'Or do you just want to take the maximum that I offer in my dumb innocence?'

'My little bird,' opens Ma. She reaches out a hand to a nearby chair and starts to stand. 'This is all wrong. Let's talk about it another day.'

'I'm staying at the PC,' I reply. 'Send me a note with a number on it for how much you want.' Shaking my head, I walk through the room, tug open the garden door and exit.

Without looking back at Ma's house again, I walk down the street and make my way towards where I'd seen some shops. I am looking for a taxi to take me back to the PC. It really is the case that I am ruined for houses and homes. I am not myself, I'm the bearer of my father's money. To anyone, that's what I am. As soon as I have passed the police barrier, I take out my phone and call Baba. The call fails. I look at the screen. The reception is fine. The battery is intact. I try again. Again the call fails. When I try a third time, the call connects to a flat unchanging tone. I call the exchange at the hotel now. 'This is Hanna,' I tell them. 'Can I speak to my father please?' There is a short pause. Clearly uncomfortable, the operator replies.

'I recognise your voice, Miss Hanna,' he says, 'but I can't connect you to the room. You're not on the list.' He's quite right. I'm not on the list. I wrote the list of the people who may be connected to Baba and I didn't put myself on it. I look at my watch and consider whether this is a time when Baba may be in the restaurant. I could ask to speak to the restaurant rather than to be connected to Baba's room. But lunchtime has passed now.

'Can you connect me to Annette?' I ask instead. Again there is a short pause.

'Yes, I can do that,' replies the operator. 'Let me find out where she is.' I keep walking while he leaves me on hold. Then there is a click on the line. 'Connecting you now,' he says.

'Hello, madam,' says Annette, adding promptly, 'Are you okay? Where are you?'

'Yes, I'm fine,' I tell her. 'They won't connect me to my father. Can you go and find him for me please?'

'I'm in his room now,' she says.

'Perfect,' I reply. 'Can you pass me over to him?'

'I can't,' she says.

'That's enough,' I tell her. 'Security is one thing, but now you're being silly.'

'I don't mean that, madam,' she says.

'What do you mean?' I say.

'He's not here,' she replies.

'He's not here?' I repeat after her.

'He left,' she says. 'We don't know when. The night porter won't say. He took a taxi.'

'He left the hotel?' I ask.

'He left last night,' she says. 'He has taken some of his clothes. His safe is empty.' I listen to these reports and find that I am completely calm. But I don't know why – I don't know why I'm staying calm.

'Call me when he comes back,' I tell Annette. I end the phone call before I say anything more foolish to her. I hold my phone against my forehead. He has taken his clothes. His safe is empty. He has terminated his mobile phone. I picture him in a taxi with the suitcase next to him on the seat, his hand on it, his other hand on the grip above the door.

I stop walking. I'm leaving Ma's house behind in a rush, and I realise that I am walking towards only an empty hotel room. But there's no reason for me to go back either. Ma isn't interested in what is happening to me. She is presiding over her own drama. I am the sole daughter of her sole daughter, as she said herself, which sounds like a precious connection, but it is also a slender one. I left Beirut. Now I have to get out of Lahore. There is nothing here any more. Baba is missing. But this time he has escaped alone. This time I'm on my own. My money is in London, the money that they all want, the money that means I'm not a real person, just a bearer. Ma and Bilal are getting nothing from me. But Alain could make big problems for Baba and me, even if all he does is put his information in the press. If I want to pay Alain, then I have to go to London. I haven't ever reached to the money before. Dozens of people will have tried to hack the account in the time since the fall of IBCD. I'll have to speak to the bank in person if I want the money. I'll have to speak to Theo, my father's banker. Uncle Terry is there in London also. Terry is the one who wasn't able to hide. I've felt sorry for him at times, that he has been the only one available to suffer the outrage due to all of them; now I'm glad that I know where he is – he is a chance to find out what's been going on, he is a destination. Though I don't know if he will speak to me. He knows from the newspapers where Baba and I have been staying. He hasn't called. And that's understandable. We haven't called him. Baba owes him a favour, for staying and taking the blame, but Baba won't recognise that. I wonder if I can. I wonder if I can speak to him and change things. In Beirut I did nothing for two years. Here is already messed up. I'll go to London. I may get better there. I may as well.

LONDON

CHAPTER 1

I 've arrived. I'm in a taxi leaving the airport. When I checked in at the airport in Lahore, they hardly looked at my passport. The woman at passport control here said 'Welcome home'. No alarm went off. No one led me behind a door without a sign on it to ask me questions about Baba. I came first class with British Airways and drank a glass of freezing cold vodka every couple of hours. That tranquillising effect is still nice to have. I am slumped across the back seat of the taxi watching the traffic absently. When we get stuck in a queue for the first time, nearing the city, I use my telephone to search the internet for recent news stories about Uncle Terry. How am I going to find him? I scan through the articles looking for clues. They mention a house in Chelsea. I've been there. There's a description of things he's had to sell, including a flat in New York. I remember that flat as well. He bought it when he spent a year teaching at Princeton. He was invited regularly to give courses of lectures at different places. He had been at the Bank of England before he came to IBCD and at the UK

193

Treasury Department before that, as well as on the boards of companies, trusts and foundations. He had published a bestselling book about the time he spent working in government, stuffed with senior anecdotes, a memoir of power, power charmed and used lightly. His year at Princeton, authorised proudly by Baba, came long before the fall of IBCD and Terry was still the expert in every regard. There's a story I was often told at dinners with him and my parents about how I was three years old and he was lying on the rug in front of the fireplace at a house they had all rented together in the Cotswolds and I spent half an hour trying to climb over him to get a closer look at the burning logs. According to the story, eventually he picked me up and told me that, if there had been a mountain in my way, I might have found a way over it, but he was more than a mountain. True or not, he was seen as a major part of IBCD's success, the rock of the intellectual credibility it did have for a long time, and Princeton wanted a piece of him. While he was at Princeton, he offered a lecture course on the history and future of international finance. It was the sort of survey course that let him show off all of his connections and talk about the insides of things that he knew: deals, decisions, institutions. He brought guest speakers to his classes, friends of his, like the President of the World Bank and the UK Chancellor of the Exchequer.

He lived a distance away from the college, plainly

in a house that he could afford only because he had other money. He held dinner parties catered by chefs from New York. He bought a Mustang sports car and a sarcastic vanity plate that read 'SEC 4EVER'. Princeton was far away from the London hub of IBCD but Uncle Terry chose to have his academic glory year in Princeton – he was made similar offers in London and Paris – because he was in between wives and he wanted to be away from both of them. He had begun the divorce proceedings against his first wife and he had met Zubaida, whom he married eighteen months after he came back. He didn't want to see either of them while he was enjoying Princeton. Princeton, he told me, was a year off from adulthood. He was like a college undergraduate with his own room for the first time and no one from the old crowd watching his moves. And so outwards they came, the women he met and seduced in Princeton, to his house in the woods, on bicycles, in taxis, in cars borrowed from other men – fathers, husbands, boyfriends. It was Uncle Terry's studly year. He was able to avoid self-caricature, he told me, like turning up to answer the front door in nothing but a silk dressing robe and with a strawberry in his mouth, but barely. He slept with about a dozen women in total that year. He slept with Gina, who had bright red hair that he was afraid to touch. He slept with Annabel, who insisted that they have sex outside in the grounds of the house, his back against a tree trunk, which he found very

195

uncomfortable, not to say demeaning. He slept with Chloe, who was a pleasure, a small, smart woman that he could have fallen in love with; she gathered herself up behind a shawl whenever she sat down, except if making an especially important point in an argument, when her right hand would emerge from under the shawl and stay dangling in the air, where he would want to grab it and kiss it; but she only came to him once, which he said was just as well. He slept with Sonia, who sang Indian movie songs aloud when riding on her bicycle, and mocked him sometimes in ribald Punjabi, using phrases that he more or less understood from his exposure to my father and some of the other IBCD South Asians. He slept with Marianne, who was black, and it was important to him, he admitted to me, that he sleep with a black woman at some point in his life.

That attractive man of power and renown doesn't exist any more. I watched his downfall on television with Baba, in Baba's room in the hotel. Terry was asked to an interview by a committee of the British Parliament. I don't think he had to go, but he did. It's as if he thought they were asking him along to explain why everyone was wrong about IBCD, to instruct them, to clear the air. That's how he seemed to approach the session, talking outside to journalists before it started. In his opening statement to the committee, he said that IBCD had had the highest capital ratio of any major bank in the world; he spoke about the investment that IBCD had made in communities; and he concluded by thanking the committee for inviting him to give evidence. Somehow he believed that he had the answer to each and every question that they might ask, that the session was going to prove their undoing, and not leave any mark on him. It was they who had overreached themselves, not the professor, the banker extraordinaire, the titan. But the questions turned out to be much more deadly than Terry had expected. It was nerve-wracking for Baba and me to watch. We didn't know how far it would go, what it would mean for the continuing investigations into Baba's own conduct. Terry was silent for a long while after the critical question was asked, the question that made it clear that all along the committee had planned a hanging, not rehabilitation. Terry lifted his hands from the table at which he was sitting and hid them. His confidence vanished. That was a surprise to me. As with Baba and Uncle Yani, Uncle Terry's confidence had always grown when challenged. But not on that day. The committee knew facts that he didn't expect them to know. As he soon discovered, they had him cornered. In the report they published afterwards, they were able to document that Terry didn't follow regulations when he was running the risk function at IBCD. They described at least three transactions that went spectacularly badly, all created by Terry during his tenure at the bank, approved by Baba, but the intellectual hubris inherent in their design belonged to Terry. Most damagingly, they linked him to several of IBCD's finance agreements with autocratic regimes, agreements that sustained those regimes beyond the time that they might otherwise have collapsed. Nothing that they established was criminal. But it was easily enough to destroy Terry's moral and intellectual reputation. The barbs first thrown by the committee were thrown again and again for many days in the media and over the internet. Just as Terry had begun to be asked to write commentary pieces in newspapers again, to show up as a talking head on Bloomberg, his resurgence was permanently halted. At the time, watching him on television losing his composure in front of the committee, I thought equally of the night that I was in his flat in New York, when his allure was stripped from me in another way. On the screen, I saw him hide his hands in the same way that he had that night. I saw the corner of his mouth twitching as it had then.

In New York, I had dinner with him at his flat. He bought it so that he could drive the Princeton women up to New York in his Mustang, for weekends or even for a single evening. He loved to hurl his fast car through the city's grid of streets, like it was a ball bearing in a handheld maze, he told me. Over dinner that night he boasted about each of his women. He may have been trying to seduce me. In fact, that's obviously what he was doing. But I noticed just in time that it was an awful idea. I was much younger than him and the daughter of his employer and one of his closest friends. Plus I wasn't even curious any more about older men. That evening with Uncle Terry came after I had made my decision about them. So I was probably quite canny for once. I knew that even an older man can wake up with a sort of panic in his eyes which he will try to mask, and even an older man can have low-level anxiety attacks while dressing up for dinner. I had found this out and it was impossible for me to see someone older than me, not sorted, not settled, not sure, and to feel the compassion for him and the admiration that building a relationship requires. I spoke of this to Terry, probably I said quite a lot about it, as I had just finished an affair with an older man about a week ago, an affair that had been my rebound after I broke up with Alain, and it affected him, Terry thought that I was talking about him, and no doubt I was to an extent, and I remember how he hid his hands and the twitch that appeared around his mouth.

I am glad that I didn't stay with him at the flat that night. If I had heard Uncle Terry moaning during sex, been under him while he pressed his body into mine, then it would be difficult to go to him for help now. It would be difficult, too, to suspect him of being complicit in violence. And yet what I've started to think now is that, if the

photograph that Baba has on his laptop is a photograph of a man that Baba had killed, if Baba is
capable of using such means, perhaps he would
have used them while IBCD was rising as well,
with Terry and Yani by his side, with *the look* in
their eyes.

I check into the Hempel Hotel. On the first day
I hardly move from my room. I venture as far as
the lobby to pick up a magazine; that's it. It's a
repeat of what I did when I arrived in Beirut for
the first time: stayed in place, pretended my room
was a home and that walking around the corridors
on my floor was a promenade. Then, on the
second day, I want to test my notoriety, so I slip
out for what I think will be a brief time but which
extends to hours. No one stares. No one stops
and harangues me in the street about the money
they lost from the collapse of IBCD. Actually the
experience is very comforting. London is as close
to home as any place ever got for me. I notice
even that hearing English is a relief. I feel
surprised whenever I step into a café and people
are talking English. In Beirut I realise now I must
have walked into cafés already having tuned out
the Arabic voices I was going to hear. I go to
Selfridges at the end of the afternoon and buy
clothes from designers that I have bought before
so that I don't have to try anything on. I pick up
two suits, two dresses, two pairs of shoes, some
tops, some underwear.

After dinner on the second day, in my hotel

room I sit back down with the laptop I got in Lahore. I look for reports about the collapse of IBCD, any mention of the names of people who predicted that it would fall, hints that there were people who made money on the day that IBCD was hollowed out. I find nothing of substance. The people who killed IBCD seem to have got away with it even more cleanly than Baba and Yani, the people who built it up. So I start to search more widely. I look through the websites of sovereign wealth funds from the Gulf and the reports written about them. These formed the gang that brought down the bank. If Baba and Yani and Terry have been seeking revenge, then people associated with these funds will have been their targets. It takes time to piece together information about them. I know some of the names of the funds. Others I have to find by reading through long reports from analysts in investment banks. Then I look for the names of their executive teams, but I also know that the decision-makers may be a different set of people entirely. I remember Baba saying that the executive teams often provided a patina of expertise, they were a roster of MBAs from prestigious schools sent in to do the first meeting with any western institutions that the fund had to deal with, whereas in fact the major players were members of the royal family, nothing to do with the financial world, appearing after long dinners in private salons to listen distractedly to the items on the term sheet while watching a girl dance on a stage or fixing travel arrangements with some family retainer. Their names I won't find anywhere. But I keep looking. I hear sirens outside and stand at the window watching for a few minutes. Then I return to the laptop. After two hours, I find news pages from Saudi Arabia reporting the disappearance of the chief executive of a Saudi fund. They're recent, from earlier in the summer. I read into them. The man's name is Faisal Bakri. I expand the picture of him from the news report, blow it up so it fills my computer screen. Here he is: I've seen this man before. This is the man who was in the photograph on Baba's laptop. I can't look at the picture for long. I close it down and look for more news stories. All that I can find out is that he is missing. No one has reported any more than this. In an Arabic language newspaper, there is a photograph of an older man next to his. I wonder if this is his father. I try to read the article but my Arabic isn't good enough; two years in Beirut didn't even fix my Arabic. If this is his father, he might still be hoping for good news about his son. Perhaps the very best thing that I can do right now is to find a way of contacting him, tell him to stop waiting.

I put the computer away and take all the little bottles of vodka out of the fridge. I pour them into a large glass and sit with it in front of the television until it's empty. I remember the vision I had of Baba shortly after I first saw the photograph on his laptop. Dressed in robes, handling the severed head, instructing someone else to take it away. By some mystery, I fall asleep.

When I wake up the next day, I don't want to stay indoors, but I'm not sure I'm ready to go and find Uncle Terry. For days I've half-believed that the photograph I saw on Baba's laptop was a threat that had been issued to him. I've been a mellow little fool. Terry will see that in me if I go and talk to him. And what do I have to ask him now? To own up? He won't. To point me to where Baba has gone? I don't know if I can bear to see Baba yet. He's a killer. What information I have points to this conclusion pretty definitively. Baba organised for a man to be killed, his head to be removed, placed on a table, a photograph taken of it. He had that photograph on his personal computer. He wanted me to see it. But was it a confession or a test? Am I wrong in thinking that it was deliberate? Or did something go wrong? Have people found out that he did this and now he is in danger? I can write down the questions and yet they don't give me a clear course of action to follow. Do I want to know the answers? Or do I want to abandon all of this, turn away from it entirely?

Eventually I get out of bed. I dress carefully, in case I do find the courage to go and look for Uncle Terry. I put on a light-grey trouser suit that I bought yesterday with a white vest top underneath, the pair of shoes that comes closest to matching the colour of the suit. I decide to visit the Victoria Miro gallery. I want to look at something else, in a familiar place. I used to come to this gallery a lot before I went to Beirut. I walk in, take off my sunglasses and say hello to the gallery assistant, who looks up at me as I walk past. Victoria Miro is a major gallery. I could easily be discovered by someone who knows me here. But I must be past caring now. On the way across, I thought even that I'll go and find Habib in a few days. He said, when I saw him in Lahore, that he will be coming here with Mudassar's mother. I'll go to the betting shop where I went to see him once with Baba. Habib suggested that.

I take out my notebook as I walk around the gallery and write notes on the pictures. It's an old habit. The artist on exhibition is Chantal Joffe. I've seen her work before. She paints women. There is a series that she made of models backstage at Paris Fashion Week. I remember reading that doing the series, she said, made her feel like Degas behind the scenes at the ballet. I stop in front of a picture called *Dungarees with Wallpaper*. The woman in it is talking on the phone, dressed in dungarees, sitting in front of a classic English wallpaper, large white flower designs on a black background. She is clearly a beautiful woman, or so it seems to me. Yet Chantal Joffe has captured her at a time, in a moment, in the midst of an activity, when her sexuality is at its lowest ebb.

The scene in the picture is not domestic, though the woman is probably at home. The only other object in the picture is the phone that she is talking on. And the point of the picture it seems to me is not at all to make the woman look ugly; she looks great. But perhaps it is to check what other forces a viewer can see in her, with the sexual ones set to one side. Or perhaps it is only me that looks at her that way, for I need to figure out what force there is in me.

As I move away from the picture, the thought of the phone in it prompts me to take out mine to look at it. I haven't heard from Baba, not once. Alain has been sending me text messages. He started on the day that I left Lahore. I read the first of them while I was boarding my flight to come here. He has gone back to Paris, he says. And he guessed that I had come to London. He repeated the threat, saying that he would make an anonymous phone call to the police in Dubai and that he would speak to a friend of his who has written about IBCD for a French newspaper in the past. I haven't been responding to him. I feel canny in thinking that I will wait for an ultimatum from him before deciding what to do.

I complete the exhibition and begin a second tour. I fantasise about buying all of the pictures. I would give the paintings as gifts to beautiful girls whom I see on the street and I would ask as a condition only that they allow me to visit them every five years and learn what has happened in their lives. I am stopped in front of *Dungarees with Wallpaper* again when I feel a tap on my shoulder. 'Hanna,' says a voice. I look around. Pen is standing behind me. Her hair is stacked on top of her head in dense curls. It is higher than I have ever seen it before. She holds out her arms and takes me into a hug.

'Pen,' I say dully, too taken aback to venture anything else.

'Oh my goodness,' says Pen. 'You're back.'

'Here I am,' I reply quietly. Suddenly I feel nervous again about being in London. My hands burrow into my pockets, as if I'm supposed to have some document in there to authorise me to be here and I had better produce it now.

'This is insane,' says Pen. 'Not an email, nothing for two years. Here you are now in flesh and blood.'

'To see Chantal Joffe.'

'To see Chantal Joffe. Isn't it absolutely amazing?' she asks.

'I'm really happy to see it,' I reply confidently. This is easier ground. I am really happy to see it.

'My god, Hanna,' says Pen. She holds out her arms again and places them on my shoulders this time. 'My god. This is a true surprise.'

'How are you?'

'When can we talk?' she says. 'What are you doing tonight?'

'Tonight?'

'Well, why not? I have some people coming for drinks and to see my latest show at the gallery.

Can you come? Can we talk after they've gone?'
I shrug my shoulders.

'Well, sure,' I tell her. I can't imagine that there
is any other reply that I could give her.

'Fantastic,' she says. 'I'm really glad. This is just
right. This could be helpful.'

'Helpful? What do you mean?' Pen waves my
question aside.

'What do you think of this picture?' she says. I
turn back to it and I stare at the woman's face.

'I like this one,' I tell her. 'It makes me think of
courage.'

'It's pricey,' she replies. 'Her prices are going up.'

We walk past another couple of pictures together,
then Pen says goodbye. She insists to me again
that I must go to her gallery tonight, takes my
phone number. I watch her leave and I feel relieved
that this has happened, that I've been recognised,
my passport was scanned at the airport, but now
I've also been recognised. Somehow it means that
the state of suspension I feel that I've been in the
last three days is over. I know this city, up and
down. It's not like Beirut, or even Lahore. I'm not
confined to a hotel room. I can go and talk to
people here. There is some force in me.

CHAPTER 2

When I leave the gallery, I find a taxi and ask the driver to take me to the road in Chelsea where I last knew Terry was living. I remember being there one morning with Baba before we took a plane to Turkey to get on our boat. Terry was coming with us, not his children, nor his wife. I sat in the garden drinking a Diet Coke that the housekeeper had given me while Terry's son played on a guitar close by and Terry argued upstairs with his wife. Baba was indoors making telephone calls for work. I am surprised by how familiar the journey across London is to me. This is the city where I've lived for most of my life, yet I thought that all that time would count for nothing, that I would start again as a stranger.

After the taxi drops me off, I walk along the street towards the house. I keep my hands in my pockets as I'm walking, as if that's the key detail that will make me look like a casual passer-by. I haven't thought about what I am going to say when I present myself to Uncle Terry at his front door so I keep walking till the end of the street

208

and then on to the next one. In fact he probably has a butler, or a security guard. They will screen me, or take my telephone number and tell me that they will call me after they've consulted with Terry. That I will speak to him right away is unlikely; and, if I did, I don't know what I would say just yet. Ultimately, I suppose that I am about to ask Terry if he and Baba are murderers. It's a different order of question to any that I have had to contemplate about them before. The bank did whatever it did, then it fell. That was like a reprieve almost, a second chance, which we took by moving away from London. By that point, Baba's requirement for self-determination had already taken him away from his family, taken my mother away from hers, vouchsafed him to run a major bank in a major way, landed him in the worldwide media as a financial villain. I have already lived with all of this. And yet if Baba feels that he is entitled to kill as well in pursuit of his own version of what is right and legitimate, then there's no limit to him. There's nothing personal about him at that point, he is a force, a phenomenon, the nameless dread that you encounter at the end of a nightmare.

I find myself on a square and along the east side of it I see a familiar car. It's the American muscle car that Terry bought during his year at Princeton with the mocking number plate. I stop and examine it. There's no cover over it, I note to myself. I suppose that means that Terry uses it quite often.

It also means that he probably still lives in the house, unless he has passed the car on to his son, or abandoned it, but that doesn't seem like him. Seeing his car gives me an idea that I could perhaps surprise him, talk to him when he isn't enclosed behind his security apparatus.

I walk to a thoroughfare and take a taxi to a car-rental office. When I return driving to the square, Terry's car is still there. I park my small plain car in a spot that he doesn't have to walk past if he's coming from the house. I've sat like this in a car waiting once before. Baba made an attempt when I was about fifteen to take away my mother's tablets. She had acquired a habit for some medical drug that boosted her, and she'd take it after lunch two or three times a week with a glass of wine or gin and then watch old films in Baba's projection room. It didn't to me seem harmful. She didn't become overwrought; on afternoons when she took the tablet, she'd take a nap from around 4pm until dinnertime and wake up fresh and normal. But Baba hated it. He referred to it as a 'dependency'. He jettisoned all the tablets he could find one day before going to work and he told me after lunch to post myself in my mother's car so that if she came out to drive to a pharmacy to buy more tablets, I could stop her. I did as he asked. I waited several hours reading a magazine, until Baba returned and told me to go inside. Later he told me that he hadn't found all the stores of tablets after all.

I wait two hours in the rental car then go to buy a bottle of water. Terry's car is still in place when I come back. I suppose Baba should not have asked me to do as he did. Children shouldn't be pressed to take the side of one parent over the other. They both did it with me. My mother often asked me to conspire with her against Baba – although it was over small things, like resisting his choice of restaurant, or persuading him to go to Lahore with us to visit my mother's family. In fact, I think that I was glad of their small plots against one another, it was proof to me that, despite all the time they spent apart and the arguments, they wanted to stay together. I remember being fearful, walking to breakfast from my bedroom, on the rare days that I knew Baba was supposed to be at home, that perhaps they wouldn't both be around the table, that he might have gone to work after all or they might have quarrelled over what to do with Baba's special day off. Thinking about them like this, I take out my phone and dial Baba's number. I remember that one night, after my mother died, I drunkenly dialled her mobile number, and there was an automatic message from the network, just as there is now when I phone Baba's number.

An hour later, I look up and there is a man by Terry's car. I glimpse him for a moment before he dips out of my view. I am alarmed that he might have seen me. Then I spy him on the other side of the car. He is examining each of the tyres in turn. He finishes and opens the driver's door. It's Uncle Terry. He has blond hair, not as much of it as he used to have, a beige overcoat, glasses. He's in the car now and he has started the engine. The lights at the back of the car come on. I wind down my window and hear the engine thrumming. I start my own car. Terry pulls out and rolls to the end of the street. I pull my car out and roll after him. I watch him turn left. I get to the end of the street and turn left as well. The light has fallen quite a bit. I hadn't noticed it's 8pm. We drive along the Embankment next to the Thames. I don't press up too close behind Terry's car; for the most part there is at least one other car between us. He drives gently except for one burst of acceleration as he turns off the Embankment north towards the City. I catch up to him at the next set of traffic lights. Eventually he parks on Old Broad Street. I idle at the side of the road to watch him and to see where he goes. I've left enough room for other cars to pass me, but the first three or four drivers beep at me anyway and try to catch my attention as they overtake me. I ignore them and watch Uncle Terry get out of his car, lock the door, straighten out his overcoat and enter a large building. It's tantalising. He might even be going to a meeting with Baba.

I decide that I can't waste time parking properly and pull my car into an empty space without checking what the notices say. I get out of the car and run across the road. I read the sign on the building as I go in: Tower 42. I enter the reception just as Uncle Terry is getting into a lift. If he had made a sideways glance, he would have seen me. Now he's in a lift and I don't know where he's going. I turn to a man dressed in a security uniform. 'Ah shit,' I tell him audaciously, pointing towards the lifts, 'he was supposed to wait for me.'

'You'll catch him up,' replies the guard cheerfully. 'Floor 24. You want the restaurant, don't you?' I nod and let him press the call button for me.

'Good evening, do you have a reservation?' the hostess asks me as I enter the restaurant.

'We didn't plan ahead,' I tell her. 'I'm meeting a friend and we thought perhaps you'd have a table.'

The hostess shakes her head. 'We're full,' she says. 'I'm really sorry.'

'Nothing at all?' I ask her, trying to look past her into the main room. 'Forget it,' I say, before she responds. 'Can I order a drink at the bar and wait for my friend?'

'Of course,' says the hostess, relieved. But her relief is a little too apparent, and I can't resist adding, 'That way, when you have a cancellation, I'll be right here to fill it.'

I take a seat at the end of the bar closest to the restaurant. While taking off my coat, I look as widely as I can into the restaurant without tripping off the hostess again. I spot Uncle Terry. He is at a table with three other people. He arrived last it seems, though there is another empty chair.

None of the three people that he's with is his wife, Zubaida; equally, none of the three people that he's with is an obvious Zubaida replacement. There's a woman at the table, small and blonde, with a black pearl necklace, but I guess that she's with the man sitting next to her because her hand is on the table and across the space where his plate will be. The other dinner guest is a man with a shaved head and glasses. He keeps his hands under the table except when he raises them to adjust his glasses on his nose. Uncle Terry has taken off his overcoat and flung it over the back of his seat, the belt of the coat has snaked out and is touching the woman sitting with her back to him at the next table. I remember this habit: Terry doesn't like to surrender any of his personal items, whether it's in a restaurant, an office or at someone's home. Coat, jacket, bag, umbrella, whatever he has, he'll hold on to it. Uncle Yani used to tease him about this. Whenever Terry visited the gents, Yani would hide his things and refuse to give them back until Terry was exasperated and threatened to leave. I feel like I could very easily go over to the table and pick up Terry's coat, hand it to a waiter, and grin at him, and he would immediately remember how well I know him, and how well he knows me, and the evenings that we had dinner together in a group that mostly isn't here. The problem is that I don't feel tender and happy about seeing him again – I don't want to procure an affectionate acknowledgement from him by doing something cute. Instead, I want to grab him by the collar and demand that he tells me about the photograph and about where Baba has gone to now. I can't do that, and yet I don't know what else to do either. Madly, I want to call Baba and get his advice on how to talk to Terry.

The hostess comes over to me again and confirms that the restaurant doesn't have a table for dinner. 'Okay,' I say, shrugging my shoulders, holding my drink, 'I'll finish this, then call my friend, and we'll go somewhere else.' She has turned away before I finish speaking. I watch, a few minutes later, as a waiter goes to Uncle Terry's table and takes orders. Uncle Terry waits until last and adds an order for wine, so this means that he is paying for dinner. It was always the key moment when it was him and Baba and Uncle Yani around the same dinner table: the person who chose the wine paid for the meal. They took it in turns, though Baba sometimes took over and paid even when it wasn't his turn. Yani used to fume about that. It was visible. Then, within a day or two, he would send an extravagant gift to my mother, worth three or four times the value of the restaurant bill that Baba had picked up out of turn.

I try to remember what wine I drank when I had dinner in Terry's flat in New York, but I draw a blank, and it would hardly be a good way to start the conversation with him tonight. I look into the dining room once again and stand up.

The hostess smiles at me as I walk towards her, assuming that I am leaving now. 'Please do reserve in future,' she says. I smile back at her dumbly, looking past her into the dining room again. 'Do you have a toilet here?' I ask her. 'The toilets are this way,' she says, indicating a door to the left of her lectern, away from the main dining room. 'There's someone inside that I know,' I say suddenly and walk past her. 'Excuse me, miss,' she calls out, but I am already in the room moving towards Terry's table. On hearing the hostess's voice at my back, the woman at Uncle Terry's table looks up at me. She watches me coming towards their table. She smiles vaguely, wondering if she ought to know me. The others at the table, including Uncle Terry, follow her gaze. I look at him. He looks back at me.

'Good evening, Terence,' I say, realising in the nick of time that to call him Uncle Terry in front of the others would make me look foolish. He nods blankly. He doesn't stand up or smile. I'm surprised. I expected some enthusiasm at seeing me, or at least acknowledgement of who I am. 'You're not going to say hello?' I say. He shrugs his shoulders.

'Are you a friend of Zubaida's?' he asks, a crease across his forehead. I feel he says this in such a way that the others at the table will realise that my connection to her is the reason why the moment is an awkward one. Now at least I know that he and Zubaida are no longer together.

'I would never do this to you,' I tell him. 'Not even when they humiliated you on television, I would never pretend not to know who you are.' I am speaking gently and soberly but I feel the heat of others' eyes on me as if I am behaving in a shocking manner. I know that I can't stand here for much longer. The hostess is next to me. She will try to move me away. Some other members of the staff may come to help her because it's noticeable that this is an odd situation, there's none of the warmth or hand-extending and glad-to-meet-yous of impromptu restaurant run-ins.

'I'm sorry,' says Terry. 'No doubt we've met but I don't remember every single one of Zubaida's friends.' I laugh at this remark despite my embarrassment and confusion, because it is funny. And it is accomplished. Terry has been a capable and successful man. He doesn't live by the one eviscerating experience of his life in front of the parliamentary committee; he lives by all the others. He isn't going to speak to me just because I turned up here. He isn't going to want to explain to these people who I am, how he knows me, why I would appear like this to be able to talk to him. He is going to speak to me, if he does at all, on his own terms. I look around at the other people on the table and raise my hand. 'My mistake,' I tell them. My difficulty is that I don't quite believe that I have it in me to turn this into a confrontation. Despite what they've done, Baba and my uncles, it's probable that I'm functioning with regret rather than anger. 'I'm sorry,' I add, towards Uncle Terry. 'I took you for someone else, I suppose.' I turn around and leave the restaurant.

I come out of the building and see my rental car parked across the street. I decide to leave it there. I walk twenty metres before I realise how futile that is; Terry, when he comes out of the restaurant, will have no idea that it is my car. But I don't want to go back for it now. I want to walk until I'm at the river and watch a boat going past. I wonder if I can get to the river quickly. I stop at a crossroads and take out from my pocket my noisy telephone. It is ringing. I check the screen but don't recognise the number. I wait for the caller to leave a message and then listen to it. It's Pen, reminding me to come and see her, detailing the address of her gallery. In relief, as quickly as I can, I stick out my hand for a taxi.

I discover that Pen's gallery is on a street of galleries. The front door is open. No one stops me or asks me who I am. There are a handful of people standing in two separate groups and I hear further voices from somewhere further back in the building. I walk around the first room. I recognise nothing. For a moment, I feel thrilled, that it is all new, new pieces, new artists, all lined up for me to make new interpretations, but the thrill passes after a moment and I experience a kind of panic instead. I've been away so long from art that perhaps I will never be able to catch up. I'll retreat into theory and nostalgic accounts of minor pictures that I saw when they were first exhibited, which have since disappeared into private collections and no one talks about any more. For almost eight years now, looking at art, reading about it, talking about it has been the main thing of interest that I have done; if I have any adulthood at all, it exists in the way I look at pictures.

I hear Pen call my name and she approaches me with her arms outstretched for the second time today. I accept her more gladly on this occasion. 'Welcome to my humble home,' she says.

'It's great to see it finally,' I tell her.

'I've been waiting for you to come,' she says. There is something like disappointment in her tone, but then she smiles.

'Just don't make a bird and nest analogy,' I reply.

'What's that?' she says.

'What a show,' I tell her, shaking my head to dispel my previous remark.

'Well, you haven't seen it yet,' she says. 'I'll show you around when it calms down a bit.'

She stretches her arm out to her left to grab an elbow and introduces me to a thin boy dressed in white called Samuel and a girl who is seventeen maximum, his girlfriend, an American; she is dressed in a red smock and wearing bright red lipstick. Pen moves away and I almost grab at her clothes as she is leaving. I realise how delicate I feel, in the wrong mood to be here among so many people who will each be brimful of news and gossip. The girl in red doesn't tell me her name and wanders off as I talk to Samuel. Two other people join us, a curator who has worked with Pen before and another artist. Ten minutes pass before I am pressed to talk about something that I have seen recently. 'I don't live here,' I tell them. 'I saw a show by Zaatari abroad. You know Zaatari?' No one does. I talk about his project with photographs of Palestinian prisoners. He has collected snapshots that men from the Palestinian resistance send to one another, to document their good health, to show off to each other the muscles developed in prison workouts. As I am describing the project, I realise that Baba might have to go to prison like those men. I might get letters from him. I might ask him for a photograph to be assured that he is healthy. I wonder if he could be in prison three nights a week and with me the rest of the time. That would be some punishment, a measure of justice, but obviously it won't happen like that.

'You live in Beirut, don't you?' says the curator.

'At the moment,' I say.

'In a hotel, right?' he says. I don't answer. Of course, for Baba, as well as any punishment, there would be the news reporting during the trial, the humiliation as well as the punishment, the glee of other people in addition to justice for the man who died. 'What do you think of the Lehman thing?' asks the curator.

'What do you mean?' I say. I shake my head at him, partly to shed my own thoughts and focus on what he is asking me.

'You didn't see the news?' he says. 'I thought you'd be glued to it.'

'What happened to Lehman?' I ask him.

'Collapsed,' he replies. 'Today. You didn't see this?'

'I haven't watched the news for a few days,' I tell him.

'All over,' he says. 'The whole day has been a video of bankers walking around with their belongings in boxes like they're the victims of an earthquake that uniquely affects people who wear chinos.'

'My cousin works at Lehman,' says Samuel.

'Well, not any more, right?' says the curator. 'What do you think about it?' he asks, looking at me.

'I told you,' I reply, 'I haven't seen the news.'

'It was this sub-prime stuff, right, buying crazy mortgage bonds with other people's money. Is that the same deal as IBCD?'

'I never worked there,' I tell him.

'Ha,' he says, laughing without laughing. 'It's not very convincing for you to plead ignorance. You're the chief exec's daughter.'

'Ignorance,' repeats Samuel softly, like he has never heard the word before. We all turn to look at him, apart from his girlfriend who has returned from her wandering and is now staring at me.

'I thought I had seen you,' she says. 'You've been in magazines.'

'Not really,' I tell her.

'You were,' she says. 'I remember. I kept that article. It was about rich women who are hiding in other countries. There were photos of dresses you own. How did they get those photos?'

'How much was your father paid in the year before the bank collapsed?' asks the curator.

'Your father worked at Lehman as well?' asks Samuel.

'Come on,' continues the curator. 'Pen told me you've dealt in art. Don't be coy. You'd ask me how much I got for a consulting job for a private foundation. Samuel would tell us how much he sold his latest piece for. How can it possibly be that the banker gets non-disclosure? Probably he made money even after the bank had collapsed,' he adds. 'He ran the thing. He must have had access to the entire secret stash.'

'Perhaps he lost everything,' suggests Samuel.

'That never happens,' says the curator.

'Why are we pretending?' I tell him. 'Why do we think that bankers are uniquely culpable? Aren't we turning them into emblems of other things that are wrong?'

'No,' he replies. 'It's a straightforward question. Did he walk away with money while others lost money or did he lose something himself as well? That's what I'm asking. I'm not saying that bankers are uniquely culpable. I'm saying that they are culpable. That's it.'

'Did your father come to London with you for the Lehman thing?' asks the girl in red. I wonder how long they might keep talking if I say nothing in reply.

'Her father doesn't work at Lehman,' says the curator. 'Lehman is the bank that collapsed today. Her father worked for a different bank.'

'My father,' I now intervene, looking at the girl in red, 'ran a bank called the International Bank of Commerce and Development. It failed about two years ago, long before the current crisis.'

'What's closer to the truth?' says the curator. 'Ten million or a hundred million?'

'Do you want a measure of how many businesses were kept going with help from IBCD because they had more generous lending policies than anyone else?' I reply.

'Not really,' he says. 'I want to know how much money your father stole.'

I turn away from him and walk away. This is what I've missed by moving away from London with Baba, this conversation a hundred times over, encounters with this fierce suspicion that is out of direct sight sometimes, but it's always there. I am surprised by my reaction to it. I am slightly thrilled. But that would change I'm sure if I had the conversation a hundred times over. And perhaps I am thrilled because of what the curator said about Lehman. I've heard stories about Lehman from Baba. He hunted them for three months when IBCD was at its peak. He and Uncle Yani in particular wanted throughout that period to bloody a large western bank. There was no business need for it. 'Pure Shia triumphalism, that's all, and it's a lot,' Baba told me. But Sherpao was still in charge then and refused to put up as much money as they needed for the sport.

I leave the gallery and walk around the corner of the street. I find an open café and read on my phone news about what has happened to Lehman. After I've gone through the first three reports, I want to call Baba – but I can't. I want to hear what he thinks about it, what he reckons will happen next, what he remembers about the fall of IBCD when he looks at the stuff about Lehman. I scroll through the rest of my phone directory. There's not much in it, though there is Alain. I want to call him almost, despite the threats he has made, despite the hands he put on me. Instead I revert to reading more stories about Lehman. Already they are quoting experts on how the financial system will be irrevocably changed after today. I remember, when IBCD fell, equally people said that it was the end of the bankers' time, their grand-seeming institutions had been shown to be, by the example of IBCD, a house of cards. But what they said didn't matter. Money is scarce. Those who manipulate it have power. That isn't changing. IBCD, now Lehman, then there will be another one. I can't rely on the system to change. I imagine the pictures on the walls in Lehman being taken down and sold, as IBCD's art collection was. I don't know what Lehman had. IBCD had the fourth-largest private collection that has ever been catalogued.

The café waitress approaches me and tells me that they are going to close. I leave and go back to the gallery. The crowd has diminished and more people are leaving as I re-enter. Pen finds me again just as quickly as before. 'I heard from Samuel that you were interrogated,' she says.

'I ran away,' I tell her meekly.

'I'm sorry,' she says. 'Richard has these radical turns occasionally, but he's a nice guy.'

'It's fine,' I say. 'I've made worse accusations against my father myself. In fact—' I begin, and then I concentrate on a picture behind her until the thought passes. 'Anyway,' I say instead, 'Richard has read what he wants and he can make up his own mind.'

'Forget about him,' says Pen. 'Tell me: where do we start?' she asks, pirouetting and smiling at me.

'I'd love to learn about everything that is on show,' I tell her. 'You can leave me here,' I add, smiling back at her. 'I'll open up in the morning.' I am genuine. I want to learn again about what is going on in London. Going to the Victoria Miro gallery in the morning has started me off. And I think what Pen is trying to achieve here is tough. It's difficult to run a new gallery in London. It's very easy to be rubbed into a stripe through the culture, the East London scene or something like that, to be associated with a particular moment in design or music or fashion; then, as soon as the moment changes, people don't know what to do about your gallery any more. It's too late then to create a distinctive identity, though equally, if you try to do it any sooner, you don't know if anyone will pay attention or if they'll keep their eyes on the stripe and never notice where you've gone.

'Well, this is Samuel's brother actually,' says Pen, pointing to a sculpture made of shredded paper, brightly coloured, hung against a wall.

'What's the name of the show?' I ask. Pen sighs.

'I couldn't name it,' she says regretfully. 'In the end, I put it just as the "Late Summer Show". I'm not too hot at theme for the moment.'

'There's a nice ambiguity in it,' I say, while looking at the paper sculpture. 'Are you going to get written up?' I ask her.

'Yes,' says Pen, 'that's going quite well really. A couple of critics visited in advance, some art agents too.' I crouch down to look at the underside of the paper sculpture. I don't like it, or see anything special in it, but it's a well-executed piece. 'What really happened, Hanna?' says Pen, tentatively. 'Can I ask you that?' I stand up and look at her.

'When?' I ask.

'You don't have to talk about it if you don't want to,' she says, waving her hand across her face.

'Two years ago, Baba came to my flat,' I tell her. 'He said let's go. We went. I didn't want him to go off alone. From my perspective, that's what happened.'

'Was it dangerous?' she asks.

'No,' I say. I can't tell what she wants to know. 'I think we got to Beirut before anyone was organised enough to try to find us. In Beirut, he's protected because they won't extradite him to face questioning. So he stays in Beirut.'

'But he knew it was going to happen in advance, didn't he?'

'What did he know?'

'That IBCD was coming down?'

'No,' I tell her, shaking my head. 'Who have you been speaking to?'

'Never mind,' says Pen. 'She is planning to make a much bigger piece using that motif and different iterations of it,' she adds, pointing to a piece that I am looking at absently.

'I like the strong colours,' I say, recovering, taking a step back to look at the picture in the whole.

'What's going on with him now?' says Pen.

'My father?'

'Sure,' she says.

'Beirut suits him well,' I tell her. 'The weather is great. He swims. The food is excellent.'

'Right,' says Pen, frowning. 'But he's not there as a tourist, is he? Some people would be shocked if you told them that he's having a good time.'

'What are you getting at?' I ask.

'I'm just curious about him,' replies Pen, raising one hand as if to stop my thoughts moving in the wrong direction. 'Really. That's all. I like him. You know that. He took us for that nice dinner when we graduated. I remember that. I'm glad that he's doing well,' she says.

'Other people think it's unfair,' I comment, holding her gaze.

'Well, you heard a lot of that from Richard,' admits Pen. 'But forget about those people. They don't know him and everyone is buzzing right now from this Lehman thing.'

'Yes,' I reply, distracted now. 'Look, I should probably go.'

'Stop, Hanna,' says Pen, coming over to me and putting her hand on my arm. 'I really don't care about all that.' She squeezes my arm. 'Anyway, I need to finish showing you the exhibition,' she says. 'Next, you should look at these.' I follow her. On the floor there are battered-looking cubes coloured in a bloody-brown red. We stand beside them and she puts an arm around my neck. 'What about a drink?' she says.

'That would be excellent,' I reply.

Pen disappears for a moment and comes back with a bottle of vodka and two plastic glasses. I watch her saying goodbye to people en route. She pours and then walks me around the rest of the show. I am drunk by the time that we stop at the last piece, the word 'Electric' written in pencil on a light grey background. The lines for the letters are made up by the word 'Electric' as well, written in different fonts, sometimes forwards, sometimes backwards, sometimes as an anagram. I take a few steps back from the piece and it is hard to read even the largest manifestation of 'Electric' due to the similarity of the colour of the pencil lines to the colour of the background. 'I like this,' I say aloud. Pen doesn't hear me. She is standing by the front door looking outside. I watch her gradually lower herself to the ground and sit with her back to the door facing the gallery. She is also quite drunk. I smile as I watch her. She sees me looking at her and raises her glass. 'Cheers,' she says with a silly smile on her face. I go over to her and put my hand on her shoulder.

'Thank you,' I tell her. She winks at me.

'I have to admit something,' she says.

'What's that?' I ask.

'Do you promise you won't hate me?' she says.

'Sure,' I reply. 'I promise.'

'Solemnly?'

'Solemnly.'

'Well,' she says. 'Do you remember that I met Yani at your twentieth birthday party?' I nod. Baba had forgotten my previous birthday. He had been abroad on IBCD business. When he came back, he announced that twenty was the most important birthday of all and told me that he would throw a big party for my twentieth. I expected him to forget that promise too, but he didn't. He invited all of my friends by email, taking their addresses by hacking into my email account (he probably had someone from the IBCD IT team do it for him). He also had someone put up posters at my university. He booked an orchestra. I remember he was very moved by their playing. And, afterwards, the musicians were the most exuberant participants in the late hours disco. I found out that this was because Baba had just given each of them a cheque for a thousand pounds on top of their fee. 'He contacted me afterwards,' continues Pen.

'Yani?'

'We went out for dinner. I'm sorry that I never told you before,' she says.

'That's okay,' I tell her.

'There's more. When I was raising money to open the gallery,' she adds, 'he became my biggest investor.'

'Yani is your biggest investor?'

'That's right.'

'You took money from Yani?'

'I didn't take it. He's an investor.'

'Wow,' I reply, 'I'm standing on IBCD ground.'

'He used money that came from his family,' replies Pen firmly. 'He didn't use money from the bank.' It's a challenge to me, or perhaps just a defence.

'How often do you see him?'

'It varies.'

'Often?' I ask relentlessly.

'Often,' she says, looking down.

'Of course he started out advising on art himself,' I tell her.

'Yes,' she says. 'I know that.'

I stand dumbly for a few moments, then the better part of me asserts itself. 'I'm glad he supported you,' I tell her.

In the taxi back to the hotel I replay the moment of saying goodbye to Pen. She was sitting on the ground next to the vodka bottle. I stood over her, touched my hand to her shoulder and she looked up at me and blew me a kiss. She said to me earlier: 'Hanna, don't disappear again.' She wasn't looking at me when she said it. She said it into the air, then turned towards me and waited for me to reply. I am surprised by her warmth towards me and the warmth I was able to express towards her, even after she told me about her involvement with Yani. Twisting in drunkenness, I feel tears accumulating in my eyes. I am quite stupid. I don't know friendship properly. This is pretty basic stuff. And yet at the same time as I touch on this feeling of friendship, I begin to imagine her together with Yani – both of them dolled up, at a prize-giving in a faraway city; standing on a hotel balcony in bathrobes; Yani closing the door after they've gone inside, Pen taking off her robe and getting into the bed – and, as I do, I see pools of dark water inside me, the surface fizzing.

On the Embankment by the river, I let the window down and feel the breeze across my face. I count the lights in the windows of tall buildings. I wonder if there are more tonight because people are staying in their offices to work out what happens next after the collapse of Lehman. I realise I don't know which way is east or which is west. I take out my phone and dial Baba's mobile phone number again. I know that it will spark a dead tone and I let it sound, as if it might contain a hidden message. 'Have you been watching the Lehman collapse?' I say into the void.

When the taxi reaches the hotel, I don't move for a few moments. 'Hotel right here,' says the taxi driver, turning in his seat to look at me. I ignore him and look out of the window. I hear him tapping on the steering wheel with his fist. He takes a mobile phone out of his pocket and reads something on its screen. 'This is a good place for a fare,' he says, 'so I can wait. Tell me if you want to go somewhere else.' I think about where else I might want to go. I think of bars I know, the private club where I am probably still enrolled as a member, but even the idea of these places makes me feel more tired. I think for a moment of going back to Pen's gallery. But I can tell that I will talk to her about Yani and I will say things that are unkind and unmeant. And I don't know what he might have said to her about Baba. Or recent events, the photograph. Is it possible that Pen knows about that? From observing the shyness that overcame her, I have assumed that her relationship with Yani isn't just a financial one over the gallery. They are sleeping together. And I didn't know about it until tonight. It makes me feel childish, makes me feel naïve. But I haven't been here. So how was I to know. Anyway, I came to London for a different reason. I didn't know that I would find a connection with Yani here. I came for Terry, because he is the fixed one, the one that I knew how to find. I did find him. I wonder if he spoke to Baba after he saw me at the restaurant. I wonder if Baba told him that I've seen the photograph. Terry might have another phone number for Baba, an alternate to the one that I have, one that Baba wouldn't disconnect. Or Baba might be right here. If he has left Beirut, then he could be anywhere and London was home for a long time. If he needs a different kind of safety now, because of what's been stirred up through the act of revenge shown in the photograph, then perhaps he will find it here.

I ask the taxi driver to take me to Terry's address. As we approach the house, I click buttons aimlessly on my phone. I have no games on it, nothing to read; I haven't prepared for anxiety, I haven't prepared for anything. When I look up, I see that the streets are lined with parked cars and empty of people. I get out, pay the driver and wait until he has gone. Then I stand and look at Terry's front door. There is no light on within the house. He may still be out. Or sleeping. I think of his bed in the flat in New York, the bed that I almost went towards. I think of the dull art in his bathroom where I dallied until I had made up my mind about what to do that night. Now I walk along the street to the square where I found his car earlier today. It is there again. I look at the high trees from the garden in the middle of the square reflected in the windscreen. I lift my foot to touch the headlight, as if it's a practise swing before I kick with force to try and break it. I reflect that my shoes are too soft at the tip. They won't absorb any shock, it will all go to my toes. I bend over and massage my foot, like I'm preparing it to do some rough work. Practically though, if I want to damage this car, I should do better than use my foot. I decide to look for a stone. I'm not as feeble now as I was earlier today when Terry ignored me. I climb over the gate in the fence around the garden square and pick up stones from the ground. I settle on my knees and sort through the stones until I have the four largest that are within reach. Leaving the garden, I feel an unfamiliar and I suppose quite misleading sort of power with the stones in my hand and a good number of shots of vodka in my stomach. I set the stones down on the bonnet of Terry's car, pick up one and throw it at the windscreen. It bounces off rather than puncturing a hole in the glass as I'd imagined. I lean back and throw the second stone. It bounces off without making any impact at all. I throw the final two stones in quick succession, aiming at the cracks made by the first stone. I lean in close and see that I have succeeded in extending them. I stand back and look at my work. This is quite good. I have done well enough for tonight. I lean in close again and then I see better. The car is not empty. Behind the windscreen into which I have instilled the cracks, there are two figures, two people, two men. The door on the driver's side of the car is pushed open from inside. A man gets out, stands up, looks at me.

'Hanna, is that you?' he says.

'Yes.'

'I apologise for earlier,' he says. 'But you shouldn't have turned up like that.' He takes a step closer to me and I can recognise him definitively now, it's Terry.

'Who's that with you in the car?' I ask. He shakes his head.

'What are you up to though?' he says. 'I thought it was a bird shitting on the car.' He advances towards me, along the front of the car. 'Look,' he says, pointing, 'you cracked the windscreen.' My first instinct is to deny that it was me who made the crack, but that's ridiculous.

'I was angry at you,' I tell him.

'That doesn't seem quite fair,' he says.

'What do you mean?' I ask.

'Never mind,' he says. 'Look, you've turned up at a terrible moment. You should get out of here. I'll give you my number. Call me tomorrow.'

'I won't fall for that,' I reply. 'You're trying to get rid of me like you did at lunch. Who is it?' I ask him. 'Who's in the car?' He shakes his head slowly and I sense that he wants to tell me. 'I can just go over and pull on the door,' I tell him.

'Please go,' he says. 'Why are you here? Why didn't your father just call me?'

'Why would he call you?' I ask. He laughs.

'He calls me whenever he wants to call me,' he replies. 'He calls me whenever he wants to shake my strings. Why does he have to send you now?'

235

I look away from him and sit down on the pavement. 'No, don't do that,' he says. 'Go.'

'You're talking in riddles,' I tell him. Also I'm drunk, but I don't admit that part.

'I take a salary,' he says. 'That's all I ever took. I take a salary and he has pushed me a long way beyond a salaryman.' He glances towards the car again.

'Did you go to Beirut in the last few months?' I ask him.

'Of course I did,' he says. 'Why are you here if you don't know about that?'

'I do know about it,' I reply. And, as I say that, the image from my father's laptop floats through my mind. The expression on the man's face has become almost familiar by now.

'And do you know,' says Terry, 'that your father asked me to come on the pretext that there was a business deal? Do you know that? I didn't know what was going to happen until it was actually happening. That's your father.'

'Why does he still pay you a salary?' I ask.

'Look, you need to go,' he repeats. 'You really need to go. Come back tomorrow.' I stand up and walk over to the car. Terry reacts too slowly to stop me. The passenger door opens before I get to it and sitting inside there is Ghalib. He doesn't make a move to get out of the car.

'Fuck off,' he says.

'Why are you here?' I ask.

'Fuck off,' he says again. 'Alain is going to ring you.'

'I'm not going to speak to Alain,' I reply.

'We have the photograph now,' he says.

'What?' I ask. Something wavers in my hips, my knees. I feel for a grip on the car door. 'What photograph?' I ask.

'Nice try,' he says immediately. 'I'm talking about the special-effects photograph, except they're not special effects, are they?'

'They could be,' I reply.

'Forget it,' he says. 'Now you're fucked. He's fucked, that idiot standing there. Your father is fucked. None of you have anywhere you can hide from this.'

'I can give you the money,' I tell him.

'Yes, I know that,' he says.

'But what do you want from him?' I ask, nodding at Terry who stands behind me, silent, looking like a man who, for once in his life, doesn't know what to do.

'He was there,' replies Ghalib. 'He was an accessory. So he's paying us as well or the photograph gets out.' I feel Terry's hand on my shoulder.

'Please, Hanna,' he says. 'You have to go.'

'Where did you get the photograph?' I ask Ghalib.

'That doesn't matter,' he says.

'Your father was there as well,' I tell him.

'You don't know that,' he says.

'Of course he was there,' I reply. 'Do you think my father would have Terry there, but not your father?'

'It doesn't matter,' he says.

'Are you going to ask your father for money as well?' I ask.

'Don't patronise me,' he replies. 'You have no idea what it's like for me at this moment. I have the shame of Habib ringing me to ask for Ma's money. I have the menace of the family retainer who works for that dick that Mudassar used to hang around with. Lehman went down today and now everyone else is spooked as well. All of my investors are calling me, all of them, every single one. They want to know when they can have their money back. Everyone wants their money where they can see it.'

'I can give you a million,' I tell him.

'No,' he says, pointing to Terry. 'He can give me a million. You and your father can give me ten million.'

'Ten million?' I exclaim. 'That's ridiculous.'

'We have the photograph now,' he says. 'Didn't you hear me? I have the photograph right here in an email on my phone. I have the attachment with the detachment.'

'My father isn't in the photograph,' I reply. 'How do you know he was there?'

'Do you want to take that chance?' he says.

'Your father must have been there as well,' I repeat.

'Great,' says Ghalib, getting out of the car. 'So he'll pay me as well.' He reaches into his coat and takes out a knife. He moves it towards my neck.

'Get out of here,' he says. 'I need to talk to Terry.' I glance at the knife and I think of the story that Yani told me about when Ghalib was caught at school with a knife, how Yani instructed him in the perils of carrying a knife by cutting him.

'Don't pay him,' I say to Terry. 'I'll talk to my father. We can get Yani to sort this out.'

'Shut up,' says Ghalib and I feel the tip of his knife nestle against my throat.

I turn around, knock my bag against the side of Ghalib's head and run. I'm not kitted for running – wrong shoes, too much alcohol in me – but I run and I am lifting my knees like I want to take off and pulling on the air with my arms to propel myself forward. I run and I hear running behind me. I hear Ghalib calling my name. I hear him swear. I hear him laugh.

I turn the corner and then I hear for the first time a repeating sound, a bell. I panic. It could be the alarm on my mobile phone. If I am carrying this sound, then it will be easy for Ghalib to follow me in the darkness even if I get a lead on him. I have to stop it. I take my phone out and press buttons on it. The sound continues, becomes louder. I am no longer breathing evenly. A numb feeling begins to cover my shins, then my thighs. I am slowing and I am giving him a beacon by which to find me. I throw my phone to the ground. There is nothing in it now. The number it carries for Baba doesn't work. I can be rid of it. Perhaps I should throw my shoes off too. I try to raise my foot high enough to grab the shoe from it while I am still moving forward. I can't. I try again. I fall. I hit the ground with my hands in front of me and I feel the skin tear on the palms. I can't stop. I can't stay here in this heap. I stand up again. I shake my hands in the air as if this will dispel the pain. I try to breathe more deeply. I'd better be moving again. I'd better be running again. I start. I lurch. Then a large arm comes around my body and, despite everything I should be feeling, I lean into it and I let it take my weight.

CHAPTER 3

I fell asleep. Or I collapsed. I should think that I collapsed. I don't open my eyes. Though I am awake, I keep them closed. We talked about the photograph. I remember that. Before I slept, Ghalib and I talked about the photograph. The attachment with the detachment, he called it. Now he has seen it too. He has the same image in his head as I do. Sometimes when I think about it, it seems that the table is draped in blood, the blood from the no-bodied head is dripping off the edges. But this is not what is in the photograph. In the photograph, I suppose the head has been placed recently on the table, after the removal from the body has been effected, after the spurting and spilling is finished. The head has been placed on the table literally for a photo opportunity. It's an add-on, a triumphal conclusion to a controlled piece of mayhem. I have woken up and this is what I have in my mind and this image is shared now, it's shared with Ghalib. So I do open my eyes. I hurl the image from my mind. I try to cut this link to Ghalib. I've known him since we were infants. Now I want to share nothing with him, least of all the knowledge of the photograph.

With my eyes open, I recognise that I am sitting inside a car. The door next to me is open. On the pavement, there is a police officer in uniform, crouching, looking in at me through the open door. A second police officer is sitting in the car in front of me. The sound that I heard earlier has vanished. In fact I realise that it was a police siren. Now the street is silent, except for the radio in the car, which suddenly transmits voices from somewhere else. It falls silent. Then there is a further volley of voices. I expect to hear one of them say my name, mispronounced in some way, but unmistakeably my name.

I look up at the police officer who is crouching on the pavement outside the door. 'I know the owner of the car,' I tell him. 'Is he okay? He's the older guy. Did you see him?'

'Which car?' says the police officer. 'There are a lot of cars here. Can you describe the car?' I look at him and he looks back at me. I climb out onto the street. We are on a corner of the square and the spot where Terry's car had been parked is empty.

'It's gone,' I tell him. 'Where did it go?'

'Can you describe the car?' he repeats. I am about to do it, then I stop. I should think a bit more now about what I want to say. I am beginning to feel more clear-headed, but in truth I know that I'm quite heavily drunk. The last time that I was drunk like this was in Beirut. I had lunch alone at the boat club while Baba was out swimming in the boat, and I drank four large glasses of wine. In the taxi on the way back to the Saint-Michel with him, I sang. When we got to the hotel, I took a stool at the bar and hurled lines at anyone that was close by. Baba came back half an hour later and took me to my room. I woke up feeling like this, but not as bad. 'You hurt your hands,' says the police officer. 'Do you remember how you did that?' I lift my hands and stare at the palms. There are long bloodied grazes. There is debris under my fingernails.

'I fell,' I tell him.

'Why were you running?' he says.

'Did you grab me while I was running?' I reply.

'You fell,' he says.

'Yes, I just said that,' I reply. 'I fell.'

'What's your name?' asks the second police officer from the front seat of the police car. I don't answer immediately. I can reel off a different name. I can refuse to answer. But they can check my bag for identity documents. The question may be a test. Probably they looked in my bag while I was sleeping.

'Hanna Mehdi,' I reply. Then, by habit, I spell my name.

'You live around here?' he says. I shake my head.

'I'm a visitor,' I say.

'Uh-huh,' he says. 'A visitor to the neighbourhood or a visitor to the city?'

243

'I'm a visitor to the country,' I tell him, plunging straight ahead. 'I arrived yesterday.'

'What are you here to do?' says the first police officer, speaking up again.

'I'm a tourist,' I reply. It's what I said to the hotel receptionist as well when I checked in.

'Do you know people in the city?' continues the first police officer.

'I'm not sure,' I say, shaking my head again. I can feel that I am heading into trouble. The radio in the car emits a couple of beeps, but no voice follows this time. 'Who called you?' I ask.

'Do you have proof of your identity?' replies the police officer inside the car. 'Your passport, driving licence, a credit card, something like that?' I find my bag on the seat inside the car and take out my wallet. I remove a credit card and show it to him.

'This says a different name,' he remarks. 'What's this name?' I take the card back from him. The card bears Baba's name. I take out a different one and show him that.

'That was a card in my father's name,' I tell him. 'This is mine.'

'Why do you have your father's card?' he says.

'He gave it to me,' I reply. He hands me back the card with my own name and I replace it in my wallet.

'Tell us about this other car,' he says.

'It's not there now,' I reply.

'Where did it go?' he says.

'I don't know,' I tell him. 'You grabbed me. I

244

slept. I don't know where it went. How long did I sleep for?'

'I didn't grab you,' says the police officer. 'You fell.'

'You did grab me,' I reply. 'I remember the feeling.'

'What have you been doing tonight?' asks the police officer from the pavement.

'You know,' I reply, 'there's a man who was in trouble in that car.' Both police officers say nothing and stare at me. 'His name is Terence Monroe,' I tell them. 'He has a house on the street over there,' I add, pointing to the turn-off from the square. 'I don't know if he's there at the moment. It's number nine. He might have left in the car. But he was possibly about to get hurt. It might be bad.'

'It couldn't be that bad if he drove away,' says the police officer from the pavement.

'No,' I tell him. 'There was another man who was driving.'

'Why was he about to get hurt?' he asks.

'I'm not sure,' I reply.

'You didn't mention the other man before,' he says.

'I'm not making this up,' I reply.

'Okay,' he says. 'That's fine. But you're not in any trouble, you know? You're hurt. It's late at night. You can just tell us what happened. What are the names of these men?'

'What will you do with that information?' I reply.

'Were you threatened?' he says. 'Is that why you

were running? And then you hurt yourself. Did these men threaten you?' I don't speak. 'We can find them, you know,' he continues. 'We can talk to them.'

As I listen to his offer, I think ahead to what will happen if they find Ghalib, if they take his mobile telephone, if they scroll through the emails and find the photograph. That's where Ghalib said it was. Actually Ghalib might show it to them right away. Ghalib wants Terry and Baba to fear discovery, that's how he will compel them to give him money. The police officer inside the car removes the radio unit from its stand. I shiver as I consider that he's going to spell my name for someone on the other end of the radio system and ask them to input the letters into a computer system. Even if they don't have an arrest warrant for me, or any other police record, someone just needs to search for my name on the internet and then this concern the police officers have for me right now will vanish and be replaced by something else.

'Where's the meeting tomorrow morning?' says the second police officer into the radio unit. I watch him waiting for a reply, but none comes. He notices me looking at him and spits out his chewing gum onto the street, then turns away from me to look out of the front of the car. The police officer who asked the questions about Ghalib and Terry is still waiting for my reply.

'I'm sorry,' I tell him. 'This is not a good night for me, but I'll be fine.'

'You're sure that there isn't anything else you want to say?' he says.

'We can get going,' says the police officer from inside the car to his colleague.

'Nothing else?' says the colleague to me.

'I'm fine,' I reply. 'I'm lucky you found me. But I'm okay now.'

'It wasn't luck,' he says, smiling.

'What do you mean?' I ask sharply.

'Well, it wasn't luck, was it?' he says.

'Were you following me?' I ask him.

'Why would we be following you?' he says, laughing. 'Someone from one of the houses hit 999. That's why we came. Were you in the garden in the middle of the square by any chance? They hate that. The garden is private, you know, residents only. That's very important to them. Whoever called told the operator there were four of you, minimum.' When I don't reply, he adds: 'This happens a lot. People don't think we'll come if they say it's one person, so they tell us it's a gang and everyone has guns or big backpacks, you know, like they might be carrying bombs. If you listened to the 999 calls, you'd think this was . . .' His last word is obscured by a burst of noise from the radio. I take a couple of steps away from the car.

'What did you say?' I ask him, taking another step when the radio is quiet.

'Oh, you know,' he says, 'it's just that to listen to the calls, you'd think that the people calling us were living in Baghdad, not in London.'

'Baghdad?'

'Yeah,' he says. 'You know, like in Iraq.' I nod and become aware of the line of sweat that sprang up across my shoulders a moment ago. I thought he said Beirut when the radio cut in. 'Don't run,' says the police officer, noticing that I am standing further away from him. He is smiling. 'We'll catch you,' he says. 'Like the last time.'

'I wasn't running away from you,' I tell him.

'No,' he says. 'Apparently you were just running. There's nothing more to it than that.'

'Let's go,' says the police officer from inside the car.

'You dropped your phone,' says the other one. 'We saw you drop it.' He reaches into his pocket. He holds my phone out to me. There is a long crack across the back. The screen is blank. 'It's broken,' he says. 'I'm sorry.'

'Thanks for finding it,' I reply, taking the phone from him.

'Do you want a lift?' he asks. I nod my head. I am insensible to offer any other response. I am tired. I am puzzled. I walk to the back door of the police car and pull on the handle.

As the car sets off, I formulate in my mind the lie that I am staying at a hotel close by. If I utter it and they drop me off there, I can turn around and go back to Terry's house. I can check if he is there, if he is all right. He might talk to me now about what's going on, what the photograph shows. I hesitate as I try to remember whether I already told the police officers the name of the hotel where I am staying. Then I decide not to make the lie as I am no good now, and Ghalib is doubtless holding on to Terry until Terry has agreed to pay him. Or they both got in the car and drove away as quickly as possible when they heard the police siren. Neither of them wants to be discovered with the photograph. In any case I can come back tomorrow if I think differently about any of this when I wake up after this night. 'How long are you staying in London?' asks the police officer who spoke the most to me earlier.

'I'm glad to be here,' I reply, slipping his question. As soon as I've made the comment, I feel like my tongue has grown heavy, like it's made of leather.

'Where's home?' he says.

'The Middle East,' I reply.

'Never been,' he says. 'Are all the women heavy drinkers?' Both he and his partner laugh. Their radio crackles and then they talk with the handset for a while instead of talking to me. At first I listen to their conversation. But then I drift away from it. I rest my head against the window and close my eyes. I remember falling asleep like this in cars when I was a child with the driver in front and my mother next to me on the back seat making telephone calls. Years later, I was in New York to attend an open house that a client was having to show off a new apartment, including the pictures I had bought for him. Parked on the street, as I was coming in, was a car with two Pakistani children asleep in the same way inside. I remember standing to look at them for a long time. My parents would have insisted that I go upstairs to the adults' event. These kids, I imagined, had come from upstate and next, when their parents returned and they woke up from their naps, they were going to Brooklyn for a meal with family friends, a clutch of children all the same age who will go into one of the bedrooms and listen to music and talk in New York accents while their parents on settees downstairs reprise Urdu expressions that they haven't used in weeks. Then they would drive home, and perhaps one sibling would talk about how the older brother of the house where they were is going to an Ivy League college, or the younger brother has made it onto the school swim team. I reflect that there would have been no demerit to feeling slightly enclosed like that for a few years when I was young. I never felt that I filled the space that I was in. It was always bigger than me. Yet perhaps I needed that sense of filling a space, even being a little restricted by it, in order to feel grown up, to feel capable, to understand at some point that there is more of me than there was perhaps two years before.

The car stops and I look out of the window. My hotel is ahead. The police officer that is driving points to it. 'Is that it?' he says.

'It must be,' I reply. I feel a dread as I think of being back in the room, no idea as to where Baba is, little chance now of speaking to Uncle Terry face to face.

'Are you okay?' asks the other police officer.

'I'm fine,' I tell him.

'You'll walk to your hotel from here?' he says. 'Don't want the concierge to see you dropped off like this.'

'That's kind,' I say.

'Well, we should get on,' says the driver. Finally I get out of the car.

'Thank you,' I say to them. As I walk to the hotel, I hear the car still idling in its spot behind me. When I peek from the hotel doors, the police officers are looking in my direction.

In my hotel room, I sleep in a thousand small intervals. I finish a large bottle of mineral water during the night, drinking in gulps each time I come out of sleep far enough to be aware of my thirst. On the briefer re-entries, I turn when I wake up, turn and start again. Twice I get out of bed and look through the gap between the curtains, searching for the police car on the street. I don't see it, then lying awake in bed at some point I remember that this room is on the opposite side of the hotel. At 5am, I give up the prospect of sleep. I take a shower. I hold both hands against my head as the hot water courses onto it. Afterwards I feel too tender to rub myself dry with the towel. I lie down on the towel on the bed and lay another towel over me. Still I can't sleep. It's like there is now a crack running through the full ambit of my skull and, every time I make the slightest move, even with each breath, the two halves of my newly bifurcated skull grind against one another. I stand up and grab things to wear from the closet. I find all the clothes I took off when I came in and stuff them into an empty drawer. Eventually housekeeping will find them and take them away for cleaning. By the time I get them back, perhaps I won't remember that I was wearing them this night.

I walk down all the stairs to the breakfast room. I pull on the doors and they don't open. Like Baba in Beirut, I've woken too early to be served breakfast. He used to sit in his room and watch the traffic while he waited. I wander outside past the night clerk on the reception desk and look out onto the street. The police car isn't standing where it dropped me off last night. In front of me there are large trees and I think of climbing one of them, hand over hand. I would lie down on a branch and the dew from the leaves above would drip onto my forehead and eradicate my headache.

I go back inside to the lounge and read the front pages of yesterday's newspapers. It hadn't happened at the point that they were written, the collapse of Lehman. This morning there will be the large headlines that take up most of the front page of the newspapers. I wasn't here when those appeared the day after IBCD fell down. We were already running. We were ahead of our notoriety by a few

252

hours; we had to be. From the news articles I read last night on my phone, I remember a photograph of the Lehman building in London. Taken from outside, it pictured Lehman staff standing with their backs to the glass. The caption suggested that they were listening to a briefing about what was happening to the bank. Baba didn't do any meetings like that on the day that IBCD collapsed. He left the building immediately and came to get me. Others stayed though. I remember reading afterwards that some people stayed until the evening. They weren't burning papers or liquidating positions; the police and the regulator were already in the building by that point. They were sitting around in groups, touring each other's offices, watching television news, talking, telling stories about things that IBCD had done in the past. When they left, they stopped by the journalists outside and told these stories and quoted from Altaf Sherpao's circulars. Some news channels used the clips, others did not. I think they found it confusing, that the failed employees of the failed bank would talk like that. The people who worked at Lehman left with their boxes. Those are the images I saw last night. I didn't see any coverage of what they said. The people who worked at IBCD couldn't take their boxes; their boxes were wanted for the investigation. They walked out of IBCD with nothing but the stories; even the money in their IBCD personal bank accounts was out of bounds for them.

I watch the doors of the breakfast room being pushed open from inside by a young waitress in a white apron with her hair tied back. She pokes a large smile towards me. I look past her into the room and it is empty. This is how Baba ate breakfast every morning in the hotel in Beirut, first in, no one else around. I enter the breakfast room and walk to a table by the window. The waitress crosses the room towards me as soon as I'm sitting down. 'Bright start,' she says, pointing outside. 'Good morning.' She hands me a menu. 'Can I get you tea or coffee to start with?' she says.

'Just water please,' I say.

I read the menu after she has gone and in turn imagine the sensation of each item in my mouth. Nothing is going to work, I can tell. I want something to fill the hole in my head and purge my blood but it will also need to seduce my stomach. If Baba were here, he would bring me a jar of Pakistani pickle from the fridge in his room. We found a supermarket in Beirut that carried it. Baba used to eat heaped spoonfuls of it at breakfast whenever he had a lot to drink, years ago. In Beirut he ate it sometimes at lunch with pitta bread. I hold an image of him eating in my mind and it reminds me what that time was like, but that time was just a few days ago. The photograph had been taken, that head had been severed from that body, yet we were living like nothing had happened. And now I'm in a hotel dining room, like I've chosen to spend this time in surroundings that will make all that has happened seem unreal. It's wrong. I'm failing. I have got to change. The waitress hasn't reappeared yet. I stand up and walk out of the breakfast room. I rush to the lift and it rushes to me when I press the call button. There are small bottles of fruit juice in the fridge in my room. I will drink one of those to dispel the weakness I feel and then I must go.

When I come out of the lift on my floor, there is a man sitting on the chair facing me. 'Hello,' he says. I make a noise. The man smiles. He's right. It was a pitiful noise. He stands up. It's Alain. He leans towards me and kisses me on one cheek and then the other. 'You must be shaken by the Lehman story,' he says, putting his hand on my shoulder. 'Everyone is over-excited by it. They think it will be the end of the world.' I throw his hand off my shoulder.

'Who told you I was here?' I ask him.

'Let's go to your room,' he says. 'It is better to speak inside.'

'No,' I reply immediately. I remember his hands on me, twice, from the night after the funeral when he came to my bedroom, from the day afterwards when he tried to intimidate me in Mudassar's office. And I remember suddenly as well the tip of Ghalib's knife against my throat. Though it rested on my skin for barely a second, I imagine that I can feel it as I swallow. I look around me in case there is some other person close by.

'Is Ghalib here as well?' I ask, walking past him

and looking down the corridors. There is no one around that I can see, not Ghalib, but no one else either.

'He's in London,' says Alain, 'but he's not here now.'

'Yes, I saw him last night,' I tell him. 'I can give you the million.'

'Ah, but one million is no longer what we want,' he says, smiling again. It's a theatrical smile, like he stood in front of the mirror earlier practising his smile for when he was going to deliver this line.

'You're even more shit at investing than you thought?' I ask him. 'You lost more money?'

'Not at all,' he says. 'In fact, we gained something. Since the last time you and I spoke, we gained something: a photograph. It's a pity for you. It's going to cost you ten million dollars.'

'What's in the photograph?' I ask him. Then it occurs to me that perhaps they don't have it. Perhaps Terry let it slip that it exists when he was talking to Ghalib last night, but they don't have it. 'Can I see it?'

Alain reaches into his pocket and takes out his telephone. 'It's right here,' he says. 'Did you forget what's in it? I don't think so. But I can refresh your memory if you like.'

'It proves nothing,' I tell him. I think of the photograph that the Arab consortium sent the members of the IBCD board when Baba turned down their offer, the photograph of IBCD HQ with the letters of the name of the bank about to fall off. 'It was done with Photoshop.' Alain just shakes his head.

'By the end of this week,' he says, 'send word via Habib that we are getting the money or both you and your father are heading to prison. That's the new deal.'

'That's not a deal,' I reply. 'That's blackmail.' I press the call button for the lift and then sit down on the chair where he was seated when I arrived. 'We're not giving you any money,' I tell him.

'We'll see,' he says. The lift bell rings.

'Fuck off,' I tell him.

'I've said what I came here to say,' he replies. Getting into the lift, he adds: 'You know, I had a good job offer from UBS after university. I should have taken it. Your world, your people are the worst.'

He turns away from me and the lift doors close. When he has gone, my body begins to shake and I cry. I slip off the chair and hold my face off the ground upon my clenched fists. All the time that I was talking to Alain I was holding myself ready I think to be struck, or to face off against a knife or even a gun. I have to start moving now. I have wasted time and now I am running a long way behind. I take long, slow, deliberate breaths, until I can stand up again. I hold my hands in front of my face and open my fists. I go quickly to my room and get dressed for going out.

★　★　★

Outside I feel flushed. It's a warm day and yet I am wearing many layers. I don't know whether I think I've put on a disguise or if the extra clothing is supposed to function as padding. I throw myself into a taxi and say Terry's address. I look through the window as we drive, deliberately keeping my eyes open, not blinking, so that they begin to hurt and the hurt obscures my other thoughts. I feel afraid now. Now I am embroiled in Baba's trouble and Terry's trouble as well as my own. None of us is safe. The anonymity and safety Baba and I found in Beirut for two years is finished. Terry was exposed by the parliamentary committee and by the media – he lost anonymity a while ago, now he has lost safety too. I want to find out what he knows. He must understand how serious matters have become. He must talk to me.

'Where do you want?' asks the taxi driver, looking over his shoulder. We are on the right street and he has slowed down. I look out for Terry's house.

'Right here,' I reply. I take a large banknote out of one of my pockets and hand it to him. 'Can I ask you a favour?' I add.

'What's that?' he says.

'Come with me while I knock on this door,' I reply. Though it isn't night this time, I don't want to encounter Ghalib on my own again. If he is still with Terry, then these streets are too private to provide me with a guarantee of help.

'Ex-boyfriend?' says the taxi driver.

'A boy,' I tell him. 'A boy who threatened me.' He turns off the engine of the taxi.

'Right,' he says, opening his door. 'Lead on.'

I go to the gate in front of the house and press the bell. The door opens within seconds and there is a man in a suit facing me. 'May I help you?' he says.

'Terence Monroe,' I say. 'Is he here?'

'Your name?' asks the man.

'Hanna Mehdi,' I reply, then spell my name. 'Is he here?' I ask again. The man at the door doesn't reply and closes the door in front of me. I look around me up and down the street just in case Alain has followed me from the hotel or if Ghalib is returning at the same time as me. The street is deserted. I look at the taxi driver.

'All right?' he says.

'I'm fine,' I reply. 'Thanks for doing this.' The door to Terry's house opens again from inside. But it isn't the same man who blocks my way now – it's Ghalib. He walks down slowly to the gate from the door. He stands behind it, carefully out of reach. 'Why are you here again?' I ask him.

'Hi to you as well,' he says. 'Who's your friend?'

'Where's Terry?' I say. Ghalib shrugs his shoulders. He looks back towards the house and makes a play of staring at each window for a couple of seconds. 'Where is he?' I repeat.

'Hanna, stop trying to track him down,' says Ghalib eventually. 'It's retarded. You're not the police.'

'Fuck you,' I tell him. 'Open the gate and let me talk to him.'

'You're too late,' says Ghalib. 'Whatever your father sent you to say to him, it's too late.'

'I want to talk to Terry,' I reply.

'He sent me,' says Ghalib. 'Talk to me.'

'Fuck you,' I tell him. 'I have nothing to say to you. I want to see him.'

'He's not going to come down,' says Ghalib.

'I'll wait here until he does,' I say. Ghalib looks away from me and sighs.

'Hanna, he can't help you,' he says softly. 'He's already agreed to pay his share. Next it's your father.'

'My father won't pay,' I tell him.

'I think he will,' he replies. 'He murdered the head of the Saudi sovereign wealth fund. That's not just murder, that's dumb murder. He can't do for anyone to find out about this. Imagine what the man's family and business pals would do to him if they found out.'

I turn away from the gate. I don't want him to see when there are tears in my eyes. I glance at the taxi driver and I can see that he is baffled, this talk of money, this talk of murder, he didn't expect to hear that talk in a conversation that I would have. He doesn't look at me. He frowns, then he turns and walks back towards his taxi. I think of calling to him, getting into the back of his car and telling him everything. I want to do that, I realise, in order to get him to say that

Baba's conduct is excusable, to place Baba above Ghalib in some strange moral ranking that I have made somewhere inside my head and I want others to endorse. I don't want Ghalib to have the last word on my father. I don't want this taxi driver to leave here with the belief that Baba is the principal villain and Ghalib is no worse than an opportunist, a parasite. I'm still the banker's daughter, even to this stranger, even at this moment when everything is unsettled.

I watch the taxi drive away. Behind me I hear the door to Terry's house close. Ghalib has gone back inside. I watch the street. A woman goes past with a small dog. Two cars drive by. I start walking towards the square where I found Terry's car yesterday. Ghalib said that Terry has paid his share. That means Terry was definitely there in the garden when the man's head was removed. Terry fears discovery too, that's why he paid. Now he can expect that it will remain a secret between a small group. He can assume that the others will be pragmatic like him, pay their share, and he can forget what happened in the garden.

It doesn't surprise me that he was there. Baba leads, but he likes to have his men beside him. And besides the victim was as much Terry's enemy as Baba's enemy. The Saudi sovereign wealth fund took all of its investment out of IBCD before it fell. The man who ran it was one of the conspirators who brought down the bank. They killed for revenge in the garden, Baba and my uncles. They were so fond of their bank, so proud, so beaten when it fell. This revenge must have been irresistible to them.

Finally I know enough. My father is a killer. The reality is that he can cope with blackmail. He doesn't need my help. Plus I've no doubt that he can produce the sum of money that they want. And, if he doesn't, then he will be arrested and put on trial. Let these brutalities end in that way. If Alain wants to tell people that I am an art fraud, then I don't care. My father is a killer. Fraud is the least I could do.

I arrive on the square and I see that Terry's car has gone. There is a smart saloon car in its place. For a brief moment, the transposition makes me wonder if I have imagined the past twenty-four hours. I'm looking for comfort, I guess, a way out, temporary insanity is easier than making the choices before me now. Expecting justice is delusional too I suppose. Ghalib hinted at it: if Baba doesn't pay, he won't send the photograph to a legal authority; he'll send it to the Saudis. They will hunt Baba, most likely with the purpose of doing the same thing to him that he did to their man. And, just as I can't reach Baba right now, I doubt that Ghalib and Alain can reach him. So I'm the one who knows about the trade that is on offer; Baba doesn't know. They are treating me as Baba's representative and I have to be the representative because, if I don't find him, or if I don't pay over the money myself, then Baba will become prey for those seeking revenge. It's only me who can stop that from happening. Whatever remonstrations I want to make to him as his daughter, first I have to avoid becoming the judge who decides that his head for the head that he took is the right punishment.

Uselessly, I take my smashed mobile phone from my pocket and check the screen. It's blank. But, even if the phone were working, I don't have a way of calling Baba and he isn't going to call me. He wanted to protect me from these choices; he doesn't know that I've hurled myself into the very heart of the situation where I must make them. What next? This at least I know. Paying the money to Ghalib and Alain is the best immediate thing for me to do, it decontaminates this, at least for the time being. It gives me the chance in slower time to make choices about the proper justice of the situation, to produce reform in the way that Baba acts. Though I hate the thought of doing it, paying them the money now is my only measure of control.

CHAPTER 4

The door of the bank is opened from inside by a man in a black suit as soon as I press the buzzer next to it. Nothing has changed. It's the same building, the same façade, the same door, the same man, as when I used to come here with instructions from Baba more than two years ago. I tell the receptionist my name and offer her the name of our personal banker, Theo. I am guided to the small salon in which I have always met him. I remember being here two or three days after my mother died. Baba didn't come. He sent me even that time. Theo didn't tip his head and ask patronising questions about how I was doing. He asked what had to happen with my mother's money and I handed over the envelope from Baba. He will help me again. He will fix this next part.

He emerges from another door a few minutes later and shakes my hand. We settle onto chairs with no desk between us. A butler brings a tray of tea things. Usually I would start these meetings by handing over the envelope from my father. Then Theo and I would chat. He had started to buy some paintings for himself. We used to talk about the latest auctions. Today I have no envelope so, after the butler has left, I say, 'Thank you for seeing me. It's kind of you.'

'I'm glad that I was available,' he says. 'It's a turbulent day. We are all watching the news about Lehman Brothers very closely. But I had a free slot.' He pauses very briefly. Usually he would ask me a question about how my work is going. I think about waiting to see what he will ask me instead, how he will manage the fact that I haven't been here to see him for two years, the knowledge that he must have and that he must know that I know he has about what happened to IBCD and where Baba and I have been ever since. But I refuse to wait. I'm worried about losing the thread that I brought into the room with me.

'I've been out of touch with you,' I say.

'Nothing to worry about,' he replies, waving an arm through the air again. 'I am pleased to see you now.'

'You're well?' I ask him.

'I am,' he says. 'How is your father?'

'He's fine,' I reply. I sit for a moment with my hands crossed in my lap. Theo sits back in his chair as well.

'He asked me to make a transfer of funds from my account,' I tell him. Theo nods. After a moment, he frowns.

'When did you speak to him?' he says.

'Oh, it was a few days ago,' I reply.

Theo smiles. 'Well, that would explain it then,'

he says. 'You see, your father sent instructions yesterday by fax. He requested the transfer on your behalf.'

'That's impossible,' I reply.

'How do you mean?' he says.

I pause and think it over. Of course it's possible that Baba would send instructions. I replied foolishly. 'Where did he send the fax from?' I ask.

'This I don't know,' replies Theo. 'It could have been from anywhere.'

'Did you speak to him?' I continue.

'I did not,' he says. He clears his throat and shifts in his seat. 'It was a large transfer that he requested,' he says.

'How did you know it was from him?' I ask.

'He has been my client for a long time,' he replies. 'I recognise his signature.'

'It could have been forged.'

'We have a software program that checks it as well. Is there a reason why you would expect someone to impersonate your father?'

'Well, there's the obvious one,' I reply. 'To take the money.'

'Well, yes,' he says. 'I see what you mean. But the signature is genuine. I can show it to you.'

'Can you please?' I ask. And, as soon as I've asked, I realise that I don't want to see it to verify it. I want to see it because I already believe that he sent the fax. I want to see a letter that he wrote and signed as a way to have contact with him.

Theo passes to the other side of the room, picks

up a telephone and speaks softly into it. He returns to his seat. After a few moments, I remark quietly: 'I'm surprised that he took money out of the account.' I have assumed always that he has plenty. He lives like he does – the hotel suite, the boat, the dinners, the expenses for me.

'I am sorry that you had to find out like this,' says Theo.

'I am sorry that you were the one who had to tell me,' I reply, smiling despite it all somehow. Yet, as I say this, I realise that the reason for the transfer may be something different. Perhaps Baba doesn't need the money, but Terry has warned him that Ghalib and Alain are making threats. Baba doesn't want to pay Ghalib and Alain. But he suspects that I will. So he took the money to make sure that I could not. He has stripped my account and diminished my agency, or restored it to where it would be if he hadn't given me the money in the first place. 'I should go,' I announce suddenly.

'My assistant will be here in just another moment,' he says.

'This is silly,' I tell him. 'I'm being silly. I don't need to see the fax. I'll call him and clear this up.'

'Of course,' he says, standing up. As I stand up as well, he adds: 'If there is anything else that I can do for you, you must tell me. There is around five hundred thousand pounds remaining in the account,' he says. 'Do you have expenses while you are in London?'

'I'm fine,' I reply. 'Thank you, Theo.'

I follow him across the room. He stands aside to allow me to pass through the door in front of him. The exit is to the right but, as I glance in the other direction, I notice a painting that is familiar. I walk over and stand in front of it. Theo joins me as I shake my head. 'You don't like it?' he says.

'No, it's not that,' I reply. 'I love it. It's Klee. It's one of the paintings in which he best expresses his approach to the natural world, remarks most clearly that it's a system quite separate from any that we have created ourselves.' This last sentence – I realise as soon as I've said it – is remembered from a description of the painting by Yani. After he had been in IBCD for a few years, he started buying up the Klee paintings that he had bought once before for the Saudi family. He wanted to have all of them in his office at the bank. This painting is one of those. They were sold off along with the rest of the bank's collection after IBCD collapsed, the biggest auction of that year both by number of lots and total sales. Soon Lehman's collection will be sold in a similar fashion I imagine.

'We acquired it last year,' he says.

'It used to be on a wall in IBCD,' I tell him.

'I didn't know that,' he says, taken aback. He frowns and I wonder if he thinks that there is something wrong with owning a painting that IBCD used to have, perhaps this means that the title to the painting might be in doubt, that for IBCD it

might have been an ill-gotten gain and that a liqui-
dator or a previous owner will turn up someday to
claim it back.

'It's a lovely painting,' I remark. 'Enjoy it.' I turn
away from it and walk this time towards the exit.

'Whenever you need anything,' Theo reminds
me, as we part at the front door of the bank. I
nod and walk away from him. I wait until I am
around the corner before taking a perfume bottle
out of my bag and smashing it on the ground. I
look down and notice that I have splashes on my
trousers. There are pieces of fine coloured glass
littered around my feet, like the debris of a
demonstration by dolls. I smell like a teenage
beauty queen. It's the perfume that Baba bought
me. It's the only one I wear. He started buying
it for me when I turned fifteen. He still buys it
for me. I still carry it around. I still wear it. I
stand and laugh at myself for a moment, but
I feel the laughter getting louder and I stop. I
look down at the pavement again and crush
underfoot the larger pieces of glass remaining
from the perfume bottle. When I have finished,
I feel like I want to walk, I want to walk for a
long time, past my old flat, perhaps all the way
to my parents' old house. Yet this would be the
worst time for someone I know to recognise me
on the street; I might tell them everything. I stick
my arm out in the air for a taxi. When the driver
asks me where I want to go, I give him the address
of Pen's gallery.

Crossing London again, I think with regret that I may have to leave the city for a second time soon. I can't pay Ghalib and Alain. Should I wait here while they decide what to do? I will be arrested if they carry out their threats, but where would I go if I made up my mind to escape? I don't know where Baba is. And I don't have a network of helpers and agents like he does to help me find another place of safety. Yani must have a way of reaching him. I want to ask Pen to let me talk to Yani. Plus I need to warn him that the photograph is out.

I ask for Pen at the front desk of the gallery. The assistant sends me through to the office at the back. 'Hanna,' says Pen urgently, as soon as I walk in. 'I've been trying to get hold of you all day.' I remove my broken phone from my pocket and show it to her. 'I need to talk to you,' she says. 'I'm really glad to see you.' I sit down in a chair close to her. 'Not here,' she says. 'I feel like I need to get out of here. Like you said last night, this is IBCD property.'

'That was a mean thing to say,' I reply. 'I shouldn't have said that. Let's stay here.'

'He owns my flat as well,' she continues. 'I should have told you that last night.'

I shrug my shoulders. 'It's okay,' I tell her.

'You know somehow,' she says, 'I was expecting you. I wasn't that surprised to find you at Victoria Miro. It's like with everything that's going on, the collapse of Lehman, it feels like time is up.

I needed to tell someone about Yani and then there you were.'

'It's really serious between the two of you,' I remark.

'He doesn't come to the city often,' she says. 'That limits things, but yes, we're close. I go to Casa every few weeks.'

'You should have told me,' I reply.

'It's hard to say these things to you.'

'Look,' I tell her, 'I almost went with Terry at one point. I didn't and that was a rare example of insight from me, but Yani isn't Terry. Yani isn't just looking for a shag. Yani has an outlook. He isn't like other bankers. He always had an outlook, even in the headiest days of the bank. Start him talking about art and it's a real pleasure to listen to him. Well, I find that anyway. Don't you? I can understand why he enjoys spending time with you. I don't have a problem with it.' I look up and I see that Pen is crying. 'What's wrong?' I ask her.

'Oh Hanna, I love this gallery.'

'Come on. It's your work that makes it what it is. It doesn't matter who owns it.'

'No,' she says. 'No, you don't understand.' I watch her while she takes a tissue from her bag and dabs at her face with it. 'Is your father coming to London as well?' she asks.

'I don't know where my father is,' I reply.

'He's not in Beirut?'

'No. He left. Do you know if Yani has spoken to him recently?'

She shakes her head. 'Why did he leave?' she asks. This is it, I suppose. I can tell her. Now that she's sleeping with Yani, she's the safest person for me to tell everything.

'The two years have been fine,' I tell her. 'You know that? They've really been fine. That's the strange thing. We left here in a rush. There was all the stuff in the news. There was Terry's parliamentary execution. Yet it's really been fine. Baba found a rhythm. I've been okay. But now it's bad. It's the worst it's ever been, it's worse than when my mother died, it's worse than when the bank collapsed.' Pen leans forward and places her hand on mine on the table. She sighs.

'There's something going on with Yani as well,' she says. 'For a few weeks now, he's been different.'

'Has he said anything?' I ask her.

'He hasn't said anything,' she says. 'I haven't asked anything, except in the generic sense: are you okay? What's wrong? That sort of thing. But I haven't asked anything. You know what I mean? I can't say that I've asked anything.' I nod and offer her a smile. 'I love my gallery,' she says, after a moment. 'I need my gallery.' She withdraws her hand and hides it behind the table. I peek at her expression and I know instantly that in fact she doesn't want me to start talking about what's wrong. If she hasn't asked Yani questions, then she isn't going to ask me. 'Can you talk to Yani?' she says.

'I'd like to,' I reply. 'I'm not sure I have the time to make a trip to Casablanca.'

272

Pen shakes her head. 'No,' she says. 'Yani's here at the moment.' She reaches into her bag and pulls out a card. She slides it across the table towards me. 'We're going to have lunch at this place tomorrow,' she says. 'Me and him. It's our regular place. He loves it. But you could go instead of me. You could meet him there.' I take the card from the table.

'Are you sure?' I ask her. She sighs. She holds the tissue in front of her eyes for a few seconds.

'I saw a photograph in his email,' she says.

'You did?'

'I check his email sometimes. He doesn't know. I guessed the password. It's my name and date of birth. Can you believe that? I check his email every time I get scared that he's cheating on me.' She stands up and pours a glass of water from a cooler in the corner. She drinks it in one shot. 'Say something,' she says.

'I've seen the photograph,' I tell her.

'What is it?' she says. 'Did Yani do it? Did your father do it? What is it?' I'm about to answer her question, but it's cruel to tell her. I could be honest. She could be a friend. She is a friend. But I know that I am going to have to leave again. I can't even offer her the exchange of my friendship for her relationship with Yani. If I still had the money in my account, I could back her in a new gallery. She could cut all her links with Yani. But I don't have the power to do even that. If I'd stayed in London, perhaps we would have set up the gallery together in the first place. Then neither of us would face these choices.

'I only have half the story,' I tell her. 'That's why I need to speak to Yani.'

'You're lying,' she says.

I shake my head. 'I have to confess something to you as well.'

'What is it?' She takes a couple of steps towards me.

'When I was selling paintings,' I reply, 'I asked someone to make some paintings in the style of someone else. I sold forgeries.'

'All the time?'

'I did it once.'

Pen laughs.

'Why do you laugh?'

She shrugs her shoulders. 'It doesn't make you the same as Yani or your father,' she says. 'Don't make the mistake of thinking that.'

'But the client found out,' I reply. 'Pen, I used to have a profession and now I've got nothing. I had my chance. I messed it up.'

'No,' says Pen. 'No, you can't think that way.'

I get up and offer myself to her in a hug. She embraces me.

'It's one o'clock tomorrow,' she says when I step back from her. She makes an empty gesture in the air, then decides to say what's on her mind. 'If he has to go somewhere right away,' she says, 'will you call me and tell me where it is? I don't think

I could bear it if he disappeared completely like your father.'

'I won't know where he's going,' I reply. 'If he decides to go somewhere, he isn't going to tell me where it is.' She nods. There's a tear creeping from her eye. I can't resist. I hold the card she gave me out to her. 'You can take it back,' I tell her. 'I don't have to go and see him.' She looks at the card, then forces herself to look away. She shakes her head.

'It'll be fine,' she says.

I take her in my arms again and then I leave the gallery. I walk towards the canal nearby. There is a swelling in my stomach, my chest, my head. I can identify it – it's not loneliness, not anger, not despair, not these companions of the past few days but, for the first time, real sadness. Like me, Pen has become a ward. My art friend who might have achieved things on her own, I thought had achieved things on her own – like me, she has her banker and, with him, she keeps herself to herself; like me, she does it with dignity, with her own spirit, but ultimately we are both weak, though she has decided that I am marginally stronger, she has strung her fate to mine.

I sit down on a bench by the water and try to collect my thoughts. I watch a man on a bicycle. He stops and fiddles with the chain, then rides on again. I watch a woman walking by with a small dog. She's familiar and it takes me several moments to work out that I saw her earlier, also with the dog, when I was standing outside Terry's house. I keep watching her after she has gone past and, just before she reaches the corner, she turns and looks at me. I get up quickly from the bench and walk in the opposite direction, take the stairs up from the canal to the street and find a taxi. I ask the driver to take me to a new hotel. I glance through the rear window a few times, but I don't know what I'm looking for. If I am being followed, then it won't be by a police car. The woman with the dog wasn't wearing a police uniform. The men who came to the hotel in Beirut never wore uniforms. Perhaps Baba already said no to Ghalib and Alain. That's why he took the money away from my account, so that I couldn't contradict him. The family or friends or organisation of the Saudi that Baba killed may have hired investigators to close in on us. Or perhaps, after my encounter with the police last night, they did work out who I am, and they think it might be useful to watch me. When the taxi drops me off at the new hotel, I go into reception and stand watching the entrance while I am checked in to a room. I look at everyone who comes in, but still I don't know what I'm looking for.

In my room, I switch on the television and change from one news channel to the next every few minutes. There is nothing about me, nothing about Baba, nothing yet. The news is all about a different crisis, unrelated to mine. I feel a tug of responsibility that I should be learning more about it, but I can't focus. There is a desk by the television and, looking at it, I go back in my mind to the discovery I made on Baba's desk in Beirut. Did he mean for me to find the photograph? It seems that he did. He wouldn't have left the laptop lying there inadvertently, not with that photograph on it. He couldn't tell me what he had done, he just showed it to me, so that I would go. But I don't know why he wanted me to go. Was it to take me out of danger, because he knew danger was imminent due to what he had done? Or was it to give himself more freedom, so that he could continue a vendetta, find and then dole out the same treatment to the other men who brought down IBCD? Mudassar's funeral took me away anyway, but I suppose I would have gone right back if Baba hadn't disappeared. Perhaps he left Beirut himself only because he could tell that the photograph had not been enough to get rid of me.

I eat dinner in my room. The television stays on all night and I flick through the news channels every time that I wake up. I turn up the volume when I start to think of Pen in the gallery after I left. In the morning, I set out too early for the lunch with Yani and so I stop to buy a book. I look at the pictures sitting in a café opposite the restaurant. I glance at everyone going in. I notice a man in a queue in the café who is the same size as Ghalib and it gives me a start and I clatter my coffee cup against the saucer, even though he's white, not an Arab, even though his face isn't

277

similar either. I stopped briefly outside a shop in the hotel foyer earlier, on my way out, because I saw a Swiss army knife and I thought about buying it and keeping it in my hand for the whole of today. But then I imagined the scene when Ghalib would find me and see the knife in my hand and how he would laugh at me.

The day reaches 1pm and I haven't seen Yani. I wait another five minutes, then I try to remember how long Yani would wait for people if they were late. I can't be so stupid as to find a way to miss him today, I can't do that. I get up from the café and cross the street. I wait in the entranceway, realising that I don't know what name to give when I go in. Yani's surname is Chalabi but I doubt that he would use it here, or anywhere in London, since the bank came down. I should have checked this detail with Pen. I think of calling her, then I peek around the corner into the dining room and start to look from table to table. I notice that there is a man at a table sitting alone who has noticed me. He stands up and I look over him and I realise that he has no hand on one side. It's Yani. He has changed completely. He has put on weight in all places, he has shaved his head. I walk towards him. 'Hanna,' he says, rubbing his head. He hardly even looks surprised.

'Someone told you to expect me?' I ask him.

'No,' he says, sitting down. 'No, they did not.'

'No hug?' I ask, sitting down as well. He was always affectionate towards me, hugged me when

278

he saw me, put his arms around me when I said something amusing.

'You don't want me to hug you,' he says. 'I think we're beyond hugs.'

'Did you come in through the back?' I ask.

'I didn't use the front door,' he says.

'I should have used your route,' I tell him. 'I'm being followed.' He frowns.

'Were you followed here?' he asks.

'I don't know,' I reply. 'I don't even know who's following me. Do you?' He shakes his head.

'I suppose Pen told you I was here,' he says. 'That was very bad of her. That's breaking the rules.'

'Don't be hard on her,' I say. 'She cares for you.'

He is silent for a moment, staring down at the fingers of his good hand. 'Cares for me or needs me?' he asks.

'You made her need you, didn't you? You gave her the money for the gallery. You gave her the flat. She didn't ask for them.'

Yani shrugs his shoulders. He reaches to the carafe of water on the table and pours himself a glass. 'What do you want?' he says.

'When did you last speak to Ghalib?' I ask him.

'Why do you ask?'

I look away, take a deep breath and then I try to keep my voice as level as possible. 'He's trying to extort five million dollars from me,' I say.

'Is he now?' replies Yani, lifting his glass to drink from it.

'He put a knife to my throat last night. Didn't he get caught with a knife at school when he was a kid?'

Yani brings the glass down on the table with a bang.

'Stupid little bitch,' he says. 'Stop your patronising routine. He's asking you for ten million dollars and you know perfectly well the story with the knife.'

'You know that he wants money from me?' I ask him. But it's a dummy question, to buy me time while I think. It was when he said you don't want me to hug you, I sensed that he was ready to speak to me, he had contemplated it and that could only be for one reason. But the reality of having this conversation with him is still different from the anticipation. I'm more afraid now that I know Yani is involved. On some level I could still be dismissive of Ghalib and Alain, but Yani is full-fledged. 'Are you involved in this with Ghalib?' I murmur, my voice trembling.

'The fruit hasn't fallen that far from the tree,' he says, but without any pride whatsoever.

'But you were there yourself,' I reply. 'You watched it happen. If this photograph gets out, you're as much in trouble as Baba.'

'I'm not in the photo,' he says.

'Neither is he.'

'But I have the proof that he organised it. He even sent me my ticket. You can't save him, Hanna. Everything that happened, happened at his request.

His fingerprints all over it.' He says these last words slowly and then smiles.

'I don't believe that you just stood there and did nothing,' I tell him. 'You took part. You're culpable.'

'When did your father ever let me do anything important?' he says. 'Did you think about that? He didn't even let me have my own revenge. Didn't even let me choose which plane to take to come and watch my revenge.'

'What do you mean your revenge? It was the bank's revenge.'

Yani shakes his head. 'It's not about the bank,' he says.

'I don't understand.'

'It's about this.'

'What?' I ask.

He pulls back the cuff on the arm that doesn't have a hand. 'It's about this,' he repeats. I say nothing. 'It's about this,' he says. 'You didn't know that. That's interesting. Through a retired spy who had done work for the bank in the past, your father got the name of the man who removed my hand. Your father—' he continues, then hesitates before thrashing on. 'Your father found out his name. He used to work for that family when he was young, then he did an MBA and became a finance guy. He's like a more ruthless version of Habib. Your father called me and told me what he was going to do. My revenge – but he had to get it for me. He couldn't stop himself. Even this he had to take away from me.'

'But you went. You knew what was going to happen.'

'Absolutely,' says Yani. 'I can't say it wasn't satisfying. Of course it was.'

'So why turn on him now?'

'It's been long enough. He's done this to me too many times. Do you have any idea how often I've thought about killing the man who cut off my hand? Can you imagine how much hatred I have for that person? And your father knew that. But he couldn't resist it. He couldn't resist being the one to organise it. He couldn't resist showing me that I am less than him in every single way. Well, you know what, I've had enough. I've had enough of him. So I took that photograph. It's time for him to pay. I didn't think of it until Ghalib came to tell me that he needs money. He'll have it from your father, not from me.'

'What if he does pay?' I reply. 'What guarantee does he have that you'll stop at ten million? What if you wait just long enough until he feels safe and then you start again?'

Yani smiles. 'You're a bright girl,' he says. 'Baba really is the lucky one.'

'You want to have some power over him,' I say softly, quietly, not particularly to him, to no one really. I watch him drink the remainder of the glass of water. 'If the photograph ends up in the wrong hands,' I continue, 'Baba will be killed. Terry will be killed. For good measure, I might be killed. They took your hand for far less provocation.'

282

'Shut the fuck up about my hand.'

'Does Terry deserve this? After he stayed and took the blame for the bank in public. He doesn't owe you anything.'

'Fuck Terry,' says Yani. 'I don't care about Terry. Pay the ten million. Save the drama.'

'But I can't,' I say. 'Yani, I don't have it. Baba emptied my account.'

'So what?' he says. 'Ask him to put the money back in.'

'I don't know where he is.'

Yani clears his throat and I see him staring at me. 'Say that again,' he says.

'He's disappeared. I don't know where he is.'

'That's bullshit,' he says.

'He's gone,' I reply.

'Well, find him, Hanna. I'm warning you. If Ghalib doesn't get that money, the photograph is going to be in the news and your Baba is going to be hunted down. If he's lucky, the police will find him. Otherwise, you don't want to imagine what will happen to him.'

I stand up, shaking my head. The thought of what might happen to Baba if someone else finds him is awful to bear. I bring my hand up to obscure my face. I don't want Yani to see me cry.

'But you will know that you did that to him,' I tell him.

'He did it to himself.'

'What happened to Shia boys stand together?' I ask. I don't wait for a reply. I turn and start walking.

I leave the restaurant through the front door. There is a gentle breeze and I feel like I am breathing in for the first time since I entered the restaurant. I look down the street and see two men standing by a car. I walk towards them. 'Are you police officers?' I ask them. They don't reply. They look at one another. 'In that restaurant, I just met Ghassan Chalabi,' I tell them. 'Do you know who that is?' After a moment, one of the men nods. 'He's going to get out through the back,' I continue. 'Be quick.' Still they hesitate.

'Please go,' I enjoin them. 'You must know that I've changed hotels. I'm in 301, Mandarin Oriental. I'll be there. Unless you hurry, you won't catch him.' I point towards the restaurant. They look at one another and then the man who nodded before does it again. They leave me and start running.

I stand still even after they have disappeared inside. I glance into the café where I was sitting before I went to meet Yani. I see my book on the table. No one has yet picked it up. I could go back, I suppose. I could sit down there again and continue reading the book. It would be a good idea to invest a lot of time in relearning London art. In a year or two, perhaps I could start working at Pen's gallery. I start to imagine myself going to work, making phone calls, talking to Pen in the evening about our artists. But at the same time I start walking, away from the café. If the police officers do catch Yani, they will soon want to speak to me as well. I don't have long left now. The police will be at my new hotel by the time that I get there. Alternatively, if I go to the hotel where I stayed before last night, then it might be Ghalib and Alain who are waiting for me. I could go back to see Theo. He could put me in a vault until Baba faxes to say what should happen to me. I have this one moment of being up, being ahead – I wrong-footed Yani, I sent the police in after him – and I don't know if I can extend it. There is no sanctuary for me, but I can think of a quiet place, a mild and kind person. I could go to see Habib in the betting shop where he goes. No one will think to look for me there.

In the taxi, the driver tries to talk to me about the collapse of Lehman Brothers. I ignore him. I think about what Alain said earlier at the hotel. He had a job offer from UBS. He didn't take it because he had become embroiled with Mudassar, Ghalib, with me, our world of severed hands and severed heads. I introduced Pen to Yani. I stayed with Baba in Beirut while he killed a man, while he humiliated his friend. Not much will change in the world after Lehman, but I can change.

When the taxi leaves me at the betting shop, I don't linger on the street. I push through the door and walk up a slope into the main part of the shop. I look across a wall of television screens tuned to different sports. There are two rows of black seats in front of the television screens. I scan through the seats and, as I'd hoped, I find Habib. He is sitting in the second row, alongside a black man with a neat beard. I see them commenting softly to each other as they watch the television screens. Habib stands up when he sees me. I move towards him.

'Dear Hanna,' he says in Urdu, shaking my hand.

'I hope you are well,' I say.

He nods and gestures towards the man sitting next to him. 'This is Lawrence,' he says, switching to English.

'Race starting soon,' says Lawrence, smiling at me. I turn around and look at the television screen he is watching.

'Nothing worth betting on in this race,' says Habib firmly to me, in Urdu again.

'Please sit down,' I say, taking the seat next to his, for I know that he won't sit down until I am sitting.

'Please don't mind me asking, Hanna,' says Habib, continuing in Urdu. 'How long have you been in London?'

I don't reply. It isn't a strange question, but he asked me urgently. The answer must matter to something. I stare at him. He doesn't flinch.

'Race starting,' says Lawrence carefully, looking at Habib and then at me.

The three of us turn to the television screens and watch the race. It lasts for several minutes, but neither Lawrence nor Habib says a word about it while the horses are running. It's as if there are only a finite number of words to be said between them and they must all be saved for the moments between races. Sure enough, as soon as the race is over, they begin to comment on the state of the racecourse and the performance of the horses. Their conversation consists almost entirely of terms and names that I don't recognise. When they stop, Lawrence stands up and walks over to the teller. Habib turns to me. I keep looking ahead at the television screens. He talks to me in Urdu. 'Is anything wrong?' he says. I don't answer. I would love to put my hand on his chest and check how hard his heart is beating. 'Would you like to make a bet on the next race?' he says eventually. I shake my head. I watch two women playing golf on one of the television screens. One of them stares towards a point that isn't shown on the screen and then speaks to the woman standing next to her.

'Here's my tip,' says Lawrence, sitting down again. He passes a slip of paper to Habib. He reads it, then passes it to me.

'Habib,' I say quietly, on an impulse, 'do you know if Ma is okay?' I hear him clear his throat.

'She is fine,' he says. 'Should I tell her that you asked?'

'I did leave suddenly,' I tell him. 'I feel bad about it.'

'It was no problem,' he says. 'Ma's judgement is poor at the moment. She shouldn't have asked you what she did.'

'I felt that I couldn't get dragged into it,' I reply.

'There isn't peace in that house,' he says,

shaking his head. 'Despite what I do, that house is falling. Your father and I have spoken about it often. He assures me that there is nothing that I can do but manage a slow decline.' I am struck by the reference to speaking to my father. He could be talking about the past, but he mentioned him deliberately I think, to test me. 'Hanna,' he says softly. I feel a touch on my hand. I look down at it and see that I have closed it into a fist with Lawrence's betting slip inside. I open my hand and I watch Habib's fingers remove the betting slip, unfurl it and return it to Lawrence. Lawrence nods at me and smiles. I smile at him too and then I lean back and run both my hands over my hair. 'Ma will recover from Mudassar's death in due course,' says Habib. 'Give her another chance soon perhaps.'

'Well, I don't have any more money,' I reply. 'She might be less interested in me in the future. My account is almost empty.'

'Who told you?' he says.

'Theo,' I reply. 'Yesterday. I went to see him,' I continue, 'to take the money out of the account, so that I could make the deal with Ghalib and Alain, but Baba had already moved it.'

'Yes,' says Habib. 'He did do that.'

'So you know about everything?' I ask. 'And you know where he is.'

He clears his throat and looks away from me. He glances at Lawrence, but Lawrence is looking straight ahead as if he hasn't heard anything. I realise that I spoke in English again. I watch Habib lean forward and put his elbows on his knees, then, as soon as he is settled in that position, he jerks backwards to sit upright again, as if someone has given him a warning about slouching.

'Why can't I be trusted?' I ask him.

'What do you mean?' he says.

'You know where Baba is,' I reply. 'Why can't I be trusted to know?'

'It's a dangerous time,' he says. 'Your father wants to protect you.'

'Well, he might not be able to any more,' I tell him.

'What do you mean?' says Habib, alarmed.

'I met Yani earlier today,' I tell him. 'Then I told the police where he was.'

'Why did you do that?' he asks, shocked. For once his urbane manner is gone.

'It's Yani who is blackmailing everyone,' I reply.

'Is that true?' he says. 'This is not what your father thinks.'

'My father is wrong,' I reply. 'It's Yani. He would have kept doing it. He has a lot that he wants back from Baba. I had to tell the police. I had to stop him.'

'I don't understand,' says Habib. 'Why has he betrayed your father now? They have been the closest of friends for many years.'

'It's not so hard to understand,' I reply. 'Yani wanted revenge for what the Saudis did to his hand. He's been living with that desire for years and years. Baba made it that he couldn't have his own revenge. Baba took over, like he always does.'

'This is an enormous betrayal,' says Habib.

'But I can understand that Yani didn't feel any fealty to him any more,' I tell him. 'Don't you see that Baba ruined his revenge?'

Habib doesn't reply. I watch him closely. He isn't going to reply. Now I imagine that he is considering how he will talk to my father about this finding, what options they have.

'We need to stop, Habib,' I tell him. 'Let's stop making our own conditions. Let's behave a bit more like normal people.'

'What do you mean?' he says.

'Habib,' I reply, 'you've always tried to help my family.'

'I have,' he says. 'It hasn't always been easy. It's my job. I've done it with pride.'

'Exactly,' I reply. 'Well, help me now. Help me to do the right thing. I want to know where my father is. I want to talk to him and tell him that I'm not going to live like this any more.'

'It's not that easy,' he says.

I shake my head. 'I have fought,' I tell him suddenly. 'I really have. Don't think that I haven't. I've fought to understand. I've fought,' I repeat, in English this time. It feels like an odd word. But I have fought, I'm right, and the time for that is over. I'm going to speak to Baba and tell him that he has done something wrong. I'm going to explain to him that I have a role to play in making it right.

I won't say that I have no choice. I do have a choice. I watch Habib knot his hands together in front of his chest. I put my hand on his shoulder. 'Will you tell me where my father is?'

EPILOGUE

SALE 2658/**LOT** 30

7 June 2012

Estimate

£40,000–£50,000

Lot Description

Ismail Gulgee (B. 1926–2007)
Three sketches of an unnamed woman
Signed and dated 'Gulgee 2002' (on the reverse
of each sketch)
Pencil on paper
29.7 x 40 cm
Drawn in 2002

Provenance

Acquired directly from the artist by the present owner

Lot Notes

This is an unusual set of portrait sketches by
Gulgee, considered by many to be the father of

modern Pakistani art. Renowned in his later career for large abstract paintings said to be inspired by the action painting movement in the US and yet grounded in the calligraphy of his Islamic Shia religious tradition, these sketches recollect the earlier phase of Gulgee's career, when he established a reputation as a portraitist. His most famous commissions from that time include portraits of members of the Afghan royal family painted in the 1950s.

The sketches were recently exhibited in a wide-ranging retrospective of the work of Gulgee curated by Hanna Mehdi. The exhibition toured major museums across Asia and the Middle East, concluding at Asia House in London. In the cata-logue to the exhibition, Ms Mehdi wrote of these sketches: 'Gulgee's famous calligraphy paintings are abstract and gestural interpretations of Arabic and Urdu letters. In these sketches, the same aesthetic instincts enter into a different form through an encounter with a woman (not a girl), a personality (not a beauty), someone whom the artist has glimpsed (but never studied). As in all his work, the lines swirl strong and free and the intimacy of the pencil has a special significance in these sketches given that, as far as we know, Gulgee was not painting any other portraits during this part of his career.'

The current owner of the sketches is Ms Mehdi's father, Mateen Mehdi, ex-chief executive and presi-dent of the International Bank of Commerce and

294

Development. Mr Mehdi was responsible for commissioning a major abstract work by Gulgee at around the same time as these sketches were made. That work was also included in the retrospective and appears in this auction as Lot 55 (Estimate: £500,000–£600,000). Commenting on the sale of the works, Ms Mehdi said: 'My father and I have enjoyed these works for a long time in private, arguably too long. The purpose of the exhibition I organised was to share them and the other Gulgee paintings that have been stuck in private collections with a wider audience. After the exhibition it doesn't make any sense to lock them inside our family vault again.'

The pieces are thought to be the last elements of the formerly vast IBCD private collection to be sold. The proceeds from the sale will be donated by Mr Mehdi to a new foundation run by Ms Mehdi that will be supporting contemporary Pakistani art.

The attribution of the sketches to Gulgee has been verified by two independent experts and their reports are available to view.

The title to the works is unaffected by the charges made against Mr Mehdi by the Islamic Kingdom of Saudi Arabia. He denies the charges. Speaking recently at an event with Ghalib Chalabi and Alain Bourely, producers of a forthcoming documentary about the 2008 financial crash, Mr Mehdi said: 'These ridiculous accusations are just the latest attempt the Saudis have made to discredit me, my colleagues and everything we achieved with IBCD. The way in which they have manipulated my dearest friend Yani and the UK government to support their campaign only strengthens my resolve to fight until my name is cleared.'